The Mood Ring

CATH WEEKS

DEDICATION

To Wilfie and Alex, my dearest boys.

Cß

A mood ring contains a thermochromic liquid crystal that causes the gemstone to change colour as temperature varies. The idea of the ring came to jewellery designer, Marvin Wernick, during the 1960's whilst witnessing his doctor friend assess a sick boy's temperature by placing a piece of thermotropic material to the child's forehead.

Some people believe that the mood ring changes to reflect its wearer's temperature and therefore their emotional state. The mood ring's powers have never been substantiated.

Cß

ACKNOWLEDGMENTS

Cover design CIF UK.
Cover photograph Carlson, Arvika, Sweden.

PROLOGUE

Daniel Trelawney used to like hanging his tongue out when it snowed. If he caught one hundred flakes in his mouth and swallowed them, his father would appear. The January he first tried this magic, his mother brought him in from the garden as the beep of the nine o'clock news sounded on the radio. Whilst the newsreader delivered the day's events – a car bombing, a woman arrested for cot death, a pensioner mugged at gun point – so Danny's eyes flitted from the hypnotising glow bars of the electric fire to his mother's sombre face as she told him, again, that his dad wouldn't be showing up tonight or any other night, no matter how many snowflakes he ate.

"Don't you ever think about him?" Danny had whispered later through the darkness to the bunched up blankets that was his brother, Erland. Erland had the weird ability to lie so still as to render him part of the room. Was he even breathing?

"Think about who?" Erland replied.

It had been a long time since Danny had thought about the snowflakes. It made him sad, thinking about how much he had wanted the magic to work back then. He shrugged away the thought by slamming the football as hard as he could into the back of the net.

"Danny, I said please stop that a moment. Come and meet Jacko." His mum was stood at the fringe of the lawn, her arms wrapped around her waist as though she were cold, despite the midday sun.

Danny was about to ignore her again and kick the ball back into the net, when a fleeting expression on his mum's face made him reconsider: a lack of confidence. In what? In him? In her new boyfriend? In herself? He trapped the ball under his foot and squinted at the man causing a hell of a shadow to fall across their garden.

"I'm Jacko," the giant said. He was about six foot four. His hands were huge, Danny noted.

"Daniel," Danny said, nodding.

"You play football?"

"Looks like it." Danny didn't need to look at his mother to see her forehead rise in subtle plea. "I play for Bath under sixteen's," he added, pulling his T-shirt away from his chest and flapping it.

"Danny's very good," his mum said, tucking her arm into Jacko's. "He's only just thirteen, but better than most of the other players who are all older than him."

"Huh," said Jacko, turning the corners of his mouth down as though impressed.

Encouraged, Danny began to header the ball whilst talking, his voice jolting with the movement. "I – support – Chelsea," he said. He could header better than anyone on his team. "Chelsea – is – the – love – of – my –"

"Girl's game," Jacko said. "Rugger's what men play."

Danny dropped the ball; it went toppling across the lawn and onto the stone path. He ran over to retrieve it, feeling every inch the child chasing butterflies. What made him tell stupid giant man about Chelsea? It wasn't as if he had asked or anything.

Danny's mum was laughing, not entirely naturally. "Oh,

don't tease him. Football's Danny's life!"

There was a creak and Danny looked in the direction of the back door in time to see Erland sliding outside surreptitiously, like a cat. Erland was heading for his chess tent, clutching a glass of milk and a stack of biscuits. He was in the middle of a tricky chess game with himself and would stop for no one. Not even for their mum's new giant man, or the ultimatum that she had delivered to them last night: behave today or grounded for a month. No one, not even Erland, wanted to be grounded on FA Cup final day, especially if you were a Chelsea fan and they were playing and you didn't own a television.

Despite all evidence to the contrary – Erland was skinny and non-syllabic – Danny envied his younger brother. Erland wouldn't have announced whom or what he loved in front of a stranger like that. He was ten years old but had lost his childishness two years previously at summer camp when he discovered pawns and rooks, in the way that anyone normal would have discovered what happens when you don't clean your teeth for a week.

Danny had replaced magic with football; Erland had replaced his entire childhood with chess. He had stale mated himself.

Lunch with the new guy was quieter than his mum would have hoped. Danny could tell that she was disappointed. Her shoulders were stiff as she placed the lasagne dish onto the mats, cursing as she burnt her thumb. If giant man hadn't been with them Danny would have asked if she was all right, but instead he fell silent and waited for the man to ask. Nothing was said.

Giant man couldn't believe that there wasn't a television anywhere in the house. He just couldn't believe it. Danny couldn't either, but not for the same reasons that this guy couldn't. Danny couldn't believe that they had to put up with going to people's houses to watch football games and had to huddle round his mum's laptop to watch DVD's on

Saturday nights. Whereas this guy couldn't *believe* it. Like it was impossible.

Wait until giant man found out that his date was eating a different portion of lasagne to the rest of them: a Quorn portion. His mum had only had two boyfriends over before and she hadn't told them about being vegetarian either. Why was that? No one came out right away and said what they liked or didn't like. He had to stop that – stop telling people about himself right away. His mother didn't do it. Erland didn't do it. Although this guy did. He was telling everyone how much he loved rugby and how great his widescreen high definition surround sound television was that had given him no change worth speaking of from four grand.

Danny kept his eyes on the mince on his plate, pronging it carefully, wondering when his mum was going to confess to being squeamish about eating lambs.

*

"I want to die! I want to die! Oh, God, let me die!" Beth had nothing left to give. Panic rose through her, causing her temporarily to forget the agony. She relaxed onto her back, just as the whole nasty circle of a contraction started again.

"Oh, no. Oh, no," she growled, her eyes fixed with horror upon a corner of the room as though her pain were crouched there, waiting to get her. She had asked for the room to be darkened, which Jacko had questioned wondering whether it might be wiser for them to see what was going on, but the midwife had pulled the giraffe-adorned curtains without hesitation, explaining that cows often retreated into darkness when giving birth.

Come fly with me, come fly let's fly away. "Turn it off, turn it *off*!" Beth shouted, gesturing at the music stereo. Jacko obliged immediately. Sinatra had been light relief at eight o'clock this morning when she was bobbing about on a birthing ball. Now, at eight minutes to ten at night, she wanted to smash his face in.

At ten past six this evening (there was a clock on the wall in front of her – as if childbirth wasn't hard enough without knowing exactly how long it had been going on for) she had been told she was going to have an emergency Caesarean section. The labour was failing to thrive; the baby was becoming distressed – its head was stuck; *mum's* blood pressure was dangerously high and *mum* was exhausted.

This was discussed by the white coats, whilst Beth wept with relief. An end to the pain! "*Mum* has refused an epidural," the midwife was telling the consultant. "She's been soldiering –"

"Beth," said Beth. "It's Beth."

The staff nodded encouragingly, as though she were doing well to remember her own name. She turned to face the clock, clutching Jacko's hand with renewed hope: at six thirty she was going to be wheeled to the operating theatre.

She was calculating how many more contractions that meant, at approximately three contractions per ten minutes...when the door opened and in brisked the chief midwife. "Good evening," the chief said, smiling.

Beth kept her eyes on the clock. She didn't like this woman. The chief had been popping in all day, looking at charts, saying things like 'chin up' and 'good work'. What was she doing now? She was down between Beth's legs. "Excuse me, dear," the chief said. "Checking progress."

Progress? What did that matter? She was getting a C-section. C-section coming right up, any minute now. An end to the pain. There went the clock hand. Six o'clock and twenty-eight minutes. "Oh no. Oh no." She began to moan. Here it came again. The bastard.

"Congratulations!" the chief said, scribbling on a chart before moving towards the door. "No need for a C.

You've progressed. Crank up the drip!"

"Wait," said Beth, trying to sit up, almost pulling the wire out of her arm. "What do you mean? I can't!"

The chief turned at the door. "You really don't want a C-section, dear. Horrible nasty things. Believe me. You'll thank me some day."

Beth turned to Jacko. "Help me. I can't do this. I really can't take any more."

"Take the epidural, Beth," he said. "Give yourself a rest."

The midwife was at his side in a second. "Yes, love," she said. "He's right."

"No," said Beth. "No way." She sank down flat, defeated, her eyes filling with tears.

"Then how about pethidine?" the midwife said, almost purring. "I've been told to increase the strength of the drip. You're going to get contractions faster and thicker now."

"Fine," said Beth, turning her face away.

At ten minutes to midnight, the baby arrived. They told Beth the head was in sight. She knew it wasn't, but she knew better than not to believe them. So she went with it and pushed some more.

As the baby emerged, all slippery feet and elbows, Beth was thinking about Hemingway's Brett Ashley. Brett Ashley had helped her push, had helped her see some kind of light in what would surely be the darkest day of her life. Brett Ashley, who had inspired women in the 1920's to bob their hair and wear masculine clothes, was the most liberated character that Beth could think of from all the lectures she had ever given. She would call her daughter Brett.

"Brett Ashley," she said aloud, straining to see what was happening beyond her. Jacko was bringing her a baby, his eyes wide open in delight, mixed messages of teary euphoria on his face.

"What a fantastic name!" he said, handing her the baby and wiping his tears with the back of his hand. "I prefer that to Jamie. Let's go for Brett Ashley Best?" He looked at her for approval.

She took her baby and stared at it. Brett was a boy.

"She's haemorrhaging!" The midwife pressed a buzzer and plucked the baby from Beth. The chief came running. Beth watched as a cannula was driven into her arm.

"Page Andy," the chief was shouting. "Now!" Beth was being wheeled at speed down the corridor, voices calling above her, white coats flapping. She felt cold. She called for Jacko, but her voice was a whisper.

She was being dragged to the darkest place they could find. Darker than the room she had given birth in. Darker than any place she had ever been before. Except one.

No....no... She tried to dig her heels into the bottom of the bed, but she had no grip. Her hands were restrained with wires and tubes. She could bite. She opened her mouth and bit wildly at nothing but air.

Oh, God. No one could help her. It was going to happen.

She held herself still. In the darkness, she could see the glow of the cigarette end – hear its crackle as it puffed itself up before dwindling again. It came closer until she felt the heat on her thigh, smelt her skin burning.

"Beth." Jacko was stroking her forehead. "It's all right." He smoothed her hair. "You've had a blood transfusion." She opened her mouth to speak. "Brett's fine," he replied, although that wasn't what she was going to ask. She was wondering where Danny and Erland were, whether they had been okay fending for themselves the whole day. Her heart twisted at the thought of Erland trying to hook his pyjamas out of the airing cupboard, of Danny rummaging through the freezer for pizza, of both of them lying in the darkness listening for the sound of the car on the driveway.

"He's right here, aren't you, son?" Jacko reached into the plastic cot by his side and placed the baby onto Beth's chest. The infant began to scream – a scream so loud that Beth's head throbbed with anxiety. She looked at Jacko for help. "He's hungry, sweetheart. We've been waiting for you to wake. The midwife thought you might like to nurse him."

He was talking as though she were on the set of the Little House of the Prairie: all rocking chairs, patchwork quilts and honey breast milk. She sat up slowly. "I'll get you one of those V-shaped cushions," said Jacko, rising.

She waited for him to leave before surveying the baby in her arms. He hadn't stopped screaming yet. His hands and feet were grey-blue; his nose was covered in tiny white spots; his pointy tongue was curled in anger and his raggedy nails were clawing at her for milk. "Welcome to our world," she murmured, untucking her nursing top.

Jacko returned with the cushion, helped settle Beth and then sat back down, looking very pleased with himself. "Fancy some toast when you're done?" he said.

PART ONE

CHAPTER ONE

Doodoo doo ah. Klaris couldn't sing, which was why she didn't bother with lyrics. If you *la la'd* and *doo be dooe'd* no one thought you were taking it seriously. But she was. Singing to Fleetwood Mac was one of her secret passions, with the sun flashing through the trees above the sky roof and the beat encouraging her to drive slightly faster than was lawful.

It was days like this, she thought, glancing in the rear view mirror at the sun lighting her hair, that you could forget that anything bad had ever happened to you.

It always surprised her that the mums didn't feel the same way in warm weather, that their problems didn't melt. Rather, the heat seemed to compound their misery in the same way that heat waves provoked riots. The mum at Klaris's last booking was red-faced, crying, sweating. *Look at the state of me,* the mum had said, running her hands through her unwashed hair, staring at her baby in horror

9

when it began to cry for milk.

Everyone was tetchy since the heat wave had begun. Two miles down the road, Klaris had just witnessed one of the worst episodes of road rage imaginable: a bare-chested man grabbed a pensioner by the throat for pulling out in front of him without indicating. It all happened so quickly, causing the traffic to halt. Necks strained to see whether a truck driver that jumped down from his tankard and was puffing up the hill shouting *stop stop!* would get there in time to prevent manslaughter.

He did. No manslaughter. Just a lot of people scowling at being detained in thirty-eight point two degrees heat. Thirty-eight point two! It was the highest temperature ever recorded in Britain.

There were few people outside today in the midday sun. It was like living somewhere like Texas, Klaris supposed. People were driving two minutes to the local Co-Op to queue for ice pops. Cars were parked skew-whiff around swimming pools and primary schools; no one was going to park properly because no one was going to be walking along to issue them a ticket. Wilting posters on telegraph poles reminded the public to use showers rather than baths and to refrain from running hosepipes unless entirely necessary.

What was entirely necessary, Klaris wondered? In her experience, people always found a way of justifying what was entirely necessary.

She pulled into Bloomsdale Rise, a tree-lined cul de sac with an exquisite view of Bath, and drove to the turning circle without glancing at her next booking's house lest she should be spotted. She parked opposite a gap in the trees and with quarter of an hour to spare unpacked a flask of strawberries and cream flavoured tea. With the air-conditioning running, she searched the radio for something cool and pacifying, settling upon a violin rendition of *Whistle down the Wind.*

She had lived in Bath for four years and still couldn't get over how pretty it was. The city lay in a valley and on a hot day like today the spires of the pale local stone wobbled in the heat haze. The scene reminded Klaris of a fairytale castle in Germany that she once visited, so long ago now that it felt as though it were someone else's memory.

The sudden sound of an ambulance speeding down the hill to the city disrupted Klaris's reverie. The noise always stirred her, made her heart beat faster – the idea that someone somewhere was in terrible danger. Her job as health visitor was a bit like being a rescue worker, she thought. Except that she dealt with people not for a few traumatic hours but upon a weekly basis, sometimes over a matter of years. Although it wasn't all car crashes and arson attacks. It was worse.

The new mothers that she dealt with had enough depression collectively that it was a wonder they didn't affect pollution levels. Yet they didn't affect anything at all. They were irrelevant: former lawyers, doctors, barmaids, students, walking the streets exhausted, unnoticed. United, they could have formed a trade union, but motherhood was a solitary, powerless occupation.

Which was why, she thought, packing her flask away and starting the car, the mums were always so pleased to see her. Here she was, the one person in the world aside from the Tesco deliveryman who knew how bad things had become.

She pulled up outside number eight and gazed at the house, which announced its birthday, 1932, on a stone above the door. The property was well maintained; bay trees stood either side of the doorsteps in the style of a boutique hotel and Laura Ashley curtains continued the theme of good taste. From the outside, it would be impossible to guess what was going on indoors.

Klaris hoisted her briefcase off the back seat of the car and with a practised movement applied lip gloss whilst ringing the doorbell. She watched as an all-white ghost-like figure approached through the frosted glass panel. Beth often wore white. Klaris didn't care for the colour herself, being too pale to carry it off with any aplomb, but on Beth it looked fresh and neat.

As the door opened, Klaris caught her breath rather too sharply. Beth looked as though she hadn't slept since their last meeting yesterday.

"Hello," Klaris said, smiling quickly and stepping into the hallway. "I would have come sooner, only my last booking over ran. Everything all right?"

"Yes…sort of…" Beth said. "Thanks for coming again. I don't know what I'd do without you. Excuse the mess."

Mess? Everything appeared wonderfully, uncannily, in order. And very quiet. Did three children not live here after all?

Klaris followed Beth into the living room, watching as she reached a tanned arm up to her hair to fix it into an alluring up-do without grips or bands. Even on the brink of despair, Beth still managed to look…Klaris tried to think of the right word but couldn't. No doubt it would be French or Italian. Perhaps a phrase. *Je ne sais quoi.*

In comparison, Klaris's new dress from the BHS sale that she had worn especially to see Beth suddenly seemed dowdy. She turned her mind to business and opened her faithful briefcase that had served her for thirty-two years this winter. She knew every crinkle in its leather, every crumb-lined nook within.

"So how is he today?" said Klaris.

"Judge for yourself," Beth said, gesturing towards the corner of the room.

"Oh?" Klaris looked where Beth was pointing. A head of blond curls was sticking out above the coffee table. Klaris knelt down, her knees clicking. "Hello, my angel," she said. "Want to play catch?" She rolled a ball so that it ventured close to Brett. A little hand reached out and the ball disappeared.

Klaris returned to the sofa. Something was different today – about the house, about Beth, about the boy. "Do you have Brett's record book?" she asked, as casually as possible.

"Of course," said Beth, jumping up to leave the room.

Quickly, Klaris approached the coffee table again. There on the left side of the toddler's forehead was a fresh red mark. She was noting this down in her file when Beth returned and handed her the record book. "So how did he hurt himself this time?" said Klaris, still writing.

Beth perched on the arm of the sofa, holding herself in her arms. "He went off on one again. He keeps doing it – having these terrible episodes where he bangs his head so violently I think he's going to…."

Klaris flicked through Brett's book, noting the head bumps that had been recorded.

"You know, Beth, sometimes toddler tantrums are a manifestation of something else."

"Hey?" said Beth, her arms falling limply from their hug around herself. "What do you mean?"

"Rarghhh." Their attention was diverted by Brett's appearance as he crawled out of his den clutching the ball in his mouth, roaring like a lion. "Rarghhhh. Rarghhh." He made towards Klaris's toes baring his teeth, so she tried to interest him in a plastic piano by tinkling the keys. Brett snatched the piano from her, thumping at the keyboard with his fat fingers.

"What I'm saying…" said Klaris, watching Brett out of the corner of her eye, "is that I want you to think about whether there's anything you or your husband are doing that might be supporting Brett's behaviour."

Beth nodded solemnly, miserably. "I hadn't thought of that." She undid her hair, twirled it round her fingers and fixed it up again.

"Don't despair," said Klaris, smiling sympathetically.

"It'll get better, I promise. Brett's going through his terrible two's, that's all."

"Do you…?" Beth began, pausing to flick away a stray tear. "Do you think this is my fault?"

"Gosh, no!" Klaris said, slipping the file back into her briefcase and smoothing out her dress.

"But what if it's all me?" said Beth, starting to cry. Klaris hated to see her mums cry.

"Chat to your husband. Think about what could be triggering Brett's episodes. He mustn't keep banging his head like this." She snapped her briefcase shut and stood up. "I'm really sorry, but I have to go. Call me any time. You know where I am." She turned to Brett. "You be a good boy now," she said, running her hand across his curls. He flicked her hand away and pouted.

As Klaris started down the steps into the blast of the afternoon heat, which she had forgotten in the coolness of the house, she turned to Beth who was leaning against the wall as cool as a lizard in the sun. It occurred to Klaris that Beth with her dark hair and eyes was a natural in this weather; barely blinking as the heat crackled on the tarmac. Her skin was already a deep tan, probably from having sunbathed once or twice – such was the Mediterranean nature of her skin. Klaris would have liked to enquire about her origins, but it didn't seem the sort of thing that you could ask in passing without seeming to be snooping.

"Remember, Beth: children are like adults. They don't do anything without a reason."

"It's just finding the reason, right?" said Beth, smiling. "You'd think I'd already know that having raised two boys. But this feels…" She shrugged, her smile fading. "…Different."

"Hang on in there," said Klaris.

Doowah yey la la la hey…As Klaris drove to her next appointment, she stopped at a set of traffic lights and watched a teenage mum who was trying to push a pram across the road whilst smoking and using a mobile phone. Beyond the teenager was a poster advertising *Panic Station*, a horror film about some kind of demonic train, by the looks of it.

Yes, that was what was different about Beth, she thought, as the traffic lights changed: with each passing day, she was looking more frightened.

"Did you ask to get down?"

Daniel was thirteen. None of his friends asked their parents if they could get down from the table. There wasn't a table to get down from. He knew because he ate meals at theirs on the sofa in front of the television. He wouldn't have told his mum this though because she would have gone nuts.

He bent double over the safety gate at the foot of the stairs to grab his rucksack and bike lock. He and Erland stored their school gear there, it being the only place that Brett couldn't reach.

"I said, did you ask to get down?"

Danny hesitated in the hallway. The tone of his mum's voice made him step back into the dining room. It was another side of himself that he was working on: the feeling sorry for everyone thing. He would never be a professional football player if he worried about every beetle that his boots mushed on the pitch.

"Mum?" He swung his rucksack onto the floor and approached, stooping to his mother's height at the table. She was crying, holding her head. He could see the veins sticking out in her bony hands. It was hot and the ceiling fan rocked and whirled, fluttering the edges of the tablecloth.

"I can't do this anymore," she said.

"Do what?" Danny said. He glanced at Erland in annoyance. His brother was reading his chess magazine silently at the table as though nothing was happening. Brett was sat by the window in his highchair wearing a bib with a goggle-eyed ant on it that said *You're bugging me*. He had a fist of mash in one hand and was using an unbreakable fish finger in his other hand to squash peas. His plate had long since dived under the table, where it lay with an upturned yogurt.

Danny shoved Erland's arm as he passed him, tumbling the magazine to the floor. "Oi!" said Erland.

"Well, get some life into you," said Danny. "Sitting there like that."

"Eh?" said Erland, frowning. Danny nodded in the direction of their mother, who was staring at the tablecloth, slotting her fingers in and out of the holes in the lace.

Danny grabbed a handful of wet wipes and scooped up the yogurt from the floorboards, feeling anger bubble close to what felt like the surface of his mouth. He was so close to yelling at his mum – at Brett, at Erland, at Jacko, at anyone who would listen – that it wasn't his frigging job to clean up after the baby all the time.

He was going out. "Clean up the rest will you, Erland?" he said, picking up his rucksack again.

"Whatever," Erland replied.

Outside in the hallway, Danny was surprised to realise that he was shaking and that as he caught a glimpse of the photograph that he couldn't ever bring himself to look at, he felt not that far away from crying.

The photograph that hung on the wall by the front door had been taken five years ago in Menorca. His mum was in the middle and he was to her left wearing an England football shirt because the World Cup was on, and Erland was to her right wearing a Brazil shirt – typical. A waiter had taken the photograph. There had been a parrot squawking in the background – a wolf-whistling parrot. They couldn't stop laughing about it and you could see in the picture that not only were they laughing hard but that they'd had a lot of sun that day: white eyes, white teeth as bright as the sun on seashells.

"I'm sorry, Danny," said his mum, close behind him. She put her arms around his waist. He could tell that she had stopped crying. Her breath was shuddery and short.

"Why isn't he ever here to help you, Mum?" he said, turning to face her and biting hard onto his bottom lip in case tears should trick him into making an appearance. At this age, emotions could do that: trick you into feeling things you didn't want to feel. He was looking forward to the day when he wouldn't have to be caught out any more. The day when he became a man, like…He couldn't think of anyone off hand that he wanted to be like.

"Because he has to work hard, sweetheart," said his mum, reaching up to smooth the front of his hair. "There's a recession on." This past year, Danny had overtaken his mother in height. It was about this time that he had started taking more care of her than her of him. He wondered whether the nurse and the patient dynamic was simply a matter of height.

Lee had told him about the patient and nurse dynamic. It was in a magazine – that every relationship was made up of a patient and a nurse looking after the patient. Lee taught Danny a lot of stuff like that – things that weren't that useful until you started to wonder about your home life and then it all became a lot clearer.

Danny pulled his bike out from underneath the stairs. He smoothed the saddle and patted it. His bike was essential to him; without it, he would be grounded. It wasn't the bike that he had wanted. He had been saving up for a Silverfox Demon with dual suspension so that he could go off-road. Not that he would do much cross-country because he would be too worried about damaging his legs before a game. But still, it was about having a choice. And now he didn't have a choice but he did have a Muddyfox Vice front suspension bike which was over a hundred pounds more expensive than the Silverfox and he had one hundred and sixty two pounds going spare in his post office savings account.

Jacko had bought him the Muddyfox as a surprise for Christmas. It was intended to buy his approval and it had worked. As far as Jacko knew.

"Are you going to Lee's again?" his mum said, with panic in her eyes. The panic was there now whenever Danny left the house, but he couldn't let it be the reason why he never went out. Erland was there, for what it was worth. "Is he your best friend now?"

"Yes," said Danny, lowering his eyes. "We have a laugh."

"You should invite him back here some time. I know things are a little…" She trailed off. "Anyway, have a good time. When do you think you'll be back?" He shrugged and pulled open the front door. "Well, I'll see you when I see you," she said, trying to smile. She turned.

"Jesus, Mum. You make it impossible for me to go out!" He grabbed for her arm, but she wouldn't turn round. She flapped him away and waved goodbye.

Danny bumped his bike down the front door steps, the strap of his rucksack hooked onto his wrist. He wore a helmet to keep his mum happy, but always took it off when he got round the corner. Today she hadn't even noticed that he wasn't wearing it.

Just as he was about to pedal off, he looked back over his shoulder at his mum. "Why don't you call Jacko and ask him to come home on time?" he said. "It's his son."

Right on cue, Brett began to scream angrily from the dining room, his voice sounding as clear as though he were right next to them. "Mama! Mama! *Mama!*"

"Call him," Danny yelled as she closed the door.

He heard a noise to his left – a foot crunching on gravel. "What are *you* looking at?" he said to Ugly Ursula, their annoying neighbour. Ursula looked stunned. Good. She was old – thirty-something – but not old enough to retire, yet she had given up work for some strange reason. Ever since, she was gaping at them all the time – her mouth hanging open, catching flies.

It *was* a bit rude, he thought, cycling away. He didn't normally have the balls to talk like that to neighbours. But the heat was making him crazy.

Beth closed the door and stood with her back to it, watching her chest move up and down. Her heart pounded whenever she was left alone with Brett now. Although she wasn't alone. She had Erland.

"Thank you, my love," she said, surveying the dining room which was now splodge free. Brett had been installed in front of CBeebies in the lounge. She hadn't been in but she could hear the awful music. She motioned for Erland to hug her. He stepped forward obligingly.

She held her son and gazed out the window at Brett's plastic windmill that she bought last week to prevent a supermarket tantrum. She had stuck it into the lawn – grinding it like a maniac into the hard earth – so that he could watch it from his highchair. But since having bought it, the windmill was getting so little action it was going to seize up. Brett seemed to sense this as some kind of failure and now a glimpse of the redundant windmill evoked rage in him. She would have to remember to remove it.

"What's wrong with Brett?" said Erland, standing so still in her arms that he might be asleep.

"I don't know," she said. "He gets really angry. It's probably just a phase."

"Is it just a phase with Jacko too?" he said.

She held him away from her with arms outstretched so that she could examine his face. "Now why would you say that?"

Erland shrugged. "He gets really angry too."

"With you?" she said, alarmed.

"No. With *you*. Don't you even notice it, Mum?"

She held him close. "No, I suppose not," she said. Then a thought occurred to her and she held Erland with her arms outstretched again. "Am I a bad mum?"

Erland looked up at her gravely, indicating that he was going to tell the truth. "You couldn't be bad. Ever."

"But that's not answering my question. You're saying I couldn't be bad, as in evil. That's not the same as being a bad mum. So am I...?"

"You're not bad, evil. You're not a bad mum either."

Beth relaxed her shoulders and Erland sighed heavily. A stranger might perceive the sigh as frustration, but Beth knew that this was contentment. Erland used to sigh over his milk as a baby and roll his eyes and point his toes – his big toe standing stiffly aside from his other digits. There wasn't much about him that she didn't know or understand. Although he spoke much less than Danny, she communicated so much more easily with him.

Erland was still, silent – a shadow of herself made in her image. She could see into his heart – all its passages and secrets, its longings and pulsations. Stood against him now like this, she felt as one with him. A child and mother whose heart beat to the same rhythm.

And Danny? She knew all about his head. He spoke whatever was on his mind so lucidly and wore his emotions so brazenly that it was impossible for a mother not to become intimate with his thoughts. Not so much lately, now that things were difficult at home, now that he was a mini-adult with feelings of his own...She gave a barely distinguishable shudder. There were things about raising boys that she had no idea how to deal with.

She often worried that the boys were too different to be close. She tried to bring them together, told them almost every day that they only had each other, that family was so important and that they had to stay friends, but as fast as she drew them in so they resisted and pulled away. It was like trying to stop water from being sucked down a plughole.

Danny's frustration with Erland was much the same as his frustration with her. Danny was so vocal that as soon as he thought it wasn't being reciprocated he became cross. And she couldn't reciprocate entirely. She hadn't ever been about the words.

Like now. She would love to have called Jacko to ask him to come home on time, like Danny suggested, except that she had no idea how to say this to a man who was trying to earn enough money for them to survive a recession.

"Can you hear anything?" said Erland, looking up at her with his deep-set eyes – a memento of the father he had inherited them from. Beth had always thought of Erland, with his dewy eyes and veiny temples, as both vulnerable and wonderfully unfathomable – his eyes so soulful that they had to be set deep by way of defence, and his eyelashes luxuriously thick for the same purpose.

"I didn't hear anything," murmured Beth.

"Exactly," said Erland.

In that moment her heart felt as though it had shot up to the back of her throat, pounding, restricting her breath. "Oh no."

She raced to the dining room door. Down the hallway she ran, the silence now so immense that she couldn't believe that they hadn't heard it until now. She pushed open the lounge door with both hands and then stopped.

"Oh my God….Oh God!" she wailed, her hands to her face. Erland came to a halt beside her. They both stared at the scene.

Brett, in his elephant shorts and top, was stood in front of Jacko's £3,900 plasma television. In his hand was a permanent marker pen. His silence had been one of concentration. Concentrating on colouring in every last centimetre of grey screen.

"Look!" he said, with delight, turning to reveal that he

had also been sucking on the pen. He laughed. "Bla!"

"Black," Beth echoed. She lowered herself onto the sofa, hands placed on her lap demurely as though about to listen to a church choir. "Can you get a cloth, Erland?" she said, knowing as she said it that a cloth and all manners of detergents were not going to remove permanent marker from this television, or any other, although she suspected that really expensive televisions would be even more adverse to disfigurement.

How to tell Jacko? If she hadn't the words to ask him to come home on time, how would she tell him that his son had ruined his precious entertainment system – that his two-year-old son had been left alone long enough to render this possible?

And then her anger rose so rapidly that she was unable to suppress it. "Get out!" she said, grabbing Brett by the wrist and yanking him away from the television. He wouldn't let go of the pen. She prized his fingers open, determined to win.

"No! No! No!" Brett was screaming, his face wrinkled in anger, his teeth and lips eerily blackened by pen, beads of sweat glistening on his nose.

"Stop it!" she shouted. "Let go!" She secured the pen and threw it across the room. Then she swung Brett onto her hip and marched up the stairs, holding him lengthways to avoid his kicking legs and slapping hands. "You're going to your room! How dare you destroy Daddy's television? I've had enough of you, you horrible child!"

She opened his bedroom door, greeted by a waft of hot air and commanded all her willpower not to toss him across the threshold. Instead she dropped him into his cot.

"Yarghhh!" Brett screamed, grabbing the rails of the cot and shaking them. "Yarghhh!" As she reached down to remove a plastic coin from the mattress, he grabbed her arm and tried to bite it.

"Get off!" She held his head away from her, using the

handoff manoeuvre that she had seen on Jacko's rugby programmes. "Calm down!" she said, pointing at him, trying her best to sound calm herself.

She turned her back to him, causing his screams to crescendo. "Mama! Mama! *Mama!*" Standing on his musical chair to reach the window to open it, she set off the woman's voice singing *when you're up you're up, and when you're down you're down and when you're only halfway up...* And then she left, without the energy to slam the door behind her.

Bye bye! the musical chair called.

Downstairs, she stood in front of the television, holding her hair out between her fingers. "Mum." Erland touched her arm. "The cloth you asked for."

"Sod the cloth!" said Beth, grabbing the rag and throwing it at the television. It splattered against the ruined screen before falling to the carpet. "Did he get the pen from you?" she said, turning on Erland. She shook him by his shoulders. "Was that your pen?"

"I..." Erland blinked rapidly. "It was in my bag. He must have taken it..." He looked confused. "I must have left it in here instead of on the stairs like normal."

"How many times have I told you to keep things out of his reach, hey?" she shouted. "You know what he's like! And what the hell were you doing with that pen anyway?"

Erland swallowed hard. "I bought it this morning..."

"What for?" she shouted, shaking him again.

"So I..." Tears began to fall down Erland's face. He hung his head. "I wanted to colour in the scratches he made on the black squares of my chess board."

Beth couldn't reply. She turned away, overcome with guilt and remorse.

No matter where she looked in the room, her eye returned to the disfigured television. Somehow over time, Jacko and that television had become one. It represented his contribution to the household. With it had come all the paraphernalia of speakers, cords, entertainment units. It was an ugly mess, Beth believed, that had changed the dynamic of their quiet home beyond recognition, but to Jacko it was the thing he most loved to behold – the thing that he looked for at the start of each day and at the end of the night.

"What am I going to tell Jacko?" she said.

"That the sound still works?" replied Erland, shrugging.

All day long and the phone hadn't rung. That had to be some kind of a record. Jacko gave his watch a long hard stare, wishing the time to rush forward to six o'clock. Not that it really mattered. As managing director, he could leave whenever he wanted, except that Matt would say he wasn't putting the hours in any more. It was true: he wasn't, because no one was frigging calling.

Jacko stifled a yawn, spun round on his chair and went out to the corridor to crank up the air conditioning. Whilst fiddling with the dial, his phone rang. He darted to his desk, straightened his tie, reached out…and saw that it was Beth calling. His hand hovered and then dropped to his lap.

He watched as the machine digested the message. It wouldn't take long because Beth normally only uttered five words at most, in which she managed to communicate that she would like to know roughly what time he'd be back for dinner. How she had managed to be a lecturer – a successful one at that, by all accounts – was a mystery.

Surprisingly, it was several minutes until the red light flashed. He was tempted to listen to the message, but couldn't bear the guilt that he would feel by doing so.

When six o'clock finally limped into place, Jacko crossed the car park to his BMW Estate, enjoying the simple but significant buzz that he got from hearing his car unlocking from a hundred yards away. He drove onto the Lower Bath Road and was relieved to leave the heavy traffic by taking the first left, following the road up the hill for a few minutes before pulling up outside a Victorian terrace house. He unwound his window, put his shades on and sat gazing in his rear view mirror, his shoulders slightly raised to put him out of view of pedestrians. You could never be careful enough.

Bang on time, give or take half a minute or so, the figure came into view. The bone-tight high-waisted skirt; the bare legs waxed to the smoothness of a Madame Taussaud's model; the eye-wateringly high heels; the crisp shirt with one button too much undone. And the hair: long, tousled, dark underneath and blond on top. It was the blatant advertising of hair dye that most caught the eye – the male eye: the fact that she wasn't going to pretend to be a natural blonde. This kind of wantonness on display was what many men dreamt of.

As the splendid young woman, Natasha, drew closer, she still looked hot. A white van tooted in testimony to this, its driver shouting something indeterminable. She was too arrogant to respond. No bashful eye fluttering or blushing. She kept her eye ahead, but betrayed the fact that she was slightly ruffled by reaching into her handbag for her menthol cigarettes. This was the kind of young woman who fooled herself into believing that menthol cigarettes were more nourishing than regular ones, and that using sun beds weren't harmful because they made her look healthier.

"Hi," she said, leaning into his car window, her sunglasses propped on her head.

This was when the fantasy almost ended. It was hard to believe that the distant goddess was the same creature up close. Her eyes were too far apart, her nose was badly hooked, her pores were large. She looked like a rather odd doll. Which was perhaps why she had to sell as much as she could from far off. By the time she was close enough for her target to smell her perfume and to spy a peep of her pink bra against her brown cleavage, he was hooked.

"You coming in?" she said, narrowing her eyes whilst

dragging on the cigarette and blowing the smoke in a neat exhalation over her shoulder.

"Can I?" he said, trying not to sound as desperate as he was.

She shrugged and nodded, extinguishing her cigarette on the pavement with a grind of her heel. "I chilled a bottle of white in case," she said.

Minutes later he was stood inside her apartment, trying to restrain himself. He glanced to the leg of his suit trousers and could see that it was obvious he was aroused. He sat down, trying to drink his wine without gulping. As he felt the first delicious sips entering his system, his thoughts raced ahead unchecked. He could drink as much as he wanted; he could ditch his car here and walk home; he could stay and make love to her all night.

"Gillian from work may be moving in," she said, joining him on the sofa with her legs tucked underneath her.

"Huh?" he said, trying not to sound too alarmed. "Then how will –?"

"…We have sex?" she said.

"That's not what I meant. This is more than sex, you know that."

"Right," she said, her voice heavy with sarcasm. She jumped up to grab her cigarettes. "I need the cash," she said.

"But Gillian will tell everyone at work."

"Yes," she said, nodding slowly.

He put his drink onto the coffee table, joined her at the window where she was leaning out to smoke and placed his hands lightly on her waist. "Please don't do this," he said, kissing the back of her neck. "I'll give you the money."

"Won't that make me some kind of a whore?" she said.

"No," he replied. "It makes me…in love."

As he said it, he regretted it and wished that he could grab the words back but it was too late. Her lit cigarette had dropped two storeys; she was kissing him, pulling at the belt of his trousers.

They made love in her bedroom, his limbs weighted with guilt. She didn't seem to notice. Gillian wasn't going to move in, she murmured. Their secret would be safe at work and their liaisons could continue for as long as he desired. Saying 'love' had bought him another couple of months. What would come next – saying that he would leave his wife and marry Natasha?

He lay on his back, his hands folded behind his head, gazing at the ceiling. "You're so yummy," she said, kissing his chest. "Did you work out today? Even in this heat?"

"I work out every day, work load permitting."

"That's what I call commitment," she said, tracing a finger along the contour of his biceps up to his shoulders. "God knows why your wife won't screw you, but it's fine by me."

"It's complicated," he said, sitting up abruptly and going through to the lounge for his clothes.

"You're going?" she said, her expression stony. She had great emotional control. It was what most attracted him to her. "Please don't go. I'm sorry."

She was topless, wearing only her knickers. Reaching up, she kissed his cheek softly. He felt her breasts touch his chest and suddenly he was kissing her lips, kissing around the back of her neck – where her hair smelt of perfume and was damp from the effort of making love in a heat wave. It was no good. He wasn't going anywhere tonight.

And then just as he pulled her tiny naked waist down on top of him, he suddenly remembered Beth's answer phone message and wondered whether he should have listened to it.

Danny always left his Muddyfox in Lee's garage. He would ring his bell in the driveway and Mrs Paris would remote control the garage door open by leaning out the window, normally with smudges of flour on her face and wearing a naff apron that said *License to Grill*, and then she would give him a wave and tell him to take his bike on in.

Lee would come to the door, her hair frizzy and loose around her face. She let her hair down at home but wore it slicked into a ponytail at school, so that no one could have guessed how big it was. It was like his mum's massive blusher brush that somehow retracted into a small metal tube when she put it away. Women's make up was one mystery that Danny didn't intend solving. Still, he liked seeing pretty things on girls – liked to scoop Lee's hair in handfuls and smell her coconut shampoo.

Lee was the prettiest girl in the world, he thought, as she pulled open the door, smiling at him to come on inside the house. She was wearing violet leggings and a Minnie Mouse T-shirt. He knew that the colour was violet because she had told him. Before Lee, he would have said it was purple.

"Hello, Daniel," said Mrs Paris. She was ironing school uniforms. "How's your mum?" Mrs Paris had never met his mum but still she asked, as though it were some housewife code of honour. His mum never asked about Mrs Paris in return. His mum didn't know about the code. It was probably because Mrs Paris didn't work. Although his mum didn't work either at the moment, but she wasn't like Mrs Paris. So what was different? Mrs P was always baking vanilla sponges, cheesy scones, shortbread. It was because Lee's Dad was American, Lee said. American men liked women to be women, you know? Maybe that was it. His mum wasn't a woman that was a woman.

Danny didn't always understand everything that Lee told him. She liked to talk a lot and some of it was very complex. She had deep discussions with her mum about relationships and television dramas. And she read a lot of magazines.

Mrs Paris was staring at him, iron raised. He realised that she was waiting for his reply about his mum. "Uh…" He paused, wondering how to answer the question honestly. "Yeah."

Mrs Paris seemed satisfied. "There's some chilled lemonade in the fridge," she called to Lee, who was already half way up the stairs. "And some cookies?"

"Thanks. Maybe later," replied Lee, a second before slamming her bedroom door shut. "So...," she said, grinning at Danny and pulling him by his T-shirt towards her. "You gonna kiss me or just stand there?"

"Actually," Danny said, pulling away, "I'd like to sit down. I'm not feeling great."

"Oh." Lee sat down cross-legged on her bed with a bounce and tapped the space next to her. "What's up?"

Despite saying that he wanted to sit down, Danny realised that what he wanted was to not be too close to anyone, not even Lee. He had wanted to see her – he always wanted to see her so badly – but now he was here he felt as though it wasn't real life being here, as though this was somehow time suspended and that real time was going on back home.

She reached for his hand, but he moved over to the window. Lee's bedroom looked out over a tree that they often climbed. He looked at the thick branch they sometimes sat on when they were pretending to read books but were really just hanging out, carving initials into the bark with their locker keys.

He suddenly felt sick that his initials were up there twelve foot in the sky on the Parises tree; that downstairs Mrs Paris was ironing and asking how his mum was; that his mum didn't even know who the hell Mrs Paris was, or about the tree, or the fact that Lee wasn't his best male friend but his girlfriend.

"Is this about your mum again?" Lee said, talking with her lips pressed against the back of his neck. She was tall – not much shorter than him. Apparently, her dad was six foot four. He was an ex-semi-professional basketball player from Kansas. Danny didn't know anything about Kansas, although his mum had told him that a giant predatory shark fossil was unearthed there recently. Somehow he didn't think that this meant a lot to Mr P, who sold the plastic chairs that people sat on in sports stadiums.

He turned to face Lee, reaching for her hands to stop them from touching his chest. He could hear the six o'clock news theme tune on Mrs Paris's television. Right now, Erland would be logging on to play cyber-chess with his internet geek friend from Aberdeen. His mum would be... Early evening was Brett's worst time.

"Why don't you just tell her about us?" she said.

Everything was so simple for Lee. Her parents loved each other – so far as he knew. Her dad lived at home and went out to work. Her mum was at home whenever Lee or her little brother needed her. And Lee was super pretty, meaning that at school she was God.

He rubbed his face, which felt hot and grimy from his cycle ride. "You wouldn't understand," he said. The thing was she probably would, given the amount of soaps that she watched on television. But more of a worry was the fact that she might not like him any more.

"Hey!" she said, reaching up to touch his chin, looking into his eyes. "This is me," she said. "*Me.*"

From somewhere out in the street, there was the sound of breaking glass. It was probably a kid kicking a bottle. And yet Danny felt his heart begin to pump and the hairs stand up on his arms. "I've gotta go," he said, grabbing his rucksack and running from the room.

"Danny?" Lee called after him. "What's going on?"

He ran in jerky strides down the stairs. "Can you do the garage for me, Mrs Paris?" he said.

"Why, yes..." Mrs Paris said, uncertainly. "Everything okay?" She looked from Danny to Lee. Lee shrugged.

"Please, just open the doors for me," said Danny. Outside, he grabbed his Muddyfox and fell off in his haste to mount it.

"Danny!" Lee yelled. Cycling away, he glanced back over his shoulder to see his rucksack stood on the pavement where he had left it.

"Bring it tomorrow!" he shouted, before turning the corner out of sight.

He had never pedalled so fast. The heat clung to him, making his eyes water, his ears burn. There was no breeze. Just a thick hot air. And a sick feeling from deep, dark in his stomach telling him that going to Lee's this afternoon was the worst thing that he could have done.

Just as the beeps of the six o'clock news sounded on the kitchen radio, Beth reached into the fridge for a bottle of Pinot Grigio and ransacked the cutlery drawer for her bottle opener. "Where the hell is it?" she said through gritted teeth, rattling the drawer demonically.

Moments later, she was sat on the bench in the garden, gazing at her lavender tubs which had recently flowered and were being courted heavily by a string of admiring bees. Like the bees and their nectar, she couldn't drink the wine fast enough. But she paced herself, feeling each sip cooling her stomach, numbing her bloodstream.

The relief that came with peace was so intense and so unexpected that she felt almost moved to tears, except that she had had enough of tears. This was quiet time. Erland was playing his friend online at chess. Brett was...

She watched a bee land neatly on a lavender flower. She didn't know what Brett was doing. She didn't care.

Or was she just saying that? She considered it for a moment. No, she was telling the truth.

Still she wondered what he could be doing. He was in his cot, where she had left him after the television disaster. He couldn't climb out yet. He wouldn't be asleep. He never slept without a huge amount of theatrically-delivered objections. This time of night was his worst time. Why the silence? Was he tantrummed out?

The screaming had gone on for a long time this afternoon. Screams that made her want to take every hair on her head and pull it out; that made her want to scratch her arms till they bled. Anything to distract her from him.

When did it get like this? When did it all get so ugly?

She cocked her head to one side to consider it. The answer came to her instantly: from the moment that Brett first screamed at her, from the moment he was born.

At that instant in the garden, she heard him begin to call for her. Quietly at first, like a nagging child tugging on her skirt – as mildly irritating as a fly buzzing around. She felt her stomach turn as though it had been prodded from slumber. Oh, God, no, she thought.

And then slowly escalating. "Mama! Mama! *Mama!*"

With each cry, so his anger built. With each cry, so she felt more desperate. She looked about her, eyes wide with panic and alarm.

What was he trying to do? Did he know that this was her first break today, that she had only wanted one moment of peace?

She threw her glass down onto the stones, the glass splintering, wine seeping into the dust. She tore through the kitchen and down the hallway, her hands clenched, her breathing tight. "Everything all right?" called Erland dreamily from beyond the lounge door, his voice indicating that he was a million miles away in Cyberland.

She didn't reply. She was heading up the stairs two at a time. Barging into his bedroom, she stood in front of the cot, waving her arms with crazed anger. "What do you want?" she screamed at him. *"Are you trying to drive me crazy? Hey?"*

She waited for him to be startled into silence, to submit. His face was wet from tears and dribble. His curly hair was a mass of ringlets, drenched in sweat. He looked exhausted, but he hadn't finished yet.

He pounded his fists on the side of the cot. "Out, out!"

he said, his eyes bulging, his hands pulling on the wooden bars. She thought for a moment that he might break the cot. Then how would she restrain him? Where could she put him? And where could she put her anger? There was nowhere for it to go. And it was so hot in the room. So hot!

What to do, now that frightening him made no difference? She paced up and down, beside herself with frustration.

And then she caught sight of something hitting the light in the evening sun's last bid for splendour. It was the gold letters that she had bought to go on Brett's wardrobe door when he was born. The letters that spelt L O V E.

She felt the tension drain out of her. Everything suddenly seemed stupid and pointless. She reached for her child, her arms open. "What are we doing?" she said. "Let's not fight. I'm your mama. I love you."

Saying *I love you* to him felt at once natural and deeply unnatural. Perhaps it had been a long time since she had said it to him. She couldn't be sure. Or maybe it was because she hadn't stopped a fight to show him affection before. Whatever it was, he stopped screaming. He was shuddering, shaking, slowly halting his rage like a car running out of petrol.

"Come here, sweetheart." She bent down to pick him up, happiness and relief flooding through her so rapidly that she didn't notice his teeth baring until they collided with her cheekbone.

The first thing Danny noticed when he got home was the television. "What the–?" He pulled off Erland's head set. What a surprise: Pink Floyd. Erland always listened to old junk whilst playing chess.

"Hey!" Erland shouted, spinning round in his swivel chair to snatch the headphones back.

"What happened to the TV?"

"Oh, that," said Erland, turning back to the laptop screen. "Mum and I had a chat about it. It's cool."

"Cool?" echoed Danny, incredulous. "Are you nuts?"

Erland shrugged, continuing to type. He was really fast at typing. Much faster than he was at talking.

"Where's Mum?" said Danny.

Erland didn't reply. Danny checked the dining room, which was as he had left it minus the yogurt spillages. He found his mum in the kitchen. She was sat in the corner near the back door, hugging her knees, her head bent.

"Mum?" He touched her shoulder. She looked up, not appearing to see him. She was looking beyond him, as though someone was stood there. Her left cheek was puffy and bloody.

"Did Brett do that to you?" he asked. She nodded. "Where is he?" She put her head down between her knees again.

He listened. There was no noise. He checked under the stairs between the prams and cosy covers where Brett liked to hide when avoiding bed time. He checked the nook behind the hallway dresser where it met the wall, and the table in the dining room corner that was covered with a cloth where his mum kept her old lecture notes.

No Brett.

As he climbed the stairs, he felt an odd sensation. He couldn't pinpoint it, having never felt it before. Afterwards he knew that it had been the sensation of realising that what you were about to find would change your life.

His baby brother was in his cot. The sun was streaming in, lighting his blonde hair. At first, he thought that Brett had fallen asleep, exhausted. His arms were thrust out behind him in the awkward way that young children slept. But he knew that Brett never slept that way. Besides, that wouldn't explain the stream of blood that was seeping across the mattress from his head.

CHAPTER TWO

Klaris had just taken her fisherman's pie ready meal out of the microwave and was trying to peel the cellophane back without scalding herself when the phone rang. She was thinking about holidays, wondering whether she should go somewhere like Cuba or Mexico this year. So she was taken aback when a faraway voice on the end of the line told her that Brett Best had been admitted to Bath Central and that her presence was required immediately.

"I'm sorry?" Klaris said, feeling her face flush.

She pictured the nurse propping the telephone under her chin in an attempt to get some paperwork completed whilst talking. That plan having failed, the nurse repeated herself, clearer now. "You're his health visitor, Klaris Shaw, right?"

"I'll be there," said Klaris. "Children's ward?"

"Yep." The line clicked dead.

Klaris dipped her fork into the corner of the pie, toying with the idea of eating it quickly but it was too hot.

She headed out, struck by the fact that this was the first time in weeks that she had heard the trees in her driveway swaying their branches. The leaves were so dry from the heat wave that they sounded like the swish of hula skirts. Seagulls were circling the air, crying. For a moment, she imagined that she had booked that holiday and was somewhere tropical by the sea, instead of setting off to the least romantic destination imaginable.

The children's ward was quiet during the handover between staff. Silence had descended, aside from the sound of a baby crying from down the corridor. Klaris always felt pricked by emotion on the ward. Pale-faced parents would pass by in search of the visitors' lounge, their eyes fixed ahead with anxiety. Whilst experiencing anguish, no one wanted to share it. Some people didn't even want to share it after the event.

As she passed the lounge, she thought she heard a voice she recognised. Hovering at the door, she saw Beth Trelawney huddled over a mug of coffee, her legs propped on the table in front of her, her sleeves pulled down over her hands. A television was on with the volume turned down. There was no one in the room with Beth. Who had she been talking to?

"Beth?"

She looked up in Klaris's direction. On her left cheek was a sore and puffy lesion. "My goodness. What happened?" Klaris sat down next to her. The sofa sagged, its stuffing hanging out as though it had absorbed so much misery in its short life that it had given up trying to hold itself together.

Beth shook her head. "I don't know. He...was unconscious. His head..." She trailed off, holding her hand to the mark on her cheek.

"Did Brett do that?" said Klaris. Beth nodded. "Is he staying in tonight for observation?" She nodded again.

Klaris knew what she was going to have to do. "I'll be back in a minute," she said, patting Beth's knee. "Do you want me to get you anything?" Beth shook her head. She seemed incapable of having a conversation.

Beth tugged on the sleeve of Klaris's winged blouse as she bent to pick up her briefcase. "Are they going to take him from me?" she whispered.

Klaris noticed a tiny emerald stud at the top of Beth's right ear. Against her dark hair and eyes, Klaris thought fleetingly that she looked gypsy-like. Once again, she realised that she knew nothing of Beth's origins – indeed of her more recent history prior to having Brett.

"Don't worry," Klaris said, trying to sound reassuring. "You take it easy. I won't be long."

As Klaris withdrew, so her smile recoiled. She headed for reception. "I need to make a phone call," she said, pointing to the ID badge on her chest.

"Ah," said a doctor, who was hovering by reception. "I'm the senior registrar. Can I have a word?"

They stepped into the corridor. "Health visitors don't normally come when a child is admitted," said the registrar, standing so close that Klaris could smell cafeteria coffee on the doctor's breath and see the pores on her cheeks. Klaris took a firm step backwards. "Why are you here?"

"Your staff called me," said Klaris, glancing down as a means of disguising her amusement. "It's standard procedure in these cases."

"What cases?" The registrar put her hands on her hips; she was clearly tired, despite it being the beginning of the night shift.

"Look," said Klaris. "I don't know what the problem is, but you're probably trying to do your job and I need to do mine so I really need to make this phone call." Klaris looked beyond the registrar to the reception. "Is there a room somewhere?"

"Follow me," said the registrar, waspishly.

Alone, Klaris put in a call to the social worker at the children's services duty desk.

For the second time that night Danny was pedalling as

fast as he could go, but this time he had to go even faster. He had sneaked out, leaving Erland on his own watching Jacko's portable television that they had taken from their mum's bedroom. When Erland got involved in a plot – it was *Miami Vice* – he wouldn't look up for anything, not even the sound of the letterbox rattling as the front door slammed shut.

Danny was supposed to be looking after Erland. His mum had made him promise to get his brother to bed before ten o'clock, that there would be no television with swearing or violence in (she didn't mention sex because she hated saying the word) and to ensure that they both cleaned their teeth and set alarms for the morning.

All this his mum had said whilst holding Brett in her arms and the taxi driver staring at her with a look that conveyed: *where you going? Why aren't you hurrying? The metre's on, you know.*

There had been no one to take them to hospital. This point alone had made Danny want to hit someone. They could have called an ambulance but Brett had come round by that point. At first Brett was woozy and then he started rubbing his eyes and their mum was trying to pull his hand away from playing with the cut on his forehead. Danny couldn't bring himself to look at that very much. It was black and congealed and his mum had stuck a bit of gauze to it that looked like it was going to have to be soaked off.

They had spent a fair amount of time running about the house, bumping into each other. They couldn't find the first aid box. They couldn't find the phone directory. They couldn't find the phone itself. His mum had decided to call a taxi and the guy showed up about three minutes after they dialled. Danny hadn't had time to say anything to his mum – to ask if she needed anything, how long she would be gone for.

As the cab pulled into their neighbour's drive to pull away, Danny saw the unmistakable form of Ursula at her window, prying. She would have seen Brett lying limp in his mother's arms, maybe even see the gash on his head. And yet she wouldn't have seen her car keys on her kitchen table, seen herself driving her neighbour to the hospital.

As Danny went to slam the front door shut, he had noticed the cab hovering in the road, his mother's head poking out the window. "Danny!" she was shouting. "Keep trying Jacko's number. Tell him to come to the Central!"

Agitated, Danny hadn't been able to settle to *Miami Vice*, even though it was about a drugs bust. Which was why he grabbed his bike and cycled off. He was thirteen. In three years time, he could marry. He had kept the peace for long enough. Now he was going to get Jacko and make him do the right thing by his mum, even if hell opened and swallowed him.

Just as his imagination conjured up flames and devils and scalding tar, so the opposite end of the universe opened up and heaven poured upon him. "Yehh!" he shouted in delight, holding his face up to the sky. "Rain!"

The weather seemed to have the same effect on everyone. Children's faces were at windows, men were stood in doorways holding out their hands palm up. Tropical rain after a four week heat wave.

As he cycled, he thought of Lee – of how much fun it would be to be out in this storm with her, of how much they had ahead of them to do together. He couldn't imagine ever being with anyone that didn't make him intensely happy. The Trelawney's – well, himself, his mum and Erland because he didn't know any others – needed to be happy. They didn't do misery very well.

Danny was going to be the one to reinstate harmony – the kind of harmony that had reigned three years ago before Jacko had entered their lives. Either Jacko was going to be a part of their happiness, or he had to leave.

By the time Danny was stood outside the office block

on Lower Bath Road gazing up at the fourth floor where Jacko worked, he didn't feel so brave. He wiped the drops off his face with the back of his hand and squinted against the rain. He felt his shoulders sink away with resignation, in the same way he had seen his mother's shoulders sink on so many occasions lately.

It was useless.

He was pushing his bike through the car park towards the ramp barrier, when a figure came out of the main office doors and strode towards the car park, keys extended before him. It was then that the obvious occurred to Danny, as he looked about for Jacko's car: it wasn't there.

He jumped on his bike and cycled over to the man who was now in his car and pulling away. "Excuse me," Danny called out. The man lowered his window. "Do you know Jacko Best?"

"I might do," the man replied. "And you are?"

"His... He's married to my mum."

"Ah," said the man, nodding slowly and looking Danny up and down as though everything now made sense.

"Do you know where he is?" asked Danny. The rain had stopped and now he felt self-consciously wet and pathetic.

"I'm afraid not."

"He's not at work?"

"No, but he could be tied up elsewhere in business-related matters." The man touched his tie and surveyed himself in his rear view mirror. "Nice talking to you," he said, before pulling away.

Danny stared at the registration plate: MAT88. That was Matt Mount, Jacko's partner. The player. Motor Mouth. All the other things Jacko said about him. It was impossible to know whether Jacko actually liked Matt or whether it was just banter. Danny hoped that he never grew up thinking that it was gay to say anything nice about anyone.

The smell of the rain on the grass was inspiring and the sound of tyres on the wet roads almost nostalgic having been withheld for so long, yet Danny had never felt so void of feeling. As he cycled forlornly up Lower Bath Road and took a left turn up Queen's Terrace, he felt as though he were cycling nowhere – his legs moving towards a goal that he was never going to reach.

Going up Queen's Terrace slowly was a challenge. It was such a steep hill that he was forced to change gear and step it up for fear of toppling off the bike. He was just standing up in order to give the hill some clout when he saw another registration plate that made his heart falter.

JACKO1

His bike fell sideways as his feet came to a halt. He tumbled onto his side and then got to his feet and stood, holding his elbow, gazing at the BMW estate. The car was glimmering with raindrops underneath the streetlight that was just starting to hold its own against the fading daylight. Black and vast, the car reminded Danny of a rubbery whale surfacing, drenched, enigmatic, impossible to pin down without the use of a harpoon.

Danny crossed the road leaving his bike on the pavement, its wheels still spinning, and surveyed the house that JACKO1 was parked outside: 89, Queen's Drive. With a quick glance around to check no one was approaching, he crouched down in front of the shrub that lined the garden wall, and peered upwards.

It was hard to see into the front room, which was set up much higher than the road. He dashed back across the road to retrieve his bike and then settled down for five minutes of surveillance – he timed it.

He was about to give up when the front window jerked open and out came an arm at the end of which was a cigarette. Danny strained to see inside the room, willing the inhabitants to flick on a light. *Please, please…*

And then he had the only bit of luck that he and his

family were going to experience that night. On came the light.

The arm and the cigarette belonged to a woman with long hair. He couldn't see much more than that. Except that she didn't have a lot on clothes-wise. He glanced around him again, in case he should be accused of being a peeping Tom.

Then he gasped and sat back onto the pavement with a bump. He could see Jacko. There was no mistaking his height and breadth, his dark fringe, his habit of throwing his head back to laugh. Whatever he was doing, he was having fun. Danny only knew about the throwing head thing from watching Jacko watch comedy on T.V. He never laughed like that with them.

He might have believed that Jacko was doing business, just like his partner said, if it weren't for the fact that he wasn't wearing a shirt or tie. And for the fact that he was a slime ball that Danny was going to punch as soon as he was big enough to reach his ugly nose.

He crossed the road and straddled the Muddyfox that Jacko had bought him, wondering how it was possible to go from feeling no emotions ten minutes earlier to now feeling so many that he felt unable to ride his bike.

As he took one more look at the room, he saw Jacko at the window looking back at him. Shocked, he felt his legs bolt to the pavement in fear. Next, the front door was opening. "Danny!" Jacko was shouting.

In that second, Danny knew that everything was Jacko's fault. At the thought of Brett lying in hospital, Danny picked up his bike and held it above his head. It was really heavy and his legs were buckling.

"Danny!" Jacko, now shirted, stopped on the opposite side of the road to let a car pass.

"Don't come near me!" Danny shouted. He took a deep breath, steadied his legs and then hurled the bike towards Jacko as far as he could, which wasn't very far. If he'd have thought about it, he would have known that this was a silly and dangerous thing to do. But as it was, there was a colossal crunch and the shrill sound of tyres swerving on tarmac. Danny's £300 Muddyfox Vice front suspension bike lay mangled.

"What the hell?" shouted a woman. Four girl Brownies were screaming in the back of her car, banging on the windows. The woman got out, leaving her car door open and stormed towards Danny.

"He's paying," said Danny, pointing at Jacko, wiping the sweat from his face and pulling his T-shirt straight. "He's gonna pay for everything."

The woman stared at Jacko, incensed.

"I'm sorry," said Jacko, defaulting to business mode and holding his hand up to the woman. "One moment, please."

He turned to Danny and spoke gently as though trying to comprehend the mind of a criminal. "What were you thinking?"

"Get stuffed," said Danny, plunging his hands in his pockets and setting up the hill on foot. Out of the corner of his eye, he saw that the woman from inside the house was hovering by her front gate. "Don't bother coming home again," he said over his shoulder.

"What the hell's going on?" said Jacko, hot-footing after him with bare feet, his shirt flapping open. He grabbed Danny's arm to halt him and pull him round. It was scary how strong the bloke was, Danny thought, imagining himself as one of those tiny men being flung about by dinosaurs in films.

But if he were scared, Danny wasn't going to show it. "Get off me," he said, pulling his arm free. "If you want to know what's going on then check your mobile. Mum's been going out of her mind, you moron."

"Why?" Jacko said, frowning, hands on hips, out of breath.

Danny paused, suddenly wanting to hit Jacko not on the

nose but right bang in the middle of his heart with an ice pick. "Because Brett banged his head and went unconscious. He's in hospital now, you idiot."

But it didn't feel as good as he imagined. Jacko sat down on the pavement, his mouth crooked with pain, with two angry women stood down the road waiting for him.

There was a song that Beth could remember from her childhood. She hadn't thought of it for over twenty years, but now it came to her and she began singing it softly, holding Brett's hand through the cot bars. She couldn't remember who had sung it to her so often that she had come to know the lyrics by heart. It seemed an odd choice of lullaby.

Her eyes were as blue as the holes in the clouds
Her voice was as gentle as a fairy child
I loved her so that my heart beat out loud
But I never could wed her 'cos her soul was wild

Brett didn't stir upon hearing the song. He was in a deep sleep wearing the *Beware: Monsters!* T-shirt that he had been admitted in. His arms were lying either side of his head on the pillow, his mouth was slightly open, his chest was shifting smoothly up and down.

Beth sighed and pushed a curl away from his eye. She realised, looking at his bulging nappy, that she hadn't changed him since before he had coloured in the television.

At the thought of Jacko's television, she winced. She hadn't managed to get hold of Jacko all evening. She had no idea what time it was now – ten o'clock at night? – or where he was. Had he discovered the television? Worse – that his son had been hospitalised?

Would it be worse, she thought? Worse for Jacko that his prized television had been ruined, or that his son whom he barely saw or seemed to have any regard for had been in an accident? It would be a close call.

Furtively – aware that staff had been giving her odd

glances since her arrival here, or was that her guilty conscience? – she dropped the side of the cot down, eased Brett's legs out from under the sheet and reached into her changing bag for a nappy and wipes. Evidently, Brett was a heavy sleeper, no matter where he was and what he had just been through. He drooled and dribbled a little as he flopped his arms outstretched, surrendering himself to his mother's work. She changed him with the expertise of a woman that had raised three children single-handedly, and then folded the sheet gently back over the sleeping boy.

She was glad that the last thing she had said to Brett was *I love you*. Not that he wasn't alive and that there would be no more words to ever say to him, but just that she suspected that when he next opened his eyes and looked at her, she might not feel the same way any more. And he might not either. Perhaps she might not even be allowed to look at him any more. He might be... She couldn't think it. It was the worst thing imaginable. No matter how hard things had become, no matter how many times of late she had wished that very thing, to have Brett removed from her would render her life as fruitless as a tree struck by lightning.

She had seen one once – a tree that had been struck by lightning. Again, it was somewhere in her childhood, but not at a moment that she could reach out with her fist to clutch and identify. She had been in a garden and the tree was stood over her – a wizened soulless being, barely able to move to defend itself against the bracing wind. The idea had frightened her rigid: of being that dead and yet appearing to still be living.

Beth watched the sun rise over the back of the children's ward, out across the car park, beyond the maternity wing and over to the hill's beyond. She longed to be over there, on the other side of her world, somewhere where she didn't know such misery.

As she watched the sun tentatively stroking pink light

across the sky as though frightened to encroach upon the night, she thought of Hemingway's *Fiesta: The Sun Also Rises* and of Brett Ashley for the first time since Brett's birth. And whereas Brett Ashley, a Tom boy and yet still wonderfully attractive, had at that time been a source of huge comfort, it surprised Beth to discover that now the same character was the cause of an intense depression that was gnawing at her internally.

The depression was born of huge remorse. Remorse that Brett Ashley was no longer a part of her life, that her life was so removed from academia. She didn't think about Brett Ashley any more because she had no cause to. She did not touch the piles of lecture material under the table in the dining room nor the books that filled an entire wall in the lounge. She had permitted Jacko to remove three shelves of books – 20th Century American literature no less – in order to make way for his DVDs and WiFi and Other Gadgets of what purpose she had absolutely no idea.

Her last day at Bath City University was the day that everything had begun to go wrong. Danny had fallen from a climbing frame at school and had broken his arm. She had to leave her very last lecture early that day to go see to him. His face had been pale, tear-washed, and even though she knew that he was in pain and needed her, she kept wishing that she could have finished that last lecture.

She could remember some of the examination questions from twenty years or so ago on her final year papers, yet she couldn't remember the details of the journey that led her to resign from her lecturing post before going on maternity leave. Jacko had convinced her – and convinced she definitely was – that her health would be at risk should she continue working whilst pregnant.

It was true: her blood pressure had been high whilst expecting Danny and Erland. They had both been premature and incubated, if only for a few weeks. Yet the consultant at Bath Central had said that there was every chance that it wouldn't happen again with this third pregnancy because there was a different father involved. Jacko had swelled with pride at this moment, she recalled – an odd detail from the blurry past suddenly stepping forward and introducing itself.

She surveyed the memory for a second: yes, he had looked proud and she had been startled. Most men would surely be displeased at not being the first man to father his wife's children. But for Jacko, she knew now, it was more important not to be first but to be the best. He would not be yielding any premature sickly boys. His seeds would be strong.

Was Professor Moss surprised when she resigned? Disappointed? Shocked?

She had worked under the professor for nine years, looking up to him as an academic father figure. He used to take great delight in relaying Beth's story to anyone who would listen, particularly to new faculty staff that walked with a swagger. This girl here, he would say, tapping Beth's shoulder, was a single mother of two boys under five when she acquired her first lecture post. She had funded herself to take GCSE's and A' levels at night school whilst working full time in a supermarket, leading her to achieve a first class honours degree in English Literature as a mature student at the University of the City of London. An outstanding scholar, she was awarded funding by the English Arts Council to study for a masters in 'Women in 20th Century American Literature'

Thinking of Professor Moss's little speech now, she barely recognised that he was alluding to her, this wisp of a woman sat in the children's ward. She was struck by the idea of phoning him and reached down towards her handbag for her mobile, before remembering that it was dawn, that she didn't work for Professor Moss any more and that Brett was going to wake any moment.

She sighed and looked out at the skyline again, noting

that the sun had inevitably won its battle and night had crept away, taking away with it all ideas of Brett Ashley and her fictional world of possibilities.

She wondered where Jacko was, why he would not have been compelled to visit them as soon as he had listened to the voice message. Was there a possibility that he hadn't heard it? No, she thought. Danny and Erland would have told him the moment he had returned home last night. Unless...her heart paused to emphasise the enormity of what she was suggesting... before beating on.

She moved over to Brett's side, lowered the cot side gently and reached forward to touch his arm. He felt hot; his cheeks were flushed so she pulled the sheet off him and tucked his curls behind his ear away from his face. He looked oddly angelic – far more angelic than she had seen him look before. Or perhaps she felt so sorry for what had passed that she was viewing him differently.

This was what she had been afraid of – that guilt and regret would cloud her eyes so bitterly that she would never be able to see her child clearly again.

And then Brett's eyes flicked opened so quickly and he fixed his gaze upon her so intently that she started in alarm.

"You're awake! How are you?" she said, obligingly, subserviently.

He didn't say anything. He just stared at her, his brow furrowed in confusion. This wasn't his usual room. This wasn't the usual smell. Where was he? Beth was about to explain when the door opened and a nurse entered.

"Morning," said Beth, trying to sound up-beat.

The nurse nodded and brisked past Beth to assess Brett. She took his blood pressure, changed the dressing on his wound and filled in the chart at the bottom of the cot bed.

She was about to go without having exchanged a word to Beth, when Beth said, "One moment," and followed the nurse to the door.

"Yes?" said the nurse, looking put out at having been

spoken to.

"I was wondering…can we go home this morning?"

The nurse gazed at her, her eyes narrowing. "It's not that simple, I'm afraid."

The sun rose through the back windows of Natasha's bedroom, lighting the blonde of her hair and the curve of her bare bottom splendidly. He felt the stirring of lust pulling against the hefty chain of responsibility. He had promised himself that he would be away by dawn, installed back home showered and shaved, ready to go to the hospital or face Beth's return – whichever occurred first.

He had wanted to be with his boy last night. He had thought of little else. Yet his moral code forbade him to even so much as glance at Beth whilst his body still smelt of Natasha. He could have returned last night, but that would have meant following in the wake of Beth's hypersensitive son, Danny, whose melodramatic scene last night Jacko was still smiting from.

He needed time to think about how Danny was going to play it. Most likely, the kid's first instinct would be to protect his mother, as he seemed to see that as his only role in life. His second instinct would be to enlighten his mother, but that instinct would no doubt only occur once Beth was back home and Brett was all sorted.

He would have to play it one step ahead of Danny. Not likely to be a problem with a child whose emotions were so transparent he may as well be wearing his organs externally.

As for Brett, he couldn't imagine how the boy had managed to sustain another head injury. He had been head banging a lot, and Beth was at her wit's end. On that score, he himself was terribly guilty.

He sat up abruptly, feeling suddenly claustrophobic in Natasha's bed.

He looked at her sleeping, her mouth squashed against the pillow, her eyes still laden with mascara. She never took her make-up off before bed; there were black and sparkly stains on her pillow-case. Beth on the other hand had always taken her make-up off, even on the first night they had slept together. What did that say, he wondered? Anything?

He missed Beth, he thought, scratching his stubbly chin miserably and easing himself to the edge of the bed away from Natasha. He looked out of the window at the hills opposite, over which the sun was rising. He had done the same thing from Beth's window on their first night of love-making, having been too thrilled to sleep. He had known then that he wanted to marry her.

He glanced over his shoulder at Natasha. Beth was far more beautiful than her; Natasha not being beautiful at all. Beth was real; Natasha was fake. Beth was high-minded, academic; Natasha was promiscuous, shallow, materialistic.

He missed being with Beth when he wasn't with her – the memory of her stinging him when he was in the oddest places: during a work out, in a meeting, sometimes whilst with Natasha. Yet he only thought of Natasha when she presented herself before him as an option that day. He knew that were she to be removed physically, so the mental image of her would melt away as simply as heating snow.

He sneaked over to the ashtray next to Natasha's sleeping head, her hair narrowly missing its contents, and plucked a cigarette from her pack. Opening the window, he leant out as far as possible to smoke so that the smell might not stir her.

He only smoked when distressed. Upon doing so now, the nicotine seized hold of his body, muddling up his blood flow, tripping his heart up, mashing his thoughts. He felt faint, but still he inhaled as punishment.

It was pathetic, he thought, how he acted out different roles for different audiences, as though his life were a series of television studios that he popped in and out of. For Natasha, he acted the part of sensitive man, deeply protective of his wife and child, a vain man with an impressive physique. At work, he was thoughtful, respected, quiet – cast opposite flamboyant Matt. At home, he was…

He knew what they thought. He knew because he had chosen the part of Alpha Male quite deliberately, from the moment he had stepped into their home and sensed the lack of testosterone. No television. No gadgets. Everything cream and floral. Vegetarian food. Books. Post-it reminders to record Woman's Hour on Radio Four.

The boys were suffocating, though they didn't know it and probably wouldn't have known it for another twenty years until they couldn't get a wife. And Beth, who probably didn't know it either, did at least recognise this on some level which was why she had brought him in, to man the place up a bit. The one condition – his one point of acquiescence – was for him to move in to *their* home. She didn't want the boys' lives disrupted too much.

She never actually said, but it was there in her eyes: she had wanted a man for her boys to look up to.

And now it was all there in her eyes again: the fact that she hadn't found such a man.

He reached forward to rub the television screen, unable to comprehend what had happened to it. Half expecting his forefinger to come away wet with black paint, he stared at his blank finger and at the screen in turn. He sniffed, pressing his nose closer. Permanent marker.

He pounded up the stairs three at a time and pushed down hard on the boys' door handle.

"What the hell has happened to my T.V?" he yelled, snapping the light on. Danny and Erland woke, squinting, until the dawn of reality straightened their backs to upright sitting positions. They squirmed, clutching sheets to their naked scrawny bodies, as Jacko towered over them, scowling. "You want to tell me what happened or shall I punch it out of you?"

He had never threatened them before and as he said the words, he knew that he had gone a step too far. As if acknowledging this, he stepped backwards in retreat, still maintaining his scowl by way of showing that they weren't off the hook.

Neither boy said anything, presumably due to lack of experience with physical threats from men twice their size.

And then Danny did something unexpected. He stood up wearing only a pair of Chelsea boxer shorts and stepped forward.

"Punch me then," Danny said. "Not Erland. He's only ten. But I'm thirteen." The boy's voice trembled as he spoke and he folded his arms to steady himself.

"Have you any idea how pathetic that sounds?" said Jacko, laughing.

"What, a thirteen-year-old boy telling a forty-something six foot man to punch him like he threatened?" said Danny, shrugging. "No, not really. In fact, it sounds…"

"Shut the hell up," said Jacko, prodding Danny so that he tumbled backwards onto the bed. "I'm not interested in fighting girls. Just tell me what happened to my T.V."

Both Danny and Erland were tight-lipped. "Fine!" Jacko said, slamming their bedroom door as hard as he could behind him. It was only then that Jacko recalled that Danny knew about him and Natasha.

He waited a minute and knocked lightly on the door before entering. He perched on the edge of Danny's bed with his hand up by way of apology. "Lads," he said. "I'm sorry. I'm worried about your mum and Brett. I shouldn't have taken it out on you."

He glanced at the boys in turn who were still sat on their beds exactly as he had left them. "You know I wouldn't ever lay a finger on either of you."

Was he saying this to reassure them or himself? There were many times he had imagined pushing Danny up against the wall or throwing Erland through the lounge window. "What are you guys up to today?"

"School," they said in unison.

"Of course. Well, let me know if you need anything." He ducked out the room in relief, knowing that his words would have rung as empty to the boys as they had to him.

After his shower, he lathered up for a shave but found that his hand was too shaky to do a smooth job. He did the best he could and was just rinsing off when a thought struck him that stopped him still. He gazed at his face in the mirror; at the clown-like image the white foam gave his lips.

What if Brett had done that to the television? And what if Beth had punished him for it?

His thoughts were interrupted by the sound of the telephone ringing. Clutching his towel, he sprinted across the landing to the bedroom, snatching up the telephone.

"Jacko?" It was Beth. "Where have you been?"

"I had a conference call last night," he replied. "I didn't pick up your message until this morning."

"Are the boys okay?"

"I just poked my head in on them now. They're fine. What's going on? How's Brett?"

"He's okay," she said, her voice sounding small. There was a long pause. "I'm not sure what's going to happen. It feels like…" Long pause again.

"Like what, honey?" He braced himself, looking out at the trees parallel with the window, nodding their heads in the wind encouragingly.

"Like they're going to take him from me," she said.

"No one's going to do that. You hear me?"

"You promise?" she said.

"Yes. You haven't done anything wrong. Have the courage of your convictions." He closed his eyes and pinched his nose.

"Can you come here now?" she said.

"Honey… I have to pop to work quickly."

"Work? How can you think about work? Have you any idea how serious this is? I can't do this alone. I don't know what's going to happen today, what they're going to—"

"There's a call that I have to take. It's a matter of keeping a roof over the boys' heads. Is anything more serious than that?"

She paused. "Just get here when you can," she said.

He stood dripping water onto the carpet, gazing out at the early morning light. He loved Brett and he loved Beth. He did want to help, to see Brett, to get Brett safely installed back at home. He just wasn't sure where the safest place was for him any more.

Beth's time was up. It seemed poetic and fitting for a former professor of literature that the moment occurred just as the sun began to set. She couldn't see it from their east facing room, but could just see a stray arm of pink reaching out to her round the corner as though throwing her a line of hope. She fancied climbing out onto the window ledge and lassoing the hope with the belt from her dress, thrusting it deep into her pocket and making off with it to the opposite hill that she had noted so enviously that morning – the hill on the other side of the world where everything was all right.

"Hello, Beth," said Rosie. Beth nodded a greeting, unsure that her vocal chords could navigate past the wall of emotion at the back of her throat. She tried to clear it away, but it remained. She would choke. She would die here on this floor, a lonely woman unable to breathe, dying of a broken heart and of the fact that no one would help her because of what she had done.

It could have been worse. Some women would have sooner ripped out their own heart than hand their child over to their mother-in-law. Yet this was the decision that Beth had reached at midday with children's services: that Brett would be placed in Rosie's care. It didn't get any worse than this, as far as family politics and humiliation went, but at the time the solution had appeared to Beth like a patch of light breaking through rain clouds.

She had been under immense stress, sat in a grey airless room with a couple of social workers and a police officer from the public protection unit. They were circumnavigating the situation, no one able to state out loud what they were all wondering: who was going to look after Brett?

At midday, the police officer fixed his eyes upon Beth and held them there as though boring into her brain for the answer.

They're going to take Brett, her mind was chanting. *They're going to take Brett. They're going to take Brett.*

"My mother-in-law can take Brett," she said. "Temporarily. To give me a break. To give everyone some time to work things out. To…" To stop you from taking my child into police protection, she thought, looking at the officer.

They liked the idea. They were all nodding.

Afterwards, Klaris had told Beth over lunch in the Friends of the Hospital café that the local authority could only place Brett with Rosie for six weeks. After which time, it would be unlawful. "After which time," Beth stated. "I will have him back."

"Of course," Klaris said, slicing her quiche. Beth didn't fancy anything except a coffee.

As Klaris ate, Beth had taken the opportunity to survey her, realising that she hadn't ever met Klaris without Brett present, without her household chaos around her. Seeing Klaris here now was like a child meeting a school teacher at the supermarket, or a work colleague spotting a co-worker whilst on holiday at the beach. Out of context, Klaris seemed shorter. More human. She had a morsel of quiche stuck to the side of her mouth. Her nails were painted coral pink, her bobbed hair was well-conditioned and neat, her make-up slightly too old for her age – what was she, late forties? Her figure was impressively slim – no bumps on her tummy or bottom; a juvenile-looking chest. She wasn't wearing a wedding ring. Did she live alone?

"Did you report me?" Beth had said suddenly. Klaris looked up, blushing, dabbing her mouth with her napkin.

"Yes. I'm sorry…"

"I don't mind," Beth found herself saying, aware that she could alienate her only friend if she didn't clarify matters. "You were just doing your job. Everyone has said that if it weren't for you, things could have ended up a lot worse."

Klaris smiled and bowed her head, modestly. "Well, I don't know about –"

"But who else reported me?" Beth interrupted. "The children's services received two calls about me yesterday."

"Oh?" said Klaris, returning her attention to her quiche. "I have no idea."

Rosie seemed to not want to see to the task in hand. Her pallor was ashen, her eyes were watery. She was hovering near the door, as though frightened to move in on Beth's territory. In the course of an afternoon, Rosie's home had been inspected, she'd been interviewed by children's services, and now faced the task of taking Brett home with her – a grandchild whom she barely knew.

In the silence of the hospital room with the sun setting behind them, everything seemed calm, simple, lucid. Beth wondered why it hadn't occurred to her before now to ask Rosie for help. Why she hadn't asked Rosie to have Brett for the night to break up the pattern that they had fallen in to, instead of waiting for disaster to occur before reaching out?

Rosie was kind, so far as Beth knew. Had Beth met her twenty years ago as a young bride, Beth might have latched onto her, hung around her kitchen learning tips about how to get cheese soufflé to rise and how to knead bread. Because Rosie was, Beth suspected, a domestic goddess. She would be expert at making jam, lemon meringue pie, caramel sauce, the perfect Victoria sandwich cake – all the tricky, slightly mysterious foods that belonged in women's kitchens because their mothers had handed their secrets down to them. All the foods that were firmly shut out to those women whose mothers had not.

Rosie was a meek person – seemingly incapable of bringing a hulk of a man like Jacko into the world via her tiny hips. Jacko's father had died when Jacko was only six years old. In Beth's limited experience of Jacko's relationship with his mother, the latter was all about the giving and the former all about the...

And there, she realised, lay the answer to her question. Jacko thought that women should serve men. His mother no doubt thought that upon some level also. There was no way that Beth was going to appear anything other than fully competent and independent in front of them. And if that meant not asking for their help, then so be it.

Did this mean, she thought, her mind racing well beyond its current capabilities, that she had lost Brett because of pride?

Not pride, she considered. Survival. Not asking for help was the only way that she had ever known to live life.

"It's only for a little while," Rosie said, edging towards Brett.

"I know," said Beth, folding her arms. "It will be nice for you to spend a day or so with him." She stated this despite the fact that the nurse was staring at her as though she were delusional. "You know absolutely nothing about me," she said, lowering her voice in hostility to the nurse. "You know nothing about what I am capable of, and what I am not capable of. I, however, know for a fact that my son is going to be back with me very soon. So I suggest that you stop gawping at me like that and take your silly fat ass somewhere else."

Had she just said that, she thought, staring at the nurse? Judging from Rosie and the nurse's blank demeanours nothing had been uttered out loud.

Rosie held her hand out to Brett. "Come on," Rosie said.

Brett stood by his cot, sucking his thumb – something that he didn't normally do. She realised that he had changed since his arrival in hospital: he was calm. He hadn't had a tantrum in almost twenty-four hours. Had that happened before?

"Go with Grandma," Beth said, tenderly, trying to keep her voice steady. "You're just going on holiday. I'll be with you soon."

She crouched down in front of Brett and folded her arms around him. For the first time in her recollection, he wrapped his arms back around her and she felt his little hands clinging to her. "I love you," she whispered into his ear.

"Mama," he said, blinking at her, before taking his grandma's outstretched hand and leaving with her.

Beth sat for a while looking at Brett's empty cot, at the wrinkled sheets where his warm body had lain, at the pillow where one of his blonde hairs remained, at the drop of blood that had marked the white linen where his wound had leaked. She reached forward for the hair and sat with it in her hand, pulling it between her fingers, seeing how much tension it could stand.

Not much. Within seconds it had snapped and wizened into a crazed spiral.

Everything had happened so quickly. Yet in a way it had been coming all along, creeping up in slow motion, moving towards her from the corner of the room – the corner of the room where pain had been crouched in the shadows on the day that Brett had been born.

She had struggled and had gone under, taking her boys with her and Brett too. And possibly her marriage. Where was Jacko now? Why wasn't he here? His absence had been noted by the social services and the police.

All day she had longed for him to be here with her, had been anxiously watching the door for his arrival. Throughout the interview she was certain that he was going to walk in and change the verdict from household violence to freakish accident. But then Rosie arrived, having picked up a few items of clothing for Brett: his dog-eared *Each Peach Pear Plum* book and Mr Rabbit, his favourite cuddly toy, and Beth realised that Jacko hadn't even wanted to be the one to assemble his son's belongings. Rosie had collected the Noddy suitcase from Danny.

Beth's stomach had twisted at the thought of Danny packing the case – of how well he would have considered every item of clothing, every toy, each of his baby brother's precious possessions. And how confused he would have been as to why the task was required of him. He wouldn't be able to concentrate on his homework. Erland would be sulking and silent. Danny wouldn't have anyone to talk to about how he felt. He would go to bed and lie in the dark, wanting to cry but not wanting Erland to hear him.

On gloomy nights before Jacko had moved in with them, Danny used to come into bed with her. He used to tell her about some magic spell that he was going to perform in order to put everything right. It would involve placing his football cards in a certain order, or surveying the Chelsea fixtures list for lucky formations such as a game that they couldn't lose or a game on his birthday.

She wondered if he still believed in lucky formations, or whether he had come to the same conclusion that she had: that there was no magic in this lonely world.

She wanted to be angry at Jacko, but despite everything she was still in love with him. She didn't love him outside of herself like she loved her boys – in a healthy, all-embracing way – the sort of unconditional love that people recognised immediately, smiling and nodding in appreciation. No, she was *in* love – enmeshed, strangled by all its confusion of wires and feelings.

She was angry at herself, not Jacko. She had allowed herself to be so fragile, so vulnerable again.

And she was angry at the universe. Because no matter how desperately she tried to alter the course of her life, things always conspired against her so that she ended up alone again.

Her anger gave way to tears. It didn't seem right being angry any more. Brett had mastered that emotion. It belonged to him and it was the reason that everything had gone so dreadfully wrong.

When her tears had all fallen, she found herself sat in the dark. Night had come and no one had been in to see her, to ask if she was all right getting home, if they could call anyone for her, if anyone would be at home waiting for her. Medical professionals were supposed to be impartial, but Beth could smell their judgement as soon as they looked at Brett's bandaged head and at her shaking hands.

She picked up her handbag, groping for it in the dark. Intuitively, she crossed over to the window. She stood looking in the direction of the hill opposite. A tiny prick of light flashed from the hill and then it was gone.

She took this as a sign – a sign from the universe that she was wrong, that she wasn't alone. She was going to do whatever it took to get Brett back, because somewhere out there was someone on her side. She just had to find out who it was.

CHAPTER THREE

"Is your mum going to prison then?"

"No," said Danny. He couldn't remember feeling angry towards Lee before, but now he wanted to push her off the wall so that she fell into the flower bed.

She squinted into the afternoon sunshine. "It's just that everyone at school…"

"How does everyone know about this?" Danny said, jumping down from the wall, his rucksack flopping against his back.

"I think Erland told someone in his tutor group."

"Erland?" Danny said, kicking the wall. He hated his shoes. They didn't fit any more and rubbed the back of his heel. "Why would *he* tell anyone?"

"Maybe he wanted to talk to someone about it."

Danny began to walk away. He had had enough. Today had been the last day of the school term and it was now the summer holidays. Last year, he had spent hours choosing what to wear in for mufti day. This year, he had to retrieve his best jeans from the dirty laundry basket and wear them creased and smelling of Erland's cross country kit.

"Danny. Wait!" Lee followed him, pulling on his arm.

"Don't run off. Come inside for a drink."

"I don't want to see your mum. She'll ask –"

"She's not there. She's taken my brother swimming."

"Oh." Danny stared at the pavement. He knew it wasn't Lee's fault, but he suddenly hated her perfect family. Her mum taking them swimming. Her dad coming home at six o'clock for steak and chips – the homemade kind of chips with the skins still on, not the one minute microwave kind that his mum had come to rely upon.

"It's not my fault," Lee said. Her voice wavered. She was sat on next door's wall, biting her bottom lip, crying. She was wearing a sparkly Barbie T-shirt – in irony, she said – and jeans and trainers. Her hair was slicked back like she always wore it for school. She had a bit of gloss on her mouth, or did have before she started chewing her lip.

He put his hands on her shoulders and hung his head low. "I know. I'm sorry. I'm being an ass. I…I really like you, Lee."

He wanted to be with Lee always, to show the world how to raise a family, how to all be together without hurting each other, how to be happy.

Lee didn't say anything. She just stood up so that her body was pressed against him and kissed him long and hard – something she had never done in view of the neighbours before.

Danny spent most of last night and his last day at school agonising over how and when to tell his mum about Jacko. During Religious Studies, he felt overcome with the pious desire to run home and confess to his mum there and then. Then during P.E. whilst being thrashed six games to love by the best tennis player in the school, he decided to stay quiet rather than suffer what Jacko would do to him as pay back.

Now on his way home from Lee's by foot because his mangled Muddyfox was presumably still lying outside 89, Queen's Drive, he realised that his mother would guess that something was up the moment he arrived home without his favourite mode of transport.

He could say it was stolen? Say he had been in a hit and run accident? Or he could say nothing because his mum wouldn't notice anything amiss.

Which was what happened.

She was sat on the sofa in the living room with her arm around Jacko – Jacko! – right by the blacked out television, as though there was nothing in the world that was peculiar about today or the fact that there were four people on the opposing sofa with files, paperwork, laptops and pens poised.

It wasn't hard to work out who they all were. The woman with the braided hair and the teeth brace, and the guy with the goatee beard and *Hope* tattoo were definitely social workers. The two blokes in policemen clothing were...

He dropped his rucksack down in the doorway. "Ah," said the teeth brace lady. "You must be Daniel. We've been waiting to talk to you."

"Really?" said Danny, his face flushing. He hadn't been expecting this. He had been expecting to sit down for a milkshake with his mum in the kitchen, for the radio to be playing softly, for his mum to tell him all about what happened two nights ago, about where Brett was, about what was going to happen to them all. For Jacko to be nowhere in sight.

He realised that Erland was knelt on the floor between the sofa and the corner bookshelf, due to lack of seating. And he could tell from the shape of his brother's panicky eyes and mouth that he had already done his interview.

Danny rubbed his face. "Can I grab a milkshake first?" he said, hoping to ignite a response in his mother, such as *I'll come with you.* He had to talk to her first, to find out what he needed to say, but his mother was sat numbly, staring ahead of her at apparently nothing. Jacko was the only person that was going to give him any pointers and judging from the fact that he was flashing a warning sign with his eyes that read something along the lines of *I'm going to beat you up*, it wasn't a very helpful pointer at that.

One of the policemen, a sandy-coloured guy – sandy freckles, sandy hair, sandy eyebrows and lashes – led Danny into the dining room, followed by the teeth-brace lady. They sat either side of him around the circular table, both with their hands folded neatly before them. This was what they were taught in order to present a non-hostile environment, he thought.

There was a knock on the door and the goatee man brought in Danny's strawberry milkshake. "I didn't know if you wanted a straw," he said, handing Danny the glass. Danny shook his head and the door closed behind goatee man.

"My name's Zoe," said the brace lady. "I'm here to try to help you. I know this is really hard, Daniel, and you probably resent us being here." She paused for his response. He said nothing. "Did you break up today?" she said, surveying his Chelsea away shirt. He nodded. "My son was a Chelsea fan," she said, smiling.

"Was?" Danny said, turning his eyes upon her.

"He supports Man U now."

"What?" said Danny, incredulous. "I thought he was dead. That's the only way that I wouldn't support Chelsea any more. And even if I was dead, I still wouldn't support Man U. Is he fickle or what?"

"Yes," she replied, quite seriously. "He is. I've told him to be more loyal, but you can't make people what they are not."

"You're loyal, aren't you, Daniel?" said the sandy policeman, leaning forward with his head cocked to one side. "Sometimes loyalty is misplaced. Sometimes you have to put what you think is loyalty aside and realise that telling the truth is more important than anything else."

Danny picked at a groove of wood in the table, running

his nail into the rut and digging to see how far he could go.

"Do you think," said Zoe, gently, "that your mum is capable of hurting anyone?"

Danny shrugged.

"Do you think that she hurt Brett?" she said.

"You don't have to say anything that you don't want to say, Daniel," said the policeman. "You have rights."

There was a silence as Danny continued picking at the groove. The policeman reached forward and covered Danny's hand with his. Danny stared at the hand – at the thick sandy hair and freckles. He wondered how many times this hand had covered the hand of a victim, of a suspect, of someone afraid to talk.

Danny looked ahead of him at the mantelpiece, at the photograph of his mum holding Brett. It was taken last year at Weston-super-Mare. It was pouring with rain and Jacko had been away on business, but his mum had promised them a trip to the beach so Weston it was. They had chips on the pier and his mum had even given them cash to spend on the machines and rides. They came home late, expecting Jacko to be anxious or annoyed even at having missed such a great day. But he wasn't there.

Danny realised now that Jacko had more than likely been at 89, Queen's Drive, with that woman. He thought of his confrontation with Jacko two nights ago and looked again at his mum's face in the photograph, at how she was smiling into the rainy camera lens, holding Brett in his yellow raincoat, her face pressed against his.

"She didn't hit him," he said, looking at the policeman and social worker in turn. "She wouldn't hurt anyone. She's a vegetarian because she's squeamish about eating animals. She can't stand blood and she won't let us have a telly because of all the violence. We're not even allowed to wear anything with camouflage on. Brett can be really annoying and I know he pushed Mum over the edge, but there is no way she would hit him. I am certain of it."

"The edge?" said Zoe, leaning forward with her eyebrows raised and her mouth forming a little 'o'.

Danny frowned at her. "We were all on the edge. Brett had these tantrums and Mum couldn't cope."

"Why didn't she ask for help?" Zoe asked.

"Ask who?"

"What about your health visitor, Klaris Shaw?"

Danny laughed. "Yeah, right. More cups of tea and pats on the back about how she can do it, how it will all work out right in the end, blah blah. Mum didn't need frilly words. She needed someone to come in and sort it all out for her."

"If it weren't for Klaris Shaw's frilly words, as you put it, Brett might be in a more serious state by now."

"Well, he's not," Danny said. He picked up his milkshake and drank it down in one.

"You speak very passionately about your mum," said Zoe.

"It's his mum," said the policeman. Danny got it: the policeman felt sorry for him, the brace lady didn't. The brace lady wanted his mum behind bars, maybe because she was ugly and his mum was pretty. Lee would have said it was as simple as that. She said some women just never got over being ugly.

"Can I go now?" said Danny. Zoe frowned and opened her mouth to reply, but the policeman held up his hand and nodded approval.

As Danny passed through the doorway, he stopped. "Have you spoken to Jacko?" he said over his shoulder.

"Yes," said the policeman. "Shortly before you arrived."

Danny smirked.

"What?" said Zoe.

"And to think that you still sat there asking me whether my mum's guilty."

"Do you fancy a Mr C's?" said Zoe, sucking on her

brace. She was hungry, having spent most of the afternoon at the Trelawney's with only a Kit Kat to keep her going. Ned could go all day without eating – which they often had to do, given their unrealistic work loads – but Zoe got all irritable and wanted to kill someone. A bit of a flaw for a social worker.

She was flawed in other ways. Everyone was. But Zoe knew that for her to be flawed in the way that she was – judgemental and resentful – was really bad in her line of business. Ned had told her so a thousand times.

Aged thirty-six, Zoe was more senior than Ned by seven years, yet when alone with him she imagined herself to be quite the little girl. He had a homeliness and wisdom about him that she found enviable as well as intimidating, as though he could see right through her immature silliness. She had had to grow up fast, having a baby on her own when she was only seventeen. Working with someone like Ned gave her the chance to sneak back to her teens every day for half an hour or so. And where was the harm in that?

She folded her arms and slumped into her seat, staring out of the car window. The heat wave had ended, the kids had finished school today for the holidays and predictably England was now trying to make its mind up what to offer weather-wise. It was neither hot, nor cold, nor muggy, nor windy, nor damp. It was just...hanging there.

"Could do," said Ned, finally. He had a habit of taking so long to reply that she had forgotten the original question. It was like the delay in communication that occurred when people were talking live on the television by satellite.

"I hate that woman," said Zoe, fiddling with a braid of her hair, curling it onto her finger and then releasing it again, only to curl it again and release.

She waited for Ned's response.

"What woman?"

"Beth Trelawney."

"Yuh, about that…" Ned glanced at her as he pulled up outside Mr C's takeaway. "I've been meaning to say to you – you're kinda hard on her, don't you think?"

Zoe unsnapped her seat belt and turned in her seat to face him. "Hard on her? How so?"

Ned shrugged, picking at a hole in his jeans. She could see his skinny knee poking through the denim. Ned was such a cliché – the tattoo, the goatee, the ripped jeans. But then she probably was too – the nose stud, the braided hair. Whatever. She didn't care what anyone thought.

"You seem to enjoy what she's going through." Ned's cheeks flushed. She had no idea how he made it through the day as a social worker, what with him being so sensitive.

"Enjoy it?" She spluttered with laughter. "You're joking. That's not enjoyment you're seeing. It's bloody scorn!"

Ned shook his head and took the keys out of the ignition. "Let's get a burger."

Zoe followed him closely, stepping on the back of his trainers.

"Doesn't she annoy you?" she said, concentrating her gaze upon the illuminated board by way of suggesting that she wasn't going to order her regular spicy bean burger with extra mayo, although that was exactly what she was intending to do.

"Nope," said Ned. "She's in trouble. How is that annoying?" He stroked his goatee whilst surveying the board. He almost never chose the same thing. Tonight he was going for a chicken supreme with garlic relish, and a banana milkshake.

"Because," said Zoe, speaking between her teeth lest the other customers should hear her (tomorrow she could be knocking on one of these loser's front doors) "she's a sanctimonious middle-class bitch who has no idea about what having a hard time actually involves. She's got guilty written all over her. I've seen her type a hundred times:

they have kids and then resent them interrupting their careers and then they have a breakdown."

"I think that's a generalisation," said Ned, muttering as he always did when annoyed. Most people raised their voices in anger, but Ned drew into himself as though anger was a private emotion that was not only rather embarrassing but deeply reprehensible. "And not only that..." He drew closer to her, narrowing his eyes at her. "I don't smell middle-class on her."

"You what?" she said, astonished. She didn't have Ned down as a class sniffing type.

"You're wrong about her," Ned said, vaguely, fixing his gaze over her shoulder as though the truth were stood there. "She's not who you think she is."

"One spicy bean burger and fries, a chicken supreme with garlic relish, and a banana milkshake?"

"Yep, that's us," said Ned, reaching out to the Mr C's assistant for the plastic carrier bag. "Cheers."

Zoe followed Ned out to the car in much the same way that she had followed him in, taking little steps (she was five foot two) to his big ones (six foot two). "What, like she's an impostor or something?" she said.

Ned plonked the carrier bag on Zoe's lap, started the car, got all the way to the end of the road and joined the dual carriageway before replying. Zoe waited patiently, the food burning her legs. "Nothing that dramatic," he said. "Just that there's something about her that we haven't found out yet."

"I guess the conference tomorrow is going to be interesting then," Zoe said, smiling and wriggling in her seat with anticipation.

She gazed out of the window at the yellow field of rape they were passing. The car was shuddering. Ned always tried to put his foot down along this stretch but his old motor only ever reached sixty-five miles per hour.

"You're evil," said Ned. She looked over at him to

laugh with him, but he didn't look remotely amused. He clicked the stereo on. He only ever listened to the Eagles, as far as she knew. It all sounded like one long boring song to her.

He took a right at the roundabout and drove along the short country lane that led to her town, Salton. He lived at the next town along from Salton, so it wasn't out of his way. It was lucky because she really didn't like driving.

She glanced sideways at him. "Can I ask you something?" she said.

She waited.

"Shoot," he said.

She looked at him sideways again. "Nothing," she said. There was no point saying anything. She couldn't risk not having a lift to work any more.

"Were you going to tell me you love me?" said Ned.

Ned never joked about. And now he was laughing his bleeding head off.

The house was unbearably quiet without Brett. Beth sat in his bedroom gazing at the empty cot, her knees pulled up in front of her as she cradled a large fluffy rabbit. The rabbit smelt of Brett – a funny little smell that only she would recognise – and its fur was spiked with areas of hardened dribble, tears and food.

"Mind if I join you?" Jacko entered the room and sat on the floor next to her, his arm around her.

He wasn't very supple and soon he was agitated, shifting about. He rose, motioning for Beth to join him on the futon. She sat down at the opposite end of the sofa, her arms folded, her jaw locked to prevent her from saying a word too much. Jacko turned on the koala nightlight and Beth watched it as it changed from red to green to blue to yellow to white and back to red again, all in a slow silent fuzzy cycle.

She glanced through the shadows at Jacko. With the

colours lighting his face, she imagined that they were parading each of the different sides to his character, sides that he didn't know that she knew about because he tried to hide them. There was red for his temper that lit up over the most trivial of things; green for his jealous side that forbade her to admire other men; blue for his composed professional side; and white for his transparency.

"Beth, honey..." He held out his hand to her. She gazed at him. His face was jaundiced, awash with yellow. What did yellow represent? Deception? Cowardice?

"No, Jacko," she said, ignoring his outstretched hand. "It's too late."

"For what?" he said, frowning.

"Are you stupid?" She pointed at the empty cot. "It's too late for everything. Where were you? Not only in the hospital, but the whole of this year just gone?"

She stood up in agitation, needing to get away from Jacko, away from Brett's bedroom. Over night the room had gone from a grubby milk-stained den where the day's screaming, anger and discord took place, to a shrine where silence had descended in the way that it did when someone you loved was missing. Beyond this room, nothing made sense. Here, she sensed Brett's presence and became focused and single-minded about the path ahead. It was her place of thought, of planning. Jacko didn't belong here. He hadn't earned a place beside her here.

She went to the door. Jacko jumped up. "Don't walk away," he said, reaching for her again.

"Don't *touch* me," she said through her teeth, pushing his hand away roughly and going downstairs to find her sons.

She didn't know what she was going to say to them, or what they would ask her. Erland was curled into a ball on the sofa watching *Family Fortunes* on a portable television which was stood on telephone directories and clothing catalogues. Danny was sprawled on a bean bag reading his

Chelsea supporters' magazine.

"Everything go okay at school, boys? Glad you've broken up?" she said, sitting down next to Erland, tapping his bottom affectionately.

"It was cool," said Danny. Erland didn't respond.

"I'm sorry I left you in the lurch. It's the first time I've ever done that. I won't let it happen—"

"It was cool," Danny repeated, glancing at her over the top of his magazine.

There was a creaking across the floorboards above them. Jacko would be lying on the bed sulking, making the point – as he so often did – that he wasn't a part of this family, particularly now that Brett wasn't at home. Beth reached for the remote control and turned the volume up on the television.

Can I have fifteen seconds on the clock, please? the presenter was saying. *Okay. Name something you can see, but you cannot touch.*

"The moon," Erland murmured.

"The sun," said Beth.

"The clouds," said Erland.

"A rainbow," said Beth.

They could have kept it up all night – watching rubbish television, breathing a quick kiss at bedtime and then parting company. But Danny lowered his magazine and his eyes were bearing upon her.

She returned his gaze, their eyes meeting. For a moment nothing happened. And then Danny looked away and began to cry.

"What's going to happen to Brett?" Danny was sobbing whole-heartedly now. "And what's going to happen to you?" He moved off the beanbag and crouched down on the carpet. She joined him and they remained fixed like that, embracing. There was a light touch upon Beth's shoulder and to her surprise, Erland crouched with them. To have cried with them would have been too much for

Erland. But crouching was a big step indeed.

Their odd formation reminded Beth of the stone figurines that stood on the patio in the garden – an ornament that Angie, a fellow professor at university had bought her, a friend whom she had lost contact with. Little men stood in a circle, each with their arms around each other. It was the Circle of Friendship. Beth sometimes lit a candle in the middle of the men and squinted a bit to imagine that the figures were primitive humans standing around a fire, the flames animating their faces.

Beth and her boys were like that circle. Except that the ornament had five people. And they were only three. That had been the problem all along: there had always seemed to be people missing from their family, no extra arms to hold them up when they were tired.

"Everything's going to be okay, boys, you hear me? We're going to get through this."

"What about the police?" said Danny, his voice sounding small as though it were being squeezed.

"What about them? I don't think they'll be too involved because that would mean they're going to press charges against me and…" Send me to prison. The four unspoken words hung in the air.

"Where's Brett?" Danny said.

"He's with Grandma Best for a couple of nights," she said. She felt Danny's arms pulling away in objection. She held him steady. "It was my idea, Danny. He's fine and he's safe."

He relaxed and wiped his eyes in the aggressive, self-loathing way that boys got rid of tears, trying to wipe away the evidence. "Grandma Best is a nice person," she said. "It's neutral territory."

"No, it's not. It's Jacko territory," said Erland. "Which doesn't make it safe at all."

Beth stared at Erland. "Why would you say that?"

Erland shrugged, his mouth flopping open.

Beth knew exactly why her son had said that. They all knew that the man who was wallowing in the room above them, a man who was privy to their secrets, witness to their weaknesses, wasn't on their side any more.

They all stared at each other, their eyes wide, thinking the same thing, unable to say it. Apart from Danny. "What are you going to do about him, Mum?"

"I don't know," she said. And she really didn't know.

The final round of interviews earlier had concluded two things: that Brett was at risk of harm and that... Beth closed her eyes momentarily, wincing. She thought again about the yellow light of Brett's lamp lingering upon her husband's face and knew that it was the colour of betrayal.

The state of her marriage, of her relationship with Jacko had been the most startling revelation of the day. Not that her little boy was considered at risk of harm, but that her marriage was a sham.

It all started to ooze out – the sticky truth – when they began to discuss the conference. Jacko had gone back to work. It was just Beth, the boys and her entourage: the two social workers and the police child abuse investigation team who had spent so much time with her lately that they moved coolly around her house saying things over her head like *coffee? Two sugars? Got any kitchen roll?*

There was going to be an emergency child protection conference tomorrow night. It was to decide whether Brett needed a child protection plan. It sounded bureaucratic and convoluted, as though administration could fix a troubled child. And yet there was something concrete and peaceable about paper and files that appealed to Beth. She knew where she was with conferences and reports. She liked things that could be categorised and filed. She just didn't like it when the thing was her child.

It had all been going okay until the social worker with the goatee told Beth that it might be nice for her to have a friend with her at the meeting – maybe a solicitor?

Hey? Beth had queried, alarmed. *Surely I can bring my husband as my friend?*

The goatee social worker and the policemen lowered their eyes. Zoe, the social worker with the teeth brace, flicked her braided hair over her shoulders and stared directly at Beth. *Ms Trelawney*, she had said quietly, *your husband thinks you're guilty.*

Beth looked now at her circle of friendship with her boys as they wobbled on their knees on the lounge floor. Their formation was fragile, about to split open.

"I know you didn't hurt Brett, Mum," said Danny, gazing at her, love twisting his face like a birth impediment.

"I know that too, Mum," said Erland.

"Thank you, boys," she said, her voice wavering.

Jacko lay on the bed gazing at the hole on the wall where his portable television used to stand. He tried to imagine what he could watch right now that might be of interest, irritation prickling him at the realisation that the US Open would be on. The boys had taken his television without asking – yet another of the multitude of signs that they neither respected him nor wanted him in their home.

He blamed their mother. Right from the start she had pledged her allegiance to the boys and not to himself and Brett. She had remained a Trelawney after they got married because she didn't want the boys to feel displaced. He had begged her to become a Best and yet she hadn't cared about having a different name from him and Brett. He had known then that Danny and Erland were always going to be her priority.

Tonight, he had known that Beth wouldn't come to him first off to talk about the situation with Brett, but that she would seek out her sons. She struggled so much to talk, it was such a premeditated thing with her that it was easy to predict what she would do. She had gone to her boys and would have spent longer with them tonight, but for the fact that there was a pressing matter to tend to with him. She would linger as long as she could, thinking of what to say, stalling in the kitchen for a glass of wine. She hated confrontations, least of all verbal ones.

So when she stood in the shadows of the bedroom doorway clutching a glass of wine and gazing beyond him to the lush summer trees moving outside the window, he was prepared.

"You didn't come because you think I did it," she said.

"What?" he said, shifting his head off the pillow to look at her. "Come where?"

"To the hospital. You stayed away the whole time because you think I did it."

"Did what?"

"Don't play dumb with me, Jacko." She hovered, uncertain whether to sit down. To do so upon their marital bed might give the wrong signal, so she pulled the stool away from her dressing table and perched on that. He couldn't see the details of her expression in the half light, but knew that she would be blank-faced, her eyes vague and faraway. She always seemed the most distant when discussing the most intensely personal subjects – a quality, or dysfunction, that she shared with Natasha.

"The social worker said that you think I'm guilty of harming Brett," she said. "How could you think that? And even if you did think it, how could you say it out loud to those people?"

He had thought a lot about what to say to this question and had decided to deny it, to say that the social worker was fabricating the truth in order to test Beth's reaction to blame. But now that the moment was upon him, he felt anger bubbling in his chest. He sat up, tossing the pillow aside, glaring at his wife.

"Because," he said, "I'm doing what's best for Brett. You can't expect me to believe that he got those injuries on his own? There's no way!"

"So the only logical explanation is that I did it?" said Beth, rising.

"Yes!" he shouted. "You hate him because you hate me! We're not as good as you and your boys. Why can't you admit it?"

"How dare you?" she shouted back. The two of them met in front of their bed. "I love Brett. I've been looking after him by myself. You're never home! We wouldn't be in this mess if you'd been around more often. I had no one to ask for help. *No one!*"

She was screaming now, her hair wild around her face, her hands flapping about.

He took a step back from her. "Just look at yourself, Beth. And you'll see what I'm saying is true."

She clasped her hand to her mouth and then turned and left the room. Her glass of wine remained on the dressing table. He snatched it up and hurled it at the closed door after her.

As he watched the wine drip down the wood onto the carpet, he heard through the open bedroom windows the sound of a car pulling up outside the house, followed by a car door slamming shut.

He stood back behind the curtains, gazing down into the road as subtly as he could. He recognised the car and its driver instantly. "Oh, God," he said, the cold sensation of shock stabbing him.

Klaris belonged to the Real Stories Club. Each month, she received a DVD of a true story film. The subject matters were varied but you could guarantee that the film would feature a female protagonist and that the viewer would be crying for at least half an hour after curtain up. Klaris kept a box of tissues on the shelf underneath her coffee table for this purpose.

On the evening that she watched the new film, she

would sit with her legs tucked beside her underneath her cosy throw with her pen and notepad held expectantly. She was on the subscriber magazine's panel of reviewers and always submitted her review by first class post the next morning. She liked to scribble notes during the film and then type the report up that night.

Sometimes she thought about ditching the review and just enjoying the film. And yet the review, if rather troublesome after a day's work, gave the film more meaning for her – made it less lonely. Her review would be published for thousands of people to read. Therefore, she wasn't really watching the film on her own.

Tonight she was watching *Framed*. An American mother was being accused of taking inappropriate photographs of her little girl playing in the bath with her best friend, a little boy. The mother, a professional photographer, maintained that the images were innocent, but the police suspected otherwise.

As the camera panned in on the mother's dark eyes, Klaris prickled with recognition. The mother's fear was palpable. It was exactly the expression that Beth Trelawney had been wearing the day that Brett was admitted to Bath Central and that she had been wearing ever since.

Klaris's thoughts strayed from the film to tomorrow's conference. She had spent the afternoon preparing notes for the chairman, Mr Langley. He had telephoned her for a chat ahead of the meeting. He seemed pleasant enough, being in possession of a charmingly temperate voice, but Klaris had felt that everything she said was being analysed and digested. Mr Langley paused before replying and fell silent when she was speaking – not even uttering an *umm* or *uh huh*. He was the sort of man to record conversations and replay them until he discovered the dust particle of information that he was seeking.

The *Framed* mother was screaming, demanding Klaris's attention. The mother calmed down as Klaris's eyes fell upon her. She wasn't just frightened of the crime that she was being accused of, she was saying. She was frightened of her past catching up with her.

Klaris considered this for a moment: the past catching up. She had always considered it an odd turn of phrase. Did the past tear along the road, reaching out, placing a heavy hand on your shoulder, heavy enough to stop your legs from moving? Did past crimes ever catch up with us? Didn't crime have to be in the present for that to happen – for the culprit to truly get their comeuppance? Nothing suggested this more markedly than the case of Nazi war criminals, Klaris thought: old men and women with sweet wistful faces who seemed incapable of catastrophic cruelties.

If the past really did catch up with us, Klaris thought, placing her notebook and pen down on the table and unfolding her legs from underneath the throw, weren't all of us running?

She felt suddenly hot. She wriggled out of the arms of her cardigan. *I'm innocent*, the mother was saying to the police interrogator. *Innocent, you hear me?*

Beth ushered the woman into the lounge. "Have I dealt with you before?" Beth said, trying to pull this girl's face out from the various children's services and medical staff faces that she had encountered in the past two days.

"No," the woman replied, looking slightly alarmed at the question. She looked about her for somewhere to sit, her eyes resting upon Danny's sprawled body momentarily before flitting away. Danny, as was typical for a boy his age, failed to show any curiosity whatsoever if it took him away from his Chelsea magazine.

"Here," said Beth, motioning for Erland to take his legs off the sofa and to sit up straight. The woman sat down, her skirt tight around her bare legs which – Beth noted – were remarkably tanned and shimmery for a social worker.

And the snakeskin heels? Was that appropriate?

Just as Beth was noting the snug fit of her visitor's blouse, so Danny looked up from his bean bag. Danny and the visitor stared at each other with reddened faces.

"Have you met before?" asked Beth, confused.

Danny looked back down at his magazine. Erland stared ahead at the television, his expression entirely unmoved by proceedings.

"Could we talk privately, please?" said the woman, placing her quilted handbag on her lap – a fashionably oversized bag that seemed too big for her skinny arm. Beth had seen this sort of thing in magazines at the doctors' surgery: pictures of celebrities wielding handbags the size of sports holdalls on their snappy wrists.

"This is as private as it gets in our house," Beth said, sitting down on the opposite sofa and placing her tongue against her top lip, gathering her thoughts. "Who are you?" she asked. " Because you're not a social worker, are you?"

"A social worker?" the woman said, attempting laughter. "I'm Natasha –"

"She's a whore!" said Danny, jumping to his feet, standing on his beloved magazine in the process, the pages all skew-whiff. Beth opened her mouth to tell Danny off, to demand an explanation, to defend the visitor against such an awful claim. But the woman was chewing her lip, her hand trembling upon her monstrous bag.

"What the hell is going on, Danny?" said Beth, standing up to meet her son head on.

Danny's eyes were red and puffy from his tears earlier. "Mum, I'm sorry to be the one–"

"You're *not* going to be the one," said Jacko, coming into the room, changing the mood as abruptly as though he had changed the channel on the giant television that was their lounge, from a daytime soap to a violent drama. Everything had felt female and under control until this point: her preoccupied sons, their glamorous visitor. Beth could sense Jacko's maleness; smell his anger, his pride, his need to defend himself. It had been like this the moment he had crossed the threshold of their home into their lives.

"Beth, there's something I have to tell you," he said.

"Oh, God," said the woman faintly, her hand rising to her mouth.

He's sleeping with her, Beth thought.

Jacko stood behind the woman as though he were backing her – backing the whore. Danny was right.

And then she realised that Danny had known. The idea that he could have betrayed her, as opposed to Jacko, was inconceivable. "Did you know about this?" she said, swinging round to face Danny in amazement, who was still stood with his bare foot screwing up his magazine.

"I found out when Brett went into hospital. I didn't know what to do." He looked as though he was about to start crying again. Beth reached forward for his hand, noting Jacko's look of disgust.

Jacko had chosen his side, she thought. And so had she.

Danny hung his head. Erland had disappeared from the room. How long had he been gone?

She turned to Jacko. "All those nights when I was struggling, all those times you were working late?..." She eyed the woman critically – her depilated legs, her tight skirt and spiky heels. "You slut," she said.

"It's not Natasha's fault," said Jacko.

Beth stared at Jacko for what felt like several minutes, her anger blocking her ears, her eyes burning. And then she reached onto the mantelpiece for a glass vase and threw it with accuracy at Jacko's head. He deflected injury with a quick move of his elbow to his face, but the second vase missile landed nicely on the woman's forehead, causing her to launch backwards in shock.

"You stupid bitch!" shouted Jacko. "You just lost Brett for good!"

"Get the hell out of my house!" Beth screamed. "*Don't*

come back!"

Erland appeared at the door, causing everyone to stop in wonder. "I've put all your things in bin liners," he said, blinking slowly. "The only thing left is this." He moved forward to the portable television, his actions so methodical and smooth that Beth didn't suspect what was to follow. He picked up the television and hurled it out of the room, his teeth clenched with the effort.

"What the–?" said Jacko, launching himself towards Erland with his fist raised.

"Babe, *no!*" screamed the woman, pulling on his arm. Jacko responded, withdrawing.

Beth stared, astounded. And then she left the room, stepping over the television in the hallway. She climbed the stairs as though each one were twice as large as it had been the last time she had climbed them. She held onto the banister, the only thing holding her up, her body being unreliable now.

She sank down onto the bed, resting her head on the one pillow that remained. How had Erland had time to be so thorough? Her eyes flitted about the room, resting on the blank spaces where fragments of Jacko had stood. Everything had gone. She pulled open the bedside drawer on Jacko's side of the bed: no handkerchiefs, no cufflinks box, no old anniversary and birthday cards. It was as if Erland had known exactly which items in the house to seize, as though he had magic vision that made the items stand out. Or as though he had planned this moment in detail over the past two years.

When the front door shut, followed by the sound of two car engines starting and pulling away, she knew that Jacko himself was now gone, in convoy with his lover. She pictured him trying to salvage the portable television, swinging his bin liners into the boot. Was that all he had brought with him into her house – a couple bin liners of belongings?

Beth hadn't been left by anyone before, having always been the one doing the leaving. She thought that it would take longer, that there would be a meaningful, heart-wrenching conversation, followed by tears, smashed crockery and punctured tyres. She hadn't thought that her husband's mistress would call for him like an after-school play date and that he would leave with her shortly after.

But perhaps there was nothing short about this. Perhaps – like Erland – Jacko had been planning this for some time.

She moaned and rolled onto the pillow with her face pressed into it. And then the telephone rang. She looked at the light flashing on the handset above the bed. The answer phone picked up.

"Beth?" It was Jacko. Without thought, she rose and answered. There was no background noise. He had pulled over. She wondered where he was, picturing him in his Nike T-shirt and tracksuit bottoms that he reserved for evenings at home. "I'm so sorry, honey. I love you."

She found herself reaching out across the dim light of the room, towards the heavy canopy of trees outside the house, towards the city lights in the valley beyond them. Somewhere out there was her husband. He was gone.

"I…" She wanted to say that she loved him too, but in that moment she realised that he couldn't love her in the same way that she loved him if he was sleeping with another woman. "How long have you been shagging that whore?" she said instead.

There was a long intake of breath before he replied. "It started last year," he replied.

"When last year?"

"Last summer."

"When last summer?"

Pause. "June."

She closed her eyes. She imagined Jacko kissing the woman – Natasha, was it? She imagined his hands caressing her throat, her neck, her breasts. Oh God.

"Honey, you were so…distant. You wouldn't let me touch you. You wouldn't –"

She opened her eyes. "This is my fault?"

"No. But it's not all my fault… Please, can we meet and talk? We're married for Christ's sake. We can't end things like this."

"We can."

"What?" He sounded incredulous. "No, Beth! We have to deal with this. I don't want to go to Natasha's –"

"Where is she now?"

"I told her to go home. I don't want to go there. Please, honey. I love you."

"You don't even realise how hypocritical you sound. It's too late, Jacko. The wall is down."

"The wall?" he said.

She paused, looking out again at the trees. Night had fallen. The trees were dark, still, soldiers guarding her secrets from the city's prying eyes. "I can't be abandoned. If it happens, the wall comes down and it can't be removed. Once you're on the other side, you can't come back."

"What are you talking about?" he said. "There is no other side, no wall. You're just putting up walls. You can control it. Bloody well smash down the wall and let me come home and talk about it."

"Goodbye, Jacko," she said, hanging up.

She sat down at her wicker dressing table, flicking on the switch at the wall so that the rose lights around the mirror glowed a warm pink. When she had bought the lights and fixed them in place, Danny had said they looked like the lights around a film star's mirror. She had liked this idea – not that she was a film star, but that she was someone worthy of illumination.

She looked at the earrings adorning the table, looped into the holes in the wicker. She had neglected them. They were dusty and some had lost their lustre. She noted the thick dust on the petals of the rose lights. When was the last time she had sat here, looking at herself in the mirror, taking care of her jewellery, of herself?

Everything had changed when she had accidentally fallen pregnant with Brett. In the few months that she had known Jacko, she had barely established herself as a confident lover, when suddenly her breasts were fattening and darkening, her knickers were damp because her bladder was weak, indigestion burned her chest. It wasn't the stuff that love nests were made of.

Jacko would come up behind her in their bedroom, behind where she was sat now. Fresh out of the shower, her hair dripping down her back onto the cushion, she would be massaging anti-stretch mark oil into her breasts and stomach, trying to take care of herself despite being full of self-repulsion. "Beautiful, Beth," he would whisper, teasing her neck with his mouth, nudging her hair away with his chin.

She would frown, reaching quickly for her nightie to cover herself up. "Sorry…I'm…"

"It's okay," he would say, turning away.

"I'll get to my sexy stage soon," she said, smiling in consolation.

She didn't ever get to that stage. It happened to other women, apparently. Angie, a fellow lecturer at university who was pregnant at the same time as Beth, confessed that she regularly sneaked home in the afternoon for lusty interludes with her husband. This had never happened to Beth, not during any of her pregnancies. And she had known all along that it wouldn't with this one either.

It hadn't helped that the start of their marriage began with a sense of failure on Beth's part: failure to feel glamorous on their wedding day, failure to know for sure whether Jacko would have proposed had it not been for the pregnancy.

She had told her wedding guests, including Jacko, that it

was the best day of her life. In truth, she had struggled not to cry, not to feel ridiculous that her swollen breasts were struggling to stay in her bra, that her thighs were rubbing together in the heat, that the cigar smoke was making her want to vomit.

They had tried to make love that night, to consummate their marriage, but she had rolled off him, tearful, overcome with failure and disappointment. They tried again the next night during their honeymoon weekend away at Burnham-on-Sea (the boys stayed with Professor Moss and his wife for the night) and were successful at last. She had vowed to herself to make an effort more often, but it was the only time they made love during her pregnancy.

She had looked forward to Brett being born, to her body being returned to her, to getting to know her husband properly. Instead, after Brett's birth she felt as though her body and its distorted parts were alien to her, as though her sexuality was an old part of her that had once mattered in another life. She waddled about, her breasts leaking milk, her infant screaming for attention, her two boys lurking in the shadows wondering when their mum was going to ask them how school was, her husband pacing up and down wondering when his wife was going to have sex with him.

This was when Jacko had started the affair, she realised now – not the physical affair itself, but the mental preparation for it. He had begun to look about, before he was even conscious that he was looking about. She remembered now, his head jerking sideways out of his car window to look at women in the street, his eye lingering a little longer than necessary on any young female within view.

Whilst he was choosing his girl, she had been having physiotherapy on her weak pelvic floor. She couldn't keep herself clean any more, she couldn't wear pretty underwear; she couldn't be the woman that Jacko wanted her to be.

He hadn't pushed her into sex, he hadn't complained.

He had just gone silent on the matter, which was worse. And now she saw that his silence was born of satisfaction.

Why had she allowed the situation to get so out of hand, out of control, she thought, looking at herself in the dusty mirror of her dressing table? This question kept being asked over and over, by herself, by the children's services. She reached forward and swept the dust off the mirror with the palm of her hand, as though doing so might reveal the answer.

The fact was, she thought, staring at her reflection, that a light layer of dust couldn't possibly conceal the truth. Because the truth was only ever one step away from making itself known. It was like a lifelong game of hide and seek between the truth and its concealer, the winner being the one who never tired.

And yet she was getting tired. She stared at herself in the mirror, at the pitted shadows underneath her eyes, at the worry lines on her forehead and around her mouth. How much longer could she play the game?

"Mum." Danny shook his mother's arm and peeled her hair away from her cheek. Good, she was still breathing. He folded back the duvet cautiously lest she should be scantily clad. Quite the reverse. She was still wearing yesterday's clothes, including her slippers. "Oh, great," he groaned. There beside her was an empty bottle of wine and a glass. The remains of the bottle had poured out onto the white sheet like a bloody stain.

He thought momentarily of the night he had found Brett. Only three nights ago, but seemingly longer. He never thought he would think this but he missed his baby brother. Still, he would be home soon. And things would be so much better now that Jacko was gone. On this last point, he felt a little doubtful – it seemed too good to be true.

Erland hadn't stopped smiling. He really hated Jacko.

"Mum." He shook her arm again. She had to wake up, if his wishes were to come true. She had to get herself together and prepare for the big meeting tonight if she was going to win Brett back.

The doorbell rang. Danny stood up straight, his heart thumping. He crossed to the window and peeked out. There was a small spearmint-green car outside that he didn't recognise. He glanced at his mum lying motionless and then raced downstairs.

He pulled open the door to see a really tall man standing there and his first thought was to wonder how on earth he managed to fit into such a small car.

"Good morning, my name is Mr Langley. I'm from the children's services in Bristol. Is Mrs Best home?" the man said, looking past Danny into the hallway.

Erland approached. He was taking a much keener interest in events now that Jacko was gone. It occurred to Danny that no one knew what Erland was like as a near-teenager without Jacko around, the latter having cast such an intimidating shadow. Perhaps Erland was chattier, more socially-adjusted than they all thought?

"She's not Mrs Best," said Erland, putting his shoulders back assertively and sniffing. "She didn't take that dumb ass's name." Erland had a cold, but he never used anything but his sleeve to wipe his nose. With or without Jacko, Erland was a loser. Danny nudged him away from the door.

"Erland didn't mean that."

"Erland?" said Mr Langley, raising an eyebrow. "That's an unusual name. I've only come across one Erland before: Erland Johnsen. Chelsea's Player of the year –"

"1995," Danny spoke in unison with the man. They stared at each other with mutual pleasure, both nodding in reverence to the great Johnsen. "Central defender. Norwegian International," Danny said.

"And you are?" said Mr Langley, peering down at

Danny enquiringly. In addition to his height, the man's nose was way too big for his face making it seem as though he was doomed to topple over at any minute. His nose – which Danny couldn't help but concentrate upon now – was so thick with tiny purple veins that it looked like a map. Danny imagined that the veins were all the problems in the world and that they all met in a knot in the middle of this man's nose – problems for him to fix. He certainly looked like he was the type of guy who took on too much and pulled his hair out a lot: it was coarse and stuck out in tufts like an overused toothbrush.

"I'm Daniel. Would you like to come in?"

"Daniel…"

"Petrescu," said Danny, smiling. "Midfielder. Always tried his best. Considered one of the best non-English players in Chelsea's history. Remained loyal to the club after transferring and even named his daughter Chelsea."

"Pretty impressive knowledge you've got there," said Mr Langley.

"It's 'cos of my dad…" said Danny. He glanced sideways at his brother. "Well, our dad… We've never met him. He was mad about Chelsea."

Danny lead the way into the lounge, noting that his rucksack was lying underneath the stairwell where his Muddyfox used to stand; that there was no baby brother to rifle through his possessions, no little pair of shoes that flashed a red light at the back when walked in.

"We have to get our brother back," Danny said, impulsively, turning on Mr Langley before they had barely gone through the lounge door. "Please. Mum hasn't done anything wrong. We really miss Brett. It's not right that he isn't with us."

Erland, who was following in Mr Langley's wake, stepped aside from the tall man to glare at Danny. The glare meant – *shut up telling everybody everything!*

Danny closed his mouth with a snap of his teeth and

stood near the window. Being reprimanded by his younger brother felt so much worse than anything else he could think of at that moment. He had to get a grip, take charge. So he remained standing whilst everyone was seated, to make the point.

"Is your mum home?" said Mr Langley, fishing into his pocket for a handkerchief which, to Danny's surprise, he handed to Erland. "Here, son. I can't abide a sniffer."

Erland's cheeks coloured as he took the handkerchief limply. Danny suppressed a smile. "So is she?" said Mr Langley again, gazing up at Danny.

"Uh...She uh... Look, to be honest, I don't think she's going to be able to..."

Danny paused, listening. He could hear something – footsteps on the stairs. Their mum entered the room, her hair up in a ponytail, her lips shimmering with gloss. She was wearing a pink blouse and ink-coloured trousers. It was what she used to wear when she lectured. She looked fresh and pretty and Danny realised that it was the first time in a long while that he had seen her looking like his mum.

"I thought I heard voices," she said, smiling lightly. "You must be Mr Langley." She reached out her hand. Mr Langley looked slightly taken aback at how nice she was, Danny thought, fantasising for a second about Mr Langley dating his mum and then moving in and them talking about Chelsea all day long. He was sure his mum could get past the big veiny nose thing.

"Have you come to bring me my paperwork so I can swot for tonight?" she said.

She sat down at the opposite sofa next to Erland, who was still sniffing despite clutching his new handkerchief.

"About that..." said Mr Langley, shifting in his seat to look at Danny's mum. "There has been a change...." He glanced at Danny and then Erland. "Are you okay with me discussing this in front of your sons?"

"Of course," said Danny's mum, smiling still, but

placing her hands out flat on her lap and holding them still. Danny knew this was his mum's way of grounding herself before a shock. It was her usual stance when he handed her his school report.

"The police are going to press charges," said Mr Langley, blowing out a little puff of breath.

"Based upon....?" said Danny's mum, still holding her hands flat but the smile having evaporated.

"Based upon your child's injuries." Mr Langley hesitated, narrowing his eyes as though trying to assess the damage that he was about to cause. "Your husband's claim that you assaulted a lady here last night hasn't helped matters. No charges are being pressed on that front, I hasten to add."

Erland moved closer to their mum who was now sat with her head bowed. "Did he mention to you that he's shagging that so called 'lady'?" said Danny. "If Mum hadn't have hit her, I would have."

"You probably think you're helping, lad," said Mr Langley, frowning, "but that kind of talk is unproductive. We don't have much time," he said, turning to Danny's mum again. "The meeting has been brought forward to two o'clock in light of the police charges. Here's a copy of the investigation report." He reached forward to ease a document onto the coffee table. "I suggest you read section 3A before the meeting. Do you have a solicitor?"

"No," she said.

"Then I'll give you the name of an excellent childcare solicitor," Mr Langley said. "Free legal representation will be available at the station as well."

"The station?" she said, her eyes frightened. Danny felt his throat tighten. They were going to take her today. What would happen to him and Erland? How long would they hold her for? She was thinking the same thing – staring at Danny, her face white, her mouth open, her cheeks looking as though someone had pinched them spitefully.

"These are serious allegations," said Mr Langley. "You must have realised the implications." Danny looked at his mum. She didn't seem to realise the implications of anything.

Mr Langley sighed and rubbed his face as though suddenly the clock had raced forward and he had found himself sat here on their couch at three in the morning.

"Look, here's what's going to happen." He crouched down on the carpet in front of Danny's mum, perhaps to try to comfort her. It was exactly what Danny's teacher had done the day he had fallen from the climbing frame and broken his arm. The teacher crouched before Danny as he howled in pain, waiting for his mum to arrive. He had never been so happy to see her.

"The chaps from the child protection unit will interview you at the station. If they have sufficient evidence, they'll charge you and fix a date for you to attend before a magistrate's court. You will more than likely be back home later tonight. I'm sure your boys can manage until then – big lads like them."

He stood up, pinching his trousers at his knees to remove the crease. "Here are my contact details should you need me." He placed his business card down on the arm of the sofa.

"Is Jacko coming to the meeting?" said Danny's mum, rising.

"I'm afraid not," said Mr Langley. "I thought it best that he stayed away, given the situation between you. I thought he might put up a fight, but surprisingly he concurred."

At this their mum crumpled, wrapping her arm around her face so that she was hidden by her sleeve. Both Danny and Erland looked at her, hands hanging by their sides, at a loss as to what to say or do.

Out in the hallway, Mr Langley turned to Danny. "It'll

be okay," he said, quietly. Danny gazed at the man's nose once more – at the metropolis of problems. "If your mum is guilty, then she needs help. If she is innocent, then the system won't let her down. The truth always outs."

"Can you help us?" said Danny, speaking before thinking.

He expected Mr Langley to start catch-phrasing, hand gesturing, like a politician who'd been told all that corny stuff about hands in a temple sign meaning honesty and that repeating words over gave the message more weight. Instead, Mr Langley stepped closer to Danny, until his veiny nose was right before Danny's nose – only much higher up, what with Mr Langley being so tall.

"Petrescu didn't see Chelsea just as his employer," Mr Langley said. "He saw it as his *life*. He displayed a heart-felt loyalty. I'm no Petrescu and this isn't Chelsea, but it is my life. And I do everything within my limited power to ensure that things work out fairly, as I see them. You understand, my son?"

Danny nodded and smiled, as he held the front door open for Mr Langley. "Make sure your mum reads Section 3A before the meeting."

Danny nodded a reply and stood blinking into the morning sunshine, watching the big man squeeze back into his small car. *My son.* Danny felt his Adam's apple react to these words. It didn't matter who said it and in what context, it always sounded bloody good.

CHAPTER FOUR

Brett had only been gone for a day and a half, but it was beginning to feel as though he had been gone for a year. Perhaps that was how long it would take for a mother to no longer be able to remember the smell of her child, the feel of his skin, the softness of the curve in the nape of his neck, the dimples in his hands, the flecks of tan in his blue irises.

She couldn't go to the conference without seeing him, without remembering everything there was to remember about him. So she was now driving to Salisbury to visit Rosie instead of reading through the investigation report. What could the report tell her that she didn't already know?

The boys had come along for the ride. Danny was sat up front, his arms tightly folded, his eyes set on the road ahead. Erland was in the back wearing his giant headphones, nodding his head to the rhythm of the music. What music, she thought? There was a time when she had known everything about her boys – every beat that they listened to, every heartbeat that they missed. Now she had no idea what was on their Ipods – whether it was *slap ma bitch up*, or some of those awful lyrics that she ran to the radio to switch off before they took up too much of the air around her.

She wanted so much for her boys to be high-minded. It was so easy to be otherwise, to give in to lazy, even dark impulses. She had fixed her gaze upon the sky many years ago and had held it there, hoping that if she ignored everything that was wrong with the world eventually it would all go away.

But teenage boys weren't known for appreciating controlled, violence-proofed lifestyles. Would her boys rebel? Get into drugs? Never come home at night?

She had lost her confidence, and was exhausted from the strain of single responsibility. And round about then she had met Jacko.

She had been with her friend, Angie, having drinks after work in the Olive bar in town. She used to go out with Angie a couple times a week; the boys were baby-sat by Professor Moss and his wife, the only people whom she ever trusted enough to sit for her. On this occasion, it was September – a new term, a new batch of students, a new sense of adventure in the air. She felt attractive and restless. The bar was empty but for two business men. They approached Beth and Angie, both men edging towards Beth's side of the table. Matt Mount was thin-faced, talkative. He chatted Beth up with assurance and charm. Jacko was handsome and quiet. He hadn't taken his eyes off her the whole time that Matt had been talking. And then when Matt went to the bar, Jacko moved closer to her and spoke to her in a low-pitched calm voice. He was steady, still, masculine, and oh so tall that he gave her the perfect excuse to continue gazing sky-bound.

Angie hadn't been able to believe that Beth was going on a date with Jacko. She thought he was a meat head. *But the boys might like him*, Beth had said.

She had messed it all up. She would make it up to her boys. She would offer a few concessions – a few gadgets in the house, a Game Boy or whatever they were called, maybe even a television.

"How's Lee?" she asked, casually, keeping her eyes upon the road ahead.

"She's cool," Danny replied automatically.

Beth sensed his face burning with guilt and shame, without seeing it. She wouldn't look over at him and let him know that she had heard the 'she' mistake. She would let him think that she didn't know, even though she had guessed that Lee was a girl over six months ago. Best friends didn't happen over night with boys – not the sort of best friends where you had to go to their house every night. His real best friend was a boy called Adrian whom he had known since he was six, whom he met on weekends to swap football cards with.

"Try Rosie's number again will you, love?" she said, handing Danny her mobile by way of distracting him. He was biting his nails. This would be her first concession: not coming down hard on him about his girlfriend. She would let it go. Let him tell her, which he would do very shortly knowing Danny.

"Still not answering," said Danny, placing the mobile back down on her lap.

Her mind whirled with possibilities of where Rosie and Brett might be this early in the morning. She had supposed that Rosie would be home all the time, shielding herself from questioning eyes about the sudden appearance of a strange child in her house. But that was a ridiculous assumption. She didn't have a clue about how Rosie would react to anything, let alone to having a child to look after. Which, Beth considered, made her feel rather uncomfortable with the set-up. She barely knew this woman and there she was looking after Brett. The fact that Rosie was related to Jacko suddenly seemed like no recommendation whatsoever.

She felt perspiration break out at the corners of her hairline. Was Brett sleeping at night? Was he eating well?

Was he frightened, calling constantly for mama?

"Try her again, Dan, and this time leave a message telling her that she won't have Brett for much longer."

"Do you think we should be saying that? I mean, it's not looking—"

"It's looking great, Danny. It's looking great."

The three of them stood in front of the door willing it to open, but it was not going to. Not if they stood there for another two hours. They had already been waiting for twenty minutes, sitting on the steps, trudging around the path to the back garden, cupping their hands against the kitchen window. Beth had glimpsed Brett's Noddy cup. The sight of it had made her want to sob, to smash her hands through the window to reach for the cup, for everything that belonged to her son – for her son himself and to run with him in her arms as far as she could run.

She wiped her forehead again. It wasn't a particularly hot day. She shuddered. Where the hell was Brett?

She dialled Rosie's number again. "We came to see Brett," she said to the answer phone machine. "You're obviously not here. We'll try again later."

They wouldn't be trying again later. She would be down at the police station chewing holes in polystyrene cups of coffee.

"Let me come with you to the conference, Mum," said Danny, as they got into the car and pulled away. "Let me be your person, your help."

There was a splutter of derisive laughter from Erland on the back seat of the car, followed by silence as he re-attached himself to his music.

"Don't be ridiculous," said Beth. "You're thirteen."

"What's ridiculous about that?" said Danny. "Mr Langley said I could go."

Beth had no idea whether that was true. It could well be. All of a sudden, she found herself not caring. She wanted to go home to bed.

"Was that a yes then?" said Danny.

"It wasn't a no," she replied, rubbing away another prickle of sweat.

Klaris sat for an indefinite amount of time watching a spider's web flapping about outside, lit by the street light that it was dangling from. The web was nature's barometer: it was shifting ever so slightly, indicating a gentle breeze, and the glistening rain drops that it was displaying revealed that a light shower had fallen not so long ago.

It was early in the morning – about four o'clock, she reckoned. Light was beginning to seep from the earth upwards; there was a halo of white brimming the tops of the trees. Klaris listened. She could hear a car roaring in the distance like the roar of the distant ocean – its sound piercing the morning silence and making its way to her like watching the dust from a vehicle on the horizon in the Outback. She saw the car's lights passing by on the road at the end of her street. It was amazing how just one car at this time of the day could make such an impression. In less than three hours, it would be a miniscule part of the summer smog and noise.

On the first day of the heat wave a few weeks ago, road works had started on the main road through Klaris's town, Bathcombe, on the outskirts of Bath. The road had been out of use except for residential traffic and in the mornings before work Klaris had marvelled over how silent her world had become. She pretended that she was living in the wilderness, cocking her ear to the solitude and peace, imagining that she was somewhere tropical where the birds were her only company, her food the fruit on the trees around her.

The road works were over now and life was back to pushing everyone along at a pace that they didn't want to go at. There was no break, no respite.

Klaris lived along a cul-de-sac containing six bungalows. Her property, at the end of the road by the turning circle, was the only house. Every year or so there was an invitation to an evening soiree, which Klaris declined.

When she had first arrived four years ago her nearest neighbour, an elderly widow, had introduced her to another neighbour as *the lady with the inheritance*: the widow's way of explaining how a single woman in Klaris's line of work managed to afford the grand house. It was shocking how money mattered so much that people made up explanations to make themselves feel better when things didn't fit. Klaris wasn't inclined to enlighten the neighbours about her financial circumstances, so didn't talk to them aside from a guarded hello.

Klaris's lack of social contact in her street was made up for by the appearance of her house – the reason why she had chosen it. It looked human, she thought – definitely male. The sentry of the street. It had a smooth smile of windows; its complexion was red-brick, its tile-hair greying; even its name was *Seymour*. Evidently, someone else had shared her whimsy.

Despite Klaris's willingness to live life with her sentry, she had been an insomniac ever since joining him. She would get off to sleep promptly and then wake with a start, frowning into the darkness, trying to perceive what it was that had woken her.

Invariably, she would be awake in the early hours of the morning. Sometimes, it was so impossible to get back to sleep that she would make a cafetiere of coffee and watch Sky News.

Today, she hadn't tried to get back to sleep. With the conference looming, her brain wasn't going to give in to rest. So she sat with her pen and notepad, making notes of preparation. She had to sort out exactly what she was going to say. Her mind was blank so she jumped on the exercise bike and cycled for three quarters of an hour. After a shower, she found the words that she needed and sat scribbling on her pad, her towel wrapped around her, drips of water from her hair splashing the ink.

The irony was that on the mornings that Klaris rose in the early hours and remained risen, she was nearly always late to work and this morning was no exception.

"I am *so* sorry," she said to her colleague, as she threw her coat and bag down, and logged onto her computer. "Any calls?"

"Yes…Mr Langley. He said it was urgent."

"Mr Langley?" said Klaris. "Oh…" She fumbled through her desk files for his telephone number.

Her colleague handed her a piece of paper. "There's his direct line."

Klaris waited for her colleague to leave the room before dialling. She was surprised to see that her hand was shaking. She held it out straight before her on the desk to steady it.

There was a new report, Mr Langley told her over the phone, that would be couriered to her within the hour. The report was much the same as the one that she already had – with one exception, he said. He wanted to draw her attention to Section 3A and ask that she might read it ahead of the meeting. It contained some new information that had been brought to his notice very lately.

Klaris cancelled her morning appointments and waited for the courier to arrive. When the jiffy bag landed on her desk, she tore at it as though it contained the answer to who shot JFK. She flicked through the report to Section 3A, sat on the edge of her desk and began to read.

She read the section through twice and then sat still, her lips pursed. She whistled softly.

Poor Beth Trelawney, she thought.

Jacko sat on the edge of the bed, his head in his hands,

lit cigarette between his fingers. He had noticed that in the space of a few hours his body had already adjusted to the nicotine and was stepping up quite nicely to the challenge of being a chain-smoker.

Natasha was stirring from sleep. She pressed against him from behind, her arms around his neck, her small breasts warm against the cold of his naked back. He fancied that she was a demon hanging from his body, dragging him into decadence.

"When you said you loved me," she said, sucking on his ear lobe. "Did you mean it?"

"Jesus, Natasha, I've only just left my wife." He shrugged her off his back and moved to the window. She sat back abruptly on her hind legs, her white pants beautifully offset against her body which was the colour of nutmeg.

"You've left her? Do you mean that?" She teaselled her mane of hair with her hand and reached for a cigarette. Her plummy accent suddenly irritated him. She was the daughter of a car mechanic, for God's sake. He flicked his cigarette out of the window and rubbed his face. He had had, what, three hours sleep, if that? He glanced at his watch. He would call Matt now.

Natasha stretched out flat on the bed. "Who you calling, babe?"

He ignored her and turned his back to her, listening to his friend's voicemail greeting.

"Hi, Matt. It's me," Jacko said. "There's something important that I need to do today. Not sure when I'll be in. I'll be in touch." He snapped his mobile shut and reached for his boxer shorts, his call to Matt making him feel very naked.

"So what's so important then?" Natasha said.

Again, he ignored her. He fumbled with his trouser belt, wondering how much notice he should give his mum. He would head over there now to catch her before she went out anywhere.

"Is this how it's going to be?" Natasha said, sat with her legs drawn up around her.

"How what's going to be?" he said.

"You – ignoring me. Keeping me in the dark."

He looked at her, trying to muster up enough pity to enable him to say the right thing. "Listen," he said, sitting down next to her. "You've got to cut me some slack. I've no idea what's going on in my life, or why I'm here."

"You've no idea why you're here?" she said, her jaw firming. "How about the fact that you said you loved me, you jerk?"

He stood up. "If you could think beyond your own face for five minutes then you'd realise that my son's welfare is hanging in the balance, not to mention my marriage."

"You make me laugh," she said, wrinkling her nose scornfully. "You say 'my marriage' as though you give a toss about it."

"Enough!" he shouted, grabbing his car keys and looking about for his suit jacket. His clothes were in a bin liner on Natasha's kitchen floor. Maybe his jacket would be there somewhere.

He stormed through to the kitchen and dropped to his hands and knees to go through the bags. Mixed up with his things was a little giraffe top of Brett's. Instinctively, he held it to his face and smelt. It smelt not of Brett but of washing powder. Without warning, he cried – silent sobs into his son's top.

Moments later, he jumped up, pressing his tear ducts to stave off any more outbursts. He wouldn't give Natasha the satisfaction of seeing him like this. She was the kind of girl that would get off on his misery, or use his weakness to manipulate him for her own gain.

As he drove to his mum's, he thought about what he might tell her about Beth. He wanted his mum to attend the conference in his place this afternoon, to represent his viewpoint. Someone had to make sure that Brett didn't get snatched up by the authorities. His mum wouldn't want to go. She hated anything controversial or even slightly awkward. As a mother and son combination – him being fickle, her being evasive – they were as deep and substantial as a raindrop.

In order to get his mum on his side, he couldn't tell her yet about living apart from Beth. She liked Beth – thought she was reliable and kind-hearted, although she didn't really know her. He wondered now that the two women hadn't had more to do with each other, his mother having always wanted a daughter, his wife having always wanted a mum. Life wasn't like that though – things fitting neatly together wherever there happened to be a gap. Things tended to slot together and then grate, rub, chafe themselves until they fell apart.

He still loved Beth. What of that? Did she love him? It was doubtful. Whilst his mother was right about Beth, the fact was that reliable, kind-hearted people tended to be the most merciless when it came to forgiving others for being cheating bastards.

Then there was Natasha. He would have to think carefully how to play it with her. He needed to keep her sweet so that he had somewhere to live that was near to work and to Beth, whilst illustrating to Beth that he wasn't setting up home with his sleazy mistress but was concentrating his sights on returning home.

It was a tough one and not something that he could think about on so little sleep. He lit a cigarette and put the radio on, only to hear a discussion about how women shouldn't forgive their cheating husbands. What were the chances of that? He glared upwards, although he didn't believe in God. He had once read in Reader's Digest that if you blamed God then you obviously believed in him. He didn't know what he believed any more.

He wondered what his mum would say if he told her

about Natasha. He always played it safe, giving his mum a version of himself that was not only cleansed but slightly muddied in order to be plausible. He didn't know whether she bought it. Most mothers knew when their sons were lying, he reckoned, but he had been lying ever since the day his dad died. Maybe his mum couldn't now tell the difference between his fabricated self and his actual self. And what's more – could he?

The first lie he had told when his father died was that he believed that his father was dead. When really he knew that his old man had left in the middle of the night leaving a note for his mum on the kitchen table.

Jacko had never let on to anyone that he knew his father wasn't dead – that he had read his goodbye note. It had been a hell of a secret to carry around with him.

Look after Jacko - he's a good kid. Don't try to replace me 'cos it won't work out for the boy. It never does. I will always love you Rosie. Or something like that.

His father's note had been at the back of his mind the day Jacko moved in to Beth's home. Kids hated replacements, particularly ones that they hadn't chosen. He had felt awkward around Beth's boys, and they in turn felt awkward around him and never failed to show this upon their immature faces. If he had stopped to think about it, he hadn't been so different to them once upon a time.

But he hadn't thought about it and he had allowed himself to hate Beth's boys and for them to hate him and for their lives to deteriorate and now he was driving out to his mum's place with his life in shreds.

As he pulled up outside the house, he switched off the engine and smoked another cigarette. It occurred to him that he didn't really know much about how his mum had handled his dad's departure, whether she knew what had provoked it. They hadn't been able to discuss it without Jacko disclosing what he knew, so it had been easier to not discuss it at all.

Perhaps this was why he had resented Danny so much. The lad knew Beth in a way that he was not only jealous of because Beth was his wife, but because he had been robbed of experiencing such congenial intimacy with his own parent.

It was never too late to get to know someone, Jacko thought, stubbing out his cigarette and locking the car. But as he rang the door bell and stepped back out of habit to glance upwards at the house at nothing at all really, he knew in his heart that habit was a powerful thing indeed.

Zoe was the first to arrive at the conference and stood twiddling her nose ring outside the meeting room door. She was wearing a suede waistcoat and a floral skirt that swept along the floor gathering dust. Her Doc Marten boots were too heavy and hot for summer, but she wanted something sturdy to stand in at such an important meeting.

She attended meetings like this all the time, but today seemed something out of the ordinary. A pampered middle-class woman had failed to cope when the going got tough and now she was going to get her comeuppance – so Zoe had thought, until the Bristol big wig, Charles Langley, rang this morning to run through some shocking changes to the conference notes.

"Hey," said Ned, raising his hand in welcome as he approached along the corridor. Zoe narrowed her eyes at him. Something was different. She cocked her head at an angle.

"No goatee!" she exclaimed, pointing at his chin.

"Yeah," he said.

"Why? I thought it was a permanent fixture, like it was sewn on."

"Itchy," he replied after some apparent thought upon the matter. He had a deep dimple on his chin. Maybe that was why he had worn the beard – to hide it. She wished he would grow the beard back. She realised that for all her anarchic tendencies, she abhorred change.

"Hey, did you see the report?" said Ned, looking down at her and grinning.

"Yeah, but what's there to smile about? I was shocked, quite frankly." Zoe fiddled with her hair braid, winding it on and off her index finger, waiting for him to reply.

"About the fact that I was right," he said. "*Yes!*" He raised his fist and pulled it down towards him like a triumphant tennis player. "I said there was something about Beth Trelawncy that we didn't know…" He trailed off, lowering his voice.

Jacko Best had arrived with an older woman in tow. It had to be his mum, Zoe thought, given the resemblance.

Jacko was the same lofty height as Ned. They greeted each other, leaving the tiny folk to knock about at their knees below. "Hello," said Zoe, reaching out her hand to her fellow dwarf. "You must be Mrs Best?"

"Yes," said Mrs Best. And no sooner had they begun their introductions when Beth Trelawney arrived, altering the mood immediately from wedding reception to funeral wake. Clutching her arm protectively was her young son, Danny. Both of them looked pale and wide-eyed, but Danny looked very much the stronger one of the two.

Zoe and Ned shuffled back against the wall and watched to see how the two parties might greet each other. Beth made no show of recognising her husband, but moved towards her mother-in-law. "I had no idea you were coming," Beth said, in a low voice.

"Nor did I," replied Mrs Best. "Jacko thought it would be best. He's not coming in." Mrs Best nudged her son's arm to involve him in the conversation, but he remained stiff, staring ahead down the corridor as though waiting for someone.

"I called at your place earlier to see Brett, but you weren't there," said Beth. "How is he?"

Mrs Best paused before answering, acknowledging how

sensitive this question was. "Just fine, Beth. He's with my next-door neighbour – a registered childminder," she added intuitively, answering Beth's next question.

Charles Langley arrived with the two officers from the child protection unit, plus a paediatrician from Bath Central whom Zoe recognised and a woman whom she didn't recognise, but judging from the unrealistic skinniness, ballet pump shoes and uninteresting necklace and earrings she was a health visitor.

Zoe and Ned were still stood by the wall and remained there whilst everyone filtered into the meeting room led by Charles, who nodded an acknowledgment and a raised eyebrow of anticipation to them.

As Beth drew parallel with Zoe, she considered for the first time how pretty Beth was – how dark and ambiguous her eyes. At the top of Beth's ear was a tiny emerald stud that flashed in the sunlight and it was at that moment that Beth's frightened eyes met Zoe's and the latter considered fleetingly that maybe the two of them weren't so different after all.

Danny had performed just about every magic ritual that he knew of in the hours preceding the meeting: donning lucky socks, lucky pants and a lucky chain; digging out a lucky Cornish pixie that he kept in a matchbox at the back of his wardrobe and kissing a four leaf clover that he had found years ago. He had tidied up his room before leaving, making sure that everything was in its right place and had left his Chelsea home shirt lying neatly on his pillow.

Erland was sat outside in the car playing on his Einstein Touch Chess – the only handheld electronic game they were allowed, aside from *Do You Sudoku* and Solitaire. Erland had wanted to be part of the meeting, but their mum didn't want him to attend as well as Danny. One of them should be spared the sorrow, she said. At this, Danny's stomach had churned.

He glanced at the clock. The meeting should have started three minutes ago. He wiped his hands on his trouser legs. He was wearing his school uniform, which had seemed right at the time but now in front of all these grown ups it seemed really immature. Had his mum been thinking straight she would have made him wear the suit that she bought him last year for a funeral and that still fitted him, just. But she hadn't been thinking straight because she wasn't dressed right either; she was wearing a baggy mohair jumper that was malting onto her chair, tufts of it escaping across the conference table like dandelion clock fluff.

He thought of Lee. She phoned just before they left the house, to wish him luck. His mum had answered the phone and had held the receiver out to him without acknowledgement of their previous conversation about Lee in the car, not that it had been a conversation at all.

He had whispered to Lee on the phone that his mum had guessed that she was a girl, not a buddy, and Lee had snapped that girls could be buddies too – the two roles being fully interchangeable. She had really accentuated *in-ter-change-ab-le*, meaning that she had just learnt the word in a magazine. Danny sighed and had gone to hang up when he heard Lee saying something. He asked her to repeat herself. She said, "good luck, *buddy*."

"No, not that bit," he said. "The other bit."

"Oh…I just said…I love you," she said, hanging up. He stared into the receiver, listening to the continuous tone. When all this was over and his mum was feeling better, he would have to ask her whether saying *I love you* counted when you were only thirteen.

A frizzy-haired woman wearing apricot lipstick came in carrying a tray of biscuits. With her was a lad aged only a few more years than Danny who went red when he saw everyone assembled at the table and put a jug of water heavily onto the table, slopping its contents. Danny gazed at the water droplets as they wobbled, catching the light.

Mr Langley, who wanted henceforth to be known as Charles, he said, was now seated with paperwork in hand, glasses perched on the end of his veiny nose. He thanked everyone for coming and went around the table doing introductions. The only person that Danny didn't know was the hospital paediatrician, a man with deeply set eyes and a long face. Some people had to go through life looking that miserable, Danny thought, and they couldn't do a thing about it. Was his face miserable because he was miserable, or was he miserable because his face was?

Today's conference wasn't to thrash over old territory and make judgements or allegations, but to decide whether there should be a child protection plan for Brett Best, Mr Langley said. Only the facts were to be considered, not opinions or theories – the facts as stated in the Section 47 enquiry report. He was pleased to see that everyone had their copies, and he wanted in particular to draw everyone's attention again to the new insertion, Section 3A.

Danny sat up straight. He hadn't read it, nor had his mum. He saw her jerk slightly, the only indication as yet that she had been paying attention. She had been pulling little balls of fur off her sleeve and watching them fall like wispy parachutes to the floor. He realised now why she was wearing the jumper: she could pick fluff, poke her nails through holes, caress the fur, snuggle down, lose herself, drift off. It was an infant security blanket in the guise of a grown up item of clothing.

At mention of Section 3A, they both casually reached for the report and bent their heads together to read, whilst pretending to listen to the chairman.

Any child protection plan regarding this case should involve an investigation into B.T's own history of physical abuse at the hand of her mother and her subsequent foster mother, and the impact that this has had upon her and her role as parent.

When their heads moved away again, Danny saw that his

mum's face was no longer the same colour. It was ash white as though every living cell on her face had been cremated and before he had time to think of what else it looked like and what he could do about it, she was lurching towards him, her eyes rolling upwards. He caught her in his arms and sat there trying to hold his mum's head upright, as everyone around the table gazed on, passively, sat with their reports propped up in front of them like news readers waiting for their cue.

"Well, get a glass of water or something, you morons!" said Danny, his mind racing with what he had read. It seemed impossible, as though it were written about someone else with the initials B.T. and not his mum whose head he was cradling.

It was Zoe, the brace lady, who first moved to help. She poured a glass of water and moved round to Danny's side, crouching before his mum, tapping her face gently and talking to her. Hushed murmurs began around the table as though the onlookers had decided that it was rude to stare and that small talk was in order. Danny heard someone mention Lanzarote and scuba diving.

He thought of the words on the page again. His mum had kept a secret from him his entire life. How could she have experienced something like that and not mentioned it to him? How come she didn't wear the memory all the time like one of those wine-coloured birth marks or bad teeth?

At that moment, his mum gained consciousness and Zoe moved her to a comfortable-looking chair at the other end of the room. His mum sat there, bewildered, looking about her, apparently not remembering for a few minutes that everyone in the room now knew exactly who she was.

When she did remember, she set her eyes upon Danny with an expression that he didn't recognise. It was only when she covered her face with her hands that he realised that she was ashamed.

He had to go to her. He knelt down beside her chair, but she wouldn't look at him. Zoe whispered something to Mr Langley and then told Danny that it would be best if his mum remained where she was. They would bring her some coffee.

Zoe returned to the table because Mr Langley had begun the conference. Danny remained with his mum, resting his hand lightly upon hers. He couldn't see her face so he stared at her hair, at a single hair that was hanging separately from the rest. He wondered at all the strands that made up a person's past and about how it could turn out that one of them had the ability to alter the present more than all the others.

Then his mum withdrew her hand. "Go listen, Dan," she said. "Go see what you can do."

Back at the table, there had been some shuffling about and Danny was now opposite Zoe. Her tooth brace was really ugly, he thought, but in light of her recent kindness he found himself thinking that her eyes were nice and that her smile, despite all the wires and wonkiness, was not all that grim. Something about her reminded him of Angie, the lady from the university that used to come to their house with her baby all the time when Brett was born. She was his mum's friend before Jacko had driven her and the other friends away. There hadn't been many friends in the first place so removing them was an easy job if you knew how, which Jacko did.

Mr Langley was talking about the child protection plan, about what it would involve if they decided to put one into action. It sounded like a lot of hard work. Poor Mr Langley. He wouldn't have time to date Danny's mum.

Lots of long words ending in *tion* were used – words that didn't ordinarily play much of a part in Danny's life. Like clarification, amplification, evaluation. It was hard for Danny to follow what was going on.

He wondered what Brett was doing now, whether he

was eating his mid-morning apple-flavoured rice cake snack or whether Rosie Brett had no idea about that. He glanced sideways at Rosie, noticing that her hands were in better condition than his mum's. Yes, they were wrinkled but they were all nicely polished and with long nails and stuff. He didn't know much about hands, but hers looked like they hadn't worked very often.

He hated Rosie all of a sudden because Jacko wasn't there for him to hate. She had brought Jacko into the world after all and there had to be some sort of pay back for that kind of a slip up.

Klaris was talking now. Danny forced himself to pay attention. He didn't like her. He couldn't see why his mum trusted her opinion so much and had let her access their private lives. She seemed wishy-washy and there was something so...he shook his head. He didn't know. She just seemed, to use an Americanism that Lee liked saying, *kinda flakey.*

Klaris was sat up as straight as the back of her chair. Her face was flushed and her hair was uncharacteristically ruffled where she had had her head in her hands, reading through her notes. She had a sort of script, it seemed, which she was reading from. She had known ever since Brett had been born that things were difficult for Beth, she was saying. She had been concerned because she knew, as a child-care practitioner, the classic signs to look out for. One such classic sign was the fact that Beth Trelawney's boys, particularly Danny, were expected to be the parent, to give love and care to their mother, rather than the other way around.

At the mention of Danny's name, Klaris lowered her notes and gazed at Danny, as though his very presence today confirmed the point she was making.

And then there was the shouting, Klaris said.

Danny sank down in his seat, his feet stretched out and thought about how often his mum had raised her voice in the past six months, about how often she had sat sobbing on the back step with her head in her hands, about how often she had threatened to leave or to kill Brett. He had no idea whether that sort of thing was normal having only ever known his mum do it, but he was fairly certain that Lee's mum had never done the V sign through the wall to her kids or called them a little shit under her breath.

The shouting had been getting worse, according to a source that wished to remain anonymous, Klaris said. Danny reeled in his legs. Who the hell was the grass? Who hated them that much?

Brett had been displaying negativism and disobedience, as many a child did at his age, Klaris said. Unfortunately, some children triggered their own physical abuse by their parents whilst undergoing this testing developmental stage, she explained. Their disobedience was a condition of their age, but the frustrated parent responded with slaps and punches to the body and head. It was Klaris's understanding that Beth had responded in this way, particularly since Rosie Best was able to confirm that his dysfunctional, hyperactive behaviour had improved drastically since having been removed from his mother's care. Wasn't that correct?

Danny winced and waited for Rosie's response as all heads turned towards her. Rosie blushed and cleared her throat, fiddling with a glass of water, turning it slowly round and round on the table. "I…" She glanced over at Danny's mum for approval. His mum nodded, sadly. "Yes…Brett has been good. Very calm. Very good."

"That might just be his natural reaction to being away from his mum," Mr Langley said. "Am I to understand that Brett isn't all that familiar with you?"

"Yes," said Rosie. "I haven't had the pleasure of knowing him that well."

"And we all know that children save their worst behaviour for those with whom they feel the most comfortable. It's rather flattering," said Mr Langley, glancing over at Danny's mum, tossing her a bone of compassion. Danny nodded in appreciation. He liked this guy. Somebody had to be on their side.

"Regardless of this," said Klaris, eager to return to her important synopsis, "it is my recommendation that Beth should work intensively with a parenting counsellor to enable her to reprogramme her parenting responses."

"Thank you, Klaris," said Mr Langley. "A cohesive summary."

Klaris stood a little and bowed, before sitting down again. Weird old bag, Danny thought, scowling at her.

In the end, it was Section 3A that made everyone's minds up. Section 3A meant that his mum was more likely to be an abuser than not. Section 3A meant that his little brother now had his own child protection plan.

Zoe was appointed as Brett's key worker and it was her responsibility to make sure that everyone kept to the plan. The plan so far consisted of their mum having therapy and parenting coaching, whatever that was; of finding ways to give her regular breaks from looking after Brett; an investigation into Brett's behaviour to see whether it was dysfunctional; plus anything else that arose at the core group meetings. Zoe would visit daily to see how things were progressing, plus Klaris was to continue to visit as often as her schedule allowed.

The police remained quiet throughout the conference. Danny had known that this was because later that night they would arrest his mum and interview her upon their own turf and terms. He had also known by the resolute look upon their faces that they would charge his mum with the offence and fix a court date for her, just like Mr Langley had said.

Rosie had stayed with them at the house with Brett whilst his mum had gone to the station. It was a bit awkward because Jacko had given Rosie a lift and then hovered around outside the house underneath the street lamp before sloping off to the local pub. At least, that was where Danny had guessed he had gone on foot, his collar turned up against the rain. The thing to do might have been to invite him in, but Danny wasn't going to show him any mercy.

Rosie wasn't so bad. And it was good spending time with Brett. Zoe was there too, plus the goatee man who turned out to be okay too. He knew quite a lot about Chelsea. He was a Liverpool fan and followed the Premiership. He said he thought that Drogba and Anelka *could* play together, and that he thought that Joe Cole coming back would give them the balance they needed. He also had a loyalty card at Mr C's so he had brought round a bucket of chicken wings, a bottle of Coke, onion rings and some apple slices. It was great. Danny and Erland had never eaten junk at home before.

Danny could see what the social workers were doing - distracting them from worrying about their mum. It wasn't difficult to distract boys their age. Erland was showing Zoe his chess magazine and Brett was refamiliarising himself with his toy basket. Rosie was watching a *Bergerac* DVD on their mum's laptop (it was as if a huge state of the art television had never entered their lives) and himself and the goatee man, Ned, were looking through his file of Chelsea programmes.

But he and Erland kept looking at each other. And Danny knew that Erland would normally have eaten way more chicken wings than that.

Ursula had started the drug therapy just after Easter. The first set of drugs were designed to suppress her hormones, followed by a course designed to super-stimulate them into egg production. And that was when her troubles had begun: the emotional outbursts, the anger, the sadness, the hot flushes, the headaches that were so debilitating that in the end she had to resign from working at the library. She couldn't stand there sweating, cursing, fighting back tears in front of the public. A woman had come in with a baby in a pushchair and Ursula had to duck behind the counter in the middle of renewing the woman's membership card in order to cry.

She resigned before the library came up with some legally permissible method of removing her.

And it wasn't just the tears. It was having to rush off during working hours for blood tests and ultrasounds. If it wasn't during working hours then it was in the middle of the night, leaving her exhausted and wired the next day at work. She and her husband were at the mercy of whenever the time was right to begin the drug cycles to have her eggs collected.

During egg collection, she went under general anaesthetic – which made her sick afterwards – whilst the doctor impaled her with a fine hollow needle. The doctor collected the eggs, mixed them with her husband's sperm, waited for fertilisation to occur and then inserted the eggs or embryos – three the last time – back into her uterus.

And then they waited….Two weeks, three days. Finally, they were informed, much to the doctor's regret, that the pregnancy had not developed.

That was last week, the day that the Trelawney boy next door was so damned rude to her. Had he not been so rude, she might have let it slide. But the fact was that the youngest boy had been crying constantly for well over an hour. Beth Trelawney had been screaming more than usual, had threatened to kill the young child, had slammed doors so loudly that the windows had rattled.

Ursula hadn't quite made up her mind about what to do about it and was hovering by her front door outside to see if she could decipher what was going on, when the eldest boy emerged and snarled at her. She retreated indoors and calmly picked up the phone and informed children's services that she was one hundred percent certain that her next door neighbour was mistreating her toddler and that he was at risk of being physically abused.

After she hung up, she poured herself a glass of gin and tonic – the only consolation of the day's news being that without a pregnancy she could enjoy the relief of alcohol. In truth, she wasn't certain which she was more rattled by – her unfruitful pregnancy or the fact that she had just jeopardised someone else's state of motherhood.

She would have loved to have told the eldest boy that she was the anonymous informer, just to see the look on his face. Instead, she satisfied herself with the knowledge that she had done the right thing. It was never a nice feeling, being a snitch. But nor was it a nice feeling knowing that some honest, kind people would pay the earth to be given the chance to have children and raise them with consideration and love, and then there were people out there who gave birth to children only to resent them. People like Beth Trelawney.

Beth stood with her hands in her pockets, looking at the rain poxing the surface of the river. She had declined the police lift home. The kind policeman with the blond hair (as opposed to his caustic partner: talk about good cop, bad cop) had pressed the matter, but she said that she wanted some time alone before facing her children. A few moments ago, she had noticed a police car cruising almost soundlessly past and she had wondered whether it was the blond police officer, following her to ensure her safe return.

It struck her that now she had been charged with child abuse, she would no longer be viewed in the same way by the police, by her boys, by anyone that read about the case in the paper or heard the gossip at the local Co-Op. She would be henceforth viewed as a fragile woman with psychological challenges – if the criticism were to be that kind. At best, she was a mess. At worst, she was a monster.

She stared downwards, wondering at what point a bad luck card ceased to be a part of the game and could be tossed away as a bad deal? People did that all the time with things – the wrong curtains, a saggy mattress, a whiny girlfriend, a defective husband. Why was it that bad luck was harder to dispose of than the lawful, binding agreement of marriage?

For it had been bad luck – mere bad luck.

She had wanted to tell Danny so many times. Not Erland and certainly not Brett. She had mostly wanted to tell Danny when he was a tiny baby because he had seemed like the sort of old worldly-wise baby that would understand and make sense of it. She used to imagine telling him the story like a fairy tale as she nursed him, stroking the tiny dent at the end of his nose, touching the dimples in his feet. In turn, when he had finished feeding he would lie in her arms, content, gurgling, full of acceptance.

He had always believed in magic.

CB

Once upon a time in Cornwall, a lonely egg bumped into a sperm and they decided to make a baby. When the time was right the baby made its eager way down the birthing canal, only to find itself in a council flat in the seaside town of Pentruthen, where it was bottle fed upon a cigarette-burnt sofa.

The baby turned into a beautiful princess who liked to put her fingers in the sofa holes and pull out the stuffing. Until one day, the little princess tripped and fell down the stairs several weeks in a row, always on a Saturday night around midnight. Suddenly, the little princess found herself in a different house that was nicer because the sofa didn't have holes in it, but that was because the lady who lived there liked using the little princess's arm as an ashtray.

One day the little princess threw the wicked lady's matches and cigarettes into the sea and began to run. As she ran, a pair of magic shoes rose from the ocean and attached themselves to her feet. As she ran further, a magic cloak dropped from the moon onto her shoulders and engulfed her. So long as she wore the shoes and the cloak she would always be safe.

But the wicked lady had tricked her. She knew the little princess would try to escape and had hidden a mood ring inside the little princess's broth. The little princess had swallowed the ring and it had nestled deep inside her heart. Far away the wicked lady laughed, knowing that she would always own the little princess's heart and that one day the circle of the ring would be complete, and she and the little princess would become One.

CB

CHAPTER FIVE

"Did your father ever touch you inappropriately?" The psychologist crunched the mint she had been sucking, as though having lost patience with it.

"I didn't have a father," said Beth.

"Oh? So who was the man that you–?"

"I didn't say he was my father. He just used to be around a lot."

"Who was he?"

"I don't know," said Beth, gazing over the psychologist's shoulder and out the window to the rooftops opposite. It was a warm afternoon. The window was one that opened from the bottom and it was half-mast. A pigeon pecked on the ledge, cooing softly. Beth normally found pigeons irritating, but sat in this office the sound of the pigeon cooing was soothing, simplistic.

"Look, I know this wasn't your idea," said the psychologist, straightening her blouse officiously. "I can tell the difference between patients who refer themselves and those who are referred as part of a programme, the latter being much more closed, but it's important that you open up."

"Open up?" said Beth, setting her eyes angrily upon her interrogator. This woman had no idea – with her glossy hair, pussy-bow blouse and pencil skirt. "You're right – I don't want to be here. I don't want to be analysed. I've made a lot of progress on my own and I –"

"Progress?" The psychologist removed her glasses. "My report states that you abused your child."

"I don't believe this," said Beth, standing up so forcibly that her chair toppled backwards. "You're judging me?"

"Too right I am. It's my job to provoke these reactions in order to tell exactly how you respond to anger."

Beth stared at her. The psychologist stared back, her lips pursed.

"I've had enough of this," said Beth, making for the door.

"Do you really want to do that?" the psychologist said. "Do you want me to conclude in my report to the children's services that you were so infuriated by my questions that you stormed out? What if I'm asked to testify?"

"Are you threatening me?" said Beth.

"For Pete's sake, Miss Trelawney." She rose and stood before Beth, holding out her hand peacefully. "I know this is an awful time for you, but I'm not here to make it worse. Please take a seat again. Let's continue where we were. I'll put the coffee on." She smiled. "This doesn't have to be awful. It could be…" She hesitated, trying to find the right word. "Fun?"

Her eyes creased in the corners. She wasn't as young as Beth had thought. Maybe early forties. She smelt of expensive perfume. Her nails were plum-coloured. It wasn't her fault that she was everything that Beth wasn't any more.

"So it wasn't your father. Was it your mother's boyfriend perhaps?"

Beth curled her legs up to the side of her. They had

moved from the upright chairs to two small adjoining sofas. "I don't think so."

"Do you think he sexually abused you?"

"No." Beth sipped her coffee. They were drinking from Denby mugs. They had the same mugs in her faculty at university, except that they hadn't had the teapot, the milk jug and sugar bowl like this lady. She sighed heavily.

"Why the sigh?" said the psychologist. "The man?"

"No," said Beth. "I think he was a good person – the only one in my life at the time. That's why I sort of remember him… I was sighing because I don't think I'll ever lecture again."

The psychologist's brow furrowed for a second and then she nodded. "Ah, yes. Your old job. You're an academic. Do you miss lecturing?"

"God, yes. You know, I don't feel as though I use my brain any more, as though I'm even alive some days. But it's not the reason that I hit Brett. I didn't do it. Do you believe me? Do I look like an abuser?"

"What does one look like, Beth?"

Beth closed her eyes and breathed out through her nose – a tight little exhalation. No matter which way Beth ran, all paths led to the road that the psychologist wanted her to take – back to that council flat in Pentruthen.

"I can't picture her face. I can see parts of the flat – men going up and down the stairs. I wonder now whether they were dealers and users. My mother was a user. Heroin, I think. At least, I heard my foster parent saying that on the phone one day, not that her opinion was to be trusted."

"How old were you when you were taken from your mother?"

"Six."

The psychologist put down her coffee cup and pushed her hair behind her ears. "Beth," she said, gently, "what did your mum do to you?"

Beth closed her eyes again. It was easier that way. She would have done the same thing when her teacher had asked her that very question after class thirty years ago. Now she could see the old flat – the brown chess board carpet, the stains on the kitchen lino; she could feel the sharp springs in her mattress, smell the off milk in the fridge.

"I was cold, hungry, smelly," she said. She smiled at the memory of herself. She had lived in squalor and had managed to get by, in the way that children often did. "She must have been suffering from withdrawal. A couple times I got thrown against the wall and down the stairs. The last time it happened, I broke my collar bone and my left wrist."

Beth looked down at her wrist. She couldn't remember breaking it. She couldn't remember who had noticed or when, or even how she knew this information. She couldn't remember leaving her mother, whether they had said goodbye. She couldn't remember whether she had ever seen her again.

It was like Brett, she thought. He had left her and one day he might not be able to recall a thing about her. He would be given fragments of information about his history, about his mother who was mentally unstable, an abuser. He would have no proof, no scars, no memories. Just an unnerving, habitual sense that all would never be right in his world. Every Christmas, every Mother's Day, every birthday for the rest of his life the unease would swell to an intensity that could not be ignored. And would then quell down to a temperate level like a tide lapping on the shore. Natural, rhythmic, intrinsic - a part of him. Every time he woke. Every time he laid his head down at night.

The psychologist was by Beth's side, handing her a tissue. "Dry your eyes, Beth. We'll leave this for today. I'll see you at the same time tomorrow. Good work."

On her way home, Beth impulsively swerved to turn off her usual route to follow a road that was so familiar she felt as though she had time travelled – her files and essay papers shifting about on the back seat of the car as she followed the winds of the rural road, the windows down, the birds singing, her head filled with the lecture ahead: *why is Dreiser's* Sister Carrie *such an important work regarding the portrayal of women in literature?* Everything – the countryside in July, her life – felt full, rich, ripe. She hadn't met Jacko yet, hadn't had Brett, was mother only to Danny and Erland. She worked whilst they were at school and had the holidays off when they were not. It all worked perfectly.

As she arrived at the campus in the present, she was disappointed to discover that Archie, the old security guard had been replaced by a young man who greeted her without expression. "Where's Archie?" she asked him, flashing her old university pass which she kept in her purse for no reason other than nostalgia.

"Retired," the lad said, sniffing. He waved her on through the barrier. She drove slowly, abiding to the ten miles per hour speed limit. From habit, she followed the road round to the right and then turned into a small forecourt before jerking to a halt. Her space outside the English faculty was filled. RESERVED: JESSICA KING.

Beth turned off the car engine, aware that the back of her car was sticking out into the road. No one would come along. She knew the workings of the university: clocks, schedules, timetables. The students were in lectures. There was a hush in the air. The only movement on campus came from flies and from the cows in the adjacent meadow.

She gripped the stirring wheel and sat with her chin resting on it, gazing up at the building. Why had she given it up?

It had happened insidiously. It was like that with babies. Everything was temporary – infants were growing, changing from day to day, and everyone was waiting for something to happen. Life was on hold. And sometimes the holding bit was so painful and so exhausting that you let go and everything drifted away.

She could have returned part time. There was a nursery on campus. She had looked around it when she first knew she was expecting, but Jacko hadn't wanted Brett to go there until he was at least two years old. The faculty couldn't have kept the post open for Beth for that long, nor would she have asked them to.

The old her would have fought Jacko. The old her wouldn't have even glanced at Jacko, let alone married him. But a decade of single motherhood had weakened her. She had felt so grateful to Jacko. He was supporting her and her boys, and he wasn't the father.

She had told the psychologist that she missed lecturing but that it wasn't the reason that things had deteriorated at home. But what if it *was* the reason? What if she had allowed it all to happen, had on some level been willing it on? Perhaps she had wanted to punish Brett for taking everything from her.

She gasped for air. She couldn't breathe. She began to panic and was about to wind down the window for air, when the faculty door swung open and out walked a young woman in a cobalt blue top and jeans. She was wearing sandals, her auburn hair was plaited, her waist accentuated with a thin gold belt. She approached the RESERVED: JESSICA KING car, glancing at Beth without recognition.

Why would they recognise each other? They had never met. It was Beth's replacement, fresh from grad school. Jessica King, King of the World, of Beth's old world.

It was like seeing herself as she had always thought she would be: unfettered, sophisticated, free from responsibility, free to make choices. Oh, God. She reversed as fast as she could, without looking, and tore off down the road. Oh, God. Oh, God. She wiped away her tears and sped up the hill to home, the speed camera flashing at her.

Klaris was trying to remember her list of Things Not to

Bother Buying Organic that was pinned to her kitchen notice board, as she surveyed the bananas. Were bananas on the list? She reckoned they were. Something to do with their skins being so thick that pesticides didn't affect them. She wasn't sure. After several moments of deliberation, she chose organic and just as she put a bunch of green bananas into her trolley her mobile phone rang.

She didn't have her reading glasses with her. She squinted at her mobile, holding it at arm's length. Even at that distance and visually impaired, she could quite clearly make it out: X X X X X X.

She toyed with the idea of not answering, but curiosity won the day. She so rarely heard from him.

"Hello?" She wanted to be one of those chic, suited women who propped their mobile under their chin whilst selecting mangoes, but she wasn't. She stood still, one hand on her trolley to defend it from the barrage of customers.

"Klaris. I'm in town."

She caught her breath. "Town?"

"Bath."

She glanced around her and lowered her voice, not worried about anyone hearing her but about being judged for being one of those people who talked too loudly on their mobile. She backed out of Fruit and Veg and wheeled herself over to Magazines and Cigarettes where it was quieter. The sort of people who came to the counter were always in a hurry – *20 Marlboros, please, oh and….*quick grab at the stand in front of them…*a Bounty bar and an* Evening Post. They weren't the slightest bit interested in a middle-aged woman's phone conversation on a hot Friday night in July.

"Why are you here?" she said.

"I had a meeting with Charles Langley."

Her mind raced and then halted abruptly, tripping over itself. "Children's services, Charles Langley?" she said.

"Yep."

She put her hand to her heart to calm herself. "Why would you be doing that?" A car had pulled up outside the supermarket, its bass pounding. She couldn't think. She moved further into the store, towards the row of magazines, surveying the covers of white teeth, red lipstick and thick hair, without taking any of it in.

"Because we work in the same line of business," he said, with a trace of sarcasm. "And because we studied at Edinburgh together?" He posed this as a question, asking her to remember pieces from her past – a past that she had done everything in her power to forget. Of course, it was impossible to do so. Bits rose up all the time and lay there lifeless, unwanted, like drowned insects in a water barrel.

"Charles and I are part of a specialist project team in the U.K – have been for the past couple of years. Ever since you and I split up, I guess…" He trailed off.

She winced, hating the casual way he spoke – the *I guesses* and *sortas* and *whaddya knows*. She had always felt like an old fuddy in his presence – even when she had been his bride. He laughed at her coyness on their wedding night, at her shyness on their honeymoon, at her sexual reticence throughout their twenty-year marriage.

She felt the anger rising. *Hang up! Hang up before it's too late!* But she had uttered the words. "How's your little slut?"

He was silent for a moment. "Don't start, hun."

"Hun?" she shouted. "*Hun?*" A woman flicking through *Marie Claire* lowered the magazine to stare at her. Klaris grabbed her handbag from the trolley and turned on her heel, abandoning her organic green bananas. She took Demon Man, her ex-husband, across the car park as fast as she could go on her cork-heeled sandals.

"Calm down," he was saying. "I was hoping we could meet for coffee whilst I'm here, but obviously not."

"Obviously not," she echoed, looking about for her car. Where the hell had she parked it? She had thought it was over in this direction near the trees in the shade, but now she was here it wasn't there. She headed off towards the trolley drop-off point instead.

"Are you ever going to forgive me?" he said, breathing into the phone. She wanted to bottle the breath and send it off somewhere for testing – to see whether you could tell beforehand whether lying breath was different to ordinary breath.

"Now, let me see….. No. No. Never. Never going to forgive you."

"Don't you think life might be easier for you if you did?" he said.

Her mouth dropped open at the cheek of the man, that he could be so flippant, dismissive, patronising. It was easy to see how he had progressed through the children's services, in a field that largely consisted of showing other people how to live their lives.

She found her car and stood with her back against it for support, her head leaning back, her eyes turned up to the sky.

She imagined how he might look now: greying for sure, but still with a generous head of black scruffy hair; jeans, navy blue sweater, checked shirt underneath. He would still be listening to Coldplay and Snow Patrol – names that she heard on the radio but whom she knew nothing about. He would be buying their albums, playing them on this stereo, running his hands through his hair, tapping his leg to the beat, reaching over to put his hand on his slim girl's knee or to stroke her pretty blonde hair.

She had no idea if the girl were blonde or pretty or slim. Just that she was a girl. To a fifty-one year old, that was enough. The young bit beat all the other categories hands down.

"Part of me still loves you, Klaris. And always will."

She stopped looking at the sky and looked ahead of her, across the car tops, at the people coming out of the supermarket – sharing carrier bag handles, holding hands, wheeling trolleys together. She had to do everything on her own now. It was likely that she would have to for the rest of her life. For twenty years, she hadn't had to, but for the next thirty or so she would.

"You are down as six x's in my phone," she said, drawing her cardigan around her. She suddenly felt chilly. A flock of birds set off from a tree top and headed off, as though thinking the same thing. "Because you've driven me to hell."

He laughed. "You always had a keen imagination, Klaris, but that's a bit dramatic isn't it? Even for you."

"This isn't my imagination," she said. "It's my life. My sad life." She began to cry. She hadn't seen it coming. If she had, she might have ended the call a while ago and jumped into her car.

"Oh, hun. Let me come over. You sound like you could use the company. We could talk about old –"

"*Fuck off!*" she screamed at her mobile, standing on tip toes to elevate her voice as much as possible. And then she turned and hurled the phone up into the air across the car park.

She had never said the F word before. She hated it. She hated what it had come to mean in today's world – the way it was bandied about by everyone in the street and on television and in the press as though it weren't one of the worst words you could say.

And now she sounded like a commoner. She didn't care any more. She got into her car, turned up her stereo and *la la la*'d to Fleetwood Mac all the way to her cul-de-sac. But as she pulled into her driveway and sat listening to the evening's silence, she felt overcome by loneliness and fear.

After all these years, she was still listening to Fleetwood Mac. She had changed the scenery, the car, the town, the house – all the big things. But hadn't changed any of the details. He would be listening to new music all the time –

buying CDs and throwing them carelessly into his stereo, snapping them out and taking them indoors to play whilst he made his morning coffee and a fry-up. Or maybe he and his girl had continental breakfasts. It all depended on what sort of a young slut she was.

They would have lots of adventurous sex. She imagined him – exuberant, released, whooping, high-fiving. He had hated her for not wanting to explore sex. It had been the single thing he most resented about her, so he had told her right after the divorce came through.

With unsatisfactory sex being hinted at as one of the reasons for her divorce, Klaris had felt utterly substandard and imperfect. Uninterested in reading women's magazines, watching soaps or having best friends to swap lascivious details with, the enormity of sex and its relevance within a marriage had completely bypassed her. She knew that it was part of marriage, like taking out the rubbish or emptying the dishwasher, but hadn't realised that failing to engage in sex regularly, even given the stresses of work and running a household, would result in a loveless life. Had she known, she might have reconsidered it. She might have obliged more often. It wasn't that they had never made love at all. It was just that she didn't initiate it. That was all.

She knew that it wasn't all, though. She knew that he thought her judgemental, old-fashioned, inhibited. They had travelled to some wonderful places whilst inter-railing around Europe and always seemed to end up in close company on a tram, in a ski-lift, with some gorgeous wide-eyed girl with hollow legs and huge lips, from Scandinavia or Bulgaria or Lithuania. The girls' broad accents, groaning, straining to find the right words, seemed almost orgasmic. Klaris always felt like a lesser being, looking down at her white legs, her nautical shorts, her floral hat. She was so…

She couldn't bear looking back at herself any more. There was a reason why the past was forbidden to her.

There was a reason she had driven two hundred miles to leave it all behind. There was no going back. Not for coffee, not for a chat, not for anything. Now that she no longer had a mobile phone with his number programmed in, it was over. The past wasn't a pool she could dip her toe into. It was a cess pit that would infect her wounds.

She locked her car, glancing about at the neighbours' houses. It was very quiet. The EastEnders theme tune was playing softly through an open window. The mere sound of it made Klaris feel comforted, although she abhorred the show; but now it made her feel part of the human race, part of a humdrum routine. Life wasn't all about blouse-ripping and keeping up with trends. Some people, like her, were happy with humdrum.

She went inside, pushing the door into something that was obstructing her entry, grating along the bottom of the door. She cursed and then laughed with delight. It was a parcel from the Real Stories Club. She tore at the wrapping and pulled out a DVD. The accompanying letter thanked Klaris for her continued support as a member of their subscriber's review panel.

She would watch the film tonight. It wasn't even a title that she had heard of. A whole host of characters that she had yet to meet – a new world to escape into.

He would be gone from her thoughts any moment now. For a few hours at least.

She realised that she didn't have any food in the house, having abandoned her shopping. She had no idea even where her list was any more.

It didn't matter. She would write a new one tomorrow.

Danny and Lee had been stood in the post office queue for fifteen minutes, staring at the sweat on the back of the man's shirt in front of them. Lee was timing their wait on her new DKNY watch that her dad had brought her back from his business trip to New York. It could go under water, Lee said, which Danny couldn't see the point of since Lee hated swimming or anything to do with water – which wasn't really an issue since Danny didn't like water either. He would have hated there to have been something really big between them like that, like one of them being a potholer and the other a claustrophobe.

Here, stood in the queue with his arm casually draped over Lee's shoulder, her hand in his shorts' back pocket, he knew that nothing was going to come between them now. That if things carried on as well, they could end up spending their lives together just like he had planned.

He had thought his mum was a big thing between them, but he knew now that she hadn't been an obstruction at any point. The obstruction had been in his mind. He had supposed that his mum would go ape at the idea of him having a girlfriend, because she was always going on at him and Erland to knuckle down at school so that they could go to university and make something of themselves. She hadn't made all these sacrifices just to have them throw it all away for some local girl that was always going to stay local.

His mum had never said anything like that, in fact. Nor had she ever told them not to have girlfriends. He had just sensed that it wasn't her bag.

Looking at Lee now, as she analysed the workings of her watch, he realised that if his mum hadn't told him not to get distracted by a local girl and throw away his future, then it had been him telling himself. What did that mean? He shrugged. He didn't want to have to worry about anything.

Everything was cool at home at the moment – as cool as it could be with a missing sibling and an impending court hearing. But cool as in quiet. His mum was mellower than he had seen her in a long time, probably because she was getting time to herself to sort things out. Without Brett she was much calmer and she was being tutored in how to keep the calm once he came home. In his house, they said that all the time – *when Brett comes home* – as though chanting it like a mantra would make it happen.

Brett had been gone nine days. They went every other day to see him at Rosie's. She wasn't so bad and made them welcome with a meal and milkshakes and cookies – she was a bit like Mrs Paris, he thought. Without Rosie, it could have been a whole lot worse.

He knew that his mum found it difficult regardless of what Rosie was like and what she had prepared for their lunch. His mum would drop to her knees and hold her arms out and say something like *come to mama* and Brett would hide his face behind Rosie's skirt, or just stand still, mouth open, motionless. He didn't smile at any of them or seem to recognise them. He couldn't not know who they were, Danny thought, could he? Lee said that she had read in a magazine that if children under three were abducted then they would never remember their real parents. This thought saddened Danny immensely, until he reminded himself that Brett hadn't been abducted but borrowed and would soon be returned.

The post office queue moved forwards an inch. "Twenty minutes," said Lee, smiling tightly, holding up her watch and tapping it.

They had just had lunch at his place for the first time with his mum and Erland. Erland kept his face near his plate and didn't say much, nor had his mum said much either. The sun had streamed in the dining room, lighting up the steaming shepherd's pie and peas. His mum hadn't gone to any trouble, which meant that she didn't see Lee's presence as a big deal – a good sign, Danny thought. Dessert was an apple and yogurt. Lee had done most of the talking and his mum had nodded thoughtfully, pronging her mash.

Lee wasn't as clever as his mum. He hadn't ever thought about this before, probably because the two of them had never met. But now at the dining table, he sensed

– slightly uncomfortably – that Lee wasn't as clever as any of them. He looked at her sweet face, her pink polo shirt unbuttoned two buttons, her arms tanned brown from her recent trip to see family in Florida. She had brought him back a pencil case with dolphins on and a plastic mug from a water park that said *Danny – a cheerful and honest friend to cherish.*

He wondered whether his mum had been quiet because she thought what Lee was saying was silly. Perhaps Erland thought this too. But a quick glance at their faces had reassured Danny that neither of them thought this at all because they weren't listening. Lee didn't realise she was rattling on unattended because his mum was nodding in all the right places, and Lee didn't expect any response from Erland because Danny had forewarned her about him.

Using Lee's presence as a softener, Danny had told his mum over lunch about what had happened to his Muddyfox. Even so, he had expected a show of anger, particularly given the events surrounding its demise, but she had just said that now he could get the bike that he really wanted: the Silverfox Demon 26 inch dual suspension bike. If he didn't have enough in his post office account, she would make up the difference – *whatever you want*, she said. But Danny reassured her that he did have enough and would even have fourteen pounds and a penny left in change.

Now they were queuing for the money and were going to get a lift down to town with his mum to the Star Buy store opposite the children's park so that he could buy his Silverfox. They had phoned ahead and the Silverfox Demon was waiting, ready for him. His mum was going to give Lee a lift home so that Danny could ride his new bike right away.

In less than an hour, he thought, squeezing Lee's shoulder as the queue moved forward a person, he would be riding the bike that he had been dreaming of for the past two years. See – dreams really could come true.

But when it got to five twenty on Lee's new watch and he was holding the money from his account firmly in his hand and his mum still hadn't picked them up outside the post office, he began to stamp his feet and curse her. If she didn't get here soon, it would be too late to get the bike. The shop closed at six o'clock and they had to take the traffic into account.

Then a thought occurred to him that stuck hard at the back of his throat. He tried to clear it away with a cough and another stamp of his feet, but there it was – stuck. His face began to burn and his body went cold all over in the early evening sun.

Whatever you want, she had said. *Whatever you want.*

His mum was never that indifferent.

Something was up with Ned. Zoe could tell it from the moment he got into the car and slumped down into his seat. He wasn't a sigher and here he was sighing away, starting the ignition, his elbow on the open window, his hand propping up his head. "What's up?" she said.

Ned wouldn't say.

"Fancy a pint at the Old Boat?" she offered. The pub was right next to where Ned lived. She would have to get a bus back home, but it was only a fifteen minute ride at most.

He probably wouldn't go for it.

"Okay," he said.

She flushed with pleasure and turned her head away to grin out the window. She glanced down at her clothes. She was wearing a yellow strappy dress with a grey holey cardigan and Doc Marten boots with grey socks. Aside from the boots – she really needed some sandals that weren't girly and didn't mess up her statement – she looked summery and okay for socialising. Social workers rarely looked like they were good at socialising, she had noticed.

At the Old Boat, Ned ordered a Guinness – meaning that he was taking it slow – and then changed his order when Zoe ordered a Katy, a local full-strength cider – meaning that she wasn't. Zoe smiled into her Katy because Ned so rarely changed his mind, and here he was altering his order to suit hers. He was drinking Hazy Mist now, a strong real ale.

It was easy to get drunk when you were a social worker, she thought, following Ned out to the beer garden – easy to want to escape what you had seen that day by drinking too much too quickly. When you were handing out ideas about clean living all day like a street canvasser, it became second nature to do a little dirty living oneself – rather like why many doctors smoked and drank.

Social workers were under more stress than most in the public services factor, given that they were all petrified to make an oversight resulting in a high publicity child abuse case. So they ran to every spark in the area, stamping it out before it became a bush fire. Two people on their team were off long-term sick with stress and one had just re-trained as a Reiki healer, and they hadn't been replaced. Zoe and Ned had made a pact not to talk about the stress they were under and to pretend instead that everything was cool. Once they acknowledged out loud that it was a crap job, they too would be headed the Reiki way.

"So I saw Beth Trelawney today," said Zoe, tossing her bag onto the bench and sitting beside it. The beer garden backed onto the canal. Reeds were growing beyond the canal, which was lit gold in the intense end of day light.

Ned sat opposite her, opening a packet of crisps and a bag of nuts and laying them open on the table between them. "Yeah? How was she?"

Zoe paused for a moment to consider this. "I don't know. Bit cagey perhaps?"

"Where were you?"

"On my lunch hour. I saw her coming out of the

chemist at the top of Rush Street. Must be her closest shop, thinking about it."

Ned took a long drink and licked his lips. He still hadn't grown his goatee back and Zoe had lost hope of him ever doing so. "So you didn't speak to her?"

"No," said Zoe, shaking her head. "I just saw her in passing."

"So how the hell can you say she was cagey?" Ned said, after some thought.

She shrugged. "I dunno." She gazed at the reeds as they bent their heads in the wind.

The first drink always went down quickly, with the conversation limp and laboured between them. The second drink was when Ned normally began to speed up his conversation a little, with fewer pauses. And the third drink was normally when he began to tell her what was wrong – if anything. Typically, the answer to this question was his love life. And tonight was no exception.

"I got dumped," said Ned, hanging his head. He was genuinely aggrieved. Women kept finishing with him because he was too kind. Too sweet. She should have been compassionate about it, but she always found it funny. She threw back her head and laughed.

"You're such a bitch," he told her, stumbling off to the toilets.

Alone, Zoe thought about this. Was she a bitch? She was told this at least every other day by Ned, or her son, or by someone else she worked with. Often the people she tried to help referred to her as such. You had to be hard to do her job, she told herself, but she didn't have to be so hard on Ned. Couldn't she offer him some support?

Ned came back and she stared at him. "What?" he said, aggressively. She had rattled him with her laughter. "Drink this." He placed two shot glasses of something murky down on the table in front of her. "I'll go first." He closed his eyes and downed the drink before slamming the glass down, shuddering.

"What is it?" she said, suspiciously.

"Thai rum."

It sounded deviant so she went for it, closing her eyes. When she opened them, Ned was sat next to her, his legs straddling the bench. "I want to make love to you tonight," he said, staring at her mouth.

She started in surprise, holding her arm out to push him away lightly. "Hey?" She laughed. And then, judging from his serious face, she stopped laughing and dropped her hands to her lap. "This is because you've been blown out again, isn't it?" she said. "You want to take it out on me."

"No," he said, still staring at her mouth. "It's not."

"Then why? This is totally out of character. You hate me!"

"Hate?" he said, looking away now. "God, Zoe." He stood up. "I show an interest in you and you think it's because I want to have some kind of sadistic sex with you. I can't believe I even tried." He reached for his wallet and pushed it into his back pocket, exposing his taut midriff. "Let's go. I'll walk you to the bus."

Zoe followed him out of the beer garden and down the path to the main road, trying to keep up with his long fast strides and to not trip on the backs of his feet. Here she was again – the little girl. Once again, she had messed up. And here was her bus, its lights juddering up and down the road as it hurtled along. Ned had his arm up in the air, flagging it for her. His front door was four houses along from the stop. The bus was starting to slow down. She grabbed at Ned's arm to yank it down to his side.

"Don't, Ned!" she shouted. The bus changed gear heavily and accelerated again. The passengers stared gormlessly at her as they passed slowly by, their eyes not seeing or understanding. "I want to stay with you."

The road had fallen silent. Ned gazed down at her. He reached for her hand noiselessly and led her to his front door. Smoothly, he pulled the key from his back pocket and moved her into the hallway. Against the wall, he bent down to kiss her – a tantalisingly well-structured kiss that was impossible to fault. Intoxicated, she followed him up the narrow stair case, watching him stoop at the top to cross the low landing through to his bedroom.

His bed was neatly made and on the bedside table was a book and a lamp. He turned the lamp on and turned its glare low against the wall, before sitting down on the bed and pulling her close to him. They looked at each other, both wordlessly acknowledging the fact that work would never be the same again, and then he put his hands up under her dress, slowly sliding up her thighs. She slipped her cardigan from her shoulders and it was only as she climbed on top of him that she realised she was still wearing her Doc Marten's.

Ned was snoring ever so softly so she sat up as gracefully as possible without disturbing him. There was still time to make the midnight bus. She sneaked downstairs and through the lounge, there being enough light from the street lamp outside for her to find her way.

Ned's lounge was nothing like she had imagined. There wasn't dope paraphernalia or a Bob Marley poster or a carved wooden Buddha or boxes of half eaten cereal and a stringless guitar lying around, as she had pictured. Rather there was a calm about the room that she might have guessed would emanate from something of Ned's creation, had she given him enough credit.

One wall was taken up entirely with a bookcase of novels and history books – he had studied history, she remembered – and there was no television. There was an armchair next to the bookcase and she imagined him sat there of an evening, reading. Next to the armchair was a photograph of two people whom upon closer inspection she reckoned to be his parents. They looked like nice folk.

Nice clean people.

As Zoe stared at the photograph, she became aware of her nose ring and braided image staring back at her in the glass reflection. She put the picture down and turned away.

She wasn't good enough for Ned, she thought, making for the door. He wasn't a stereotype. When he got home, he stepped out of his Right On clothes and got on with his humble, thoughtful world. She was the stereotype – a social worker who dressed like an anarchist and hadn't yet learnt that no one else gave a toss how she dressed, and that it might be okay every now and then to let the act go.

She let herself out of the front door and out into the night. She could never come here again. She could never tell Ned that she loved him with all her wicked black heart.

The bus arrived on time and as it pulled away with her on board, she jerked towards the nearest seat, clutching for the metal rail to sit down.

Outside, the world was black. All she could see through the window was her mean face staring back at her and the faces of the handful of passengers around her who were probably wondering what a woman was doing out on her own at this time of night.

And that was when she realised: Beth Trelawney had bought something at the chemist shop and had been looking furtive about it.

Zoe pulled out her mobile phone. "Come on, Ned, come on, pick up," she murmured, picturing his phone ringing on the table next to his bed where he had left it.

She hung up and tried again. And again.

Finally, he picked up.

"What?"

"Jesus Christ, Ned," she said. "She's gonna kill herself."

Beth sat up with a fright, drawing her knees to her stomach in her long nightie, clutching the blanket close to her chin. The blanket was scratchy and hairy. She suppressed a sneeze, squeezing her eyes tight and holding her breath. She couldn't see anything. There was no light in this room at the back of the house. She stared ahead at the blackness, listening intently.

From beyond the open door, down the stairway, came the sound of creaking floorboards. Then the sound of wheezing, quiet cursing. Beth held herself taut, her skin breaking out in goosebumps. The wheezing was getting louder, then the floorboard at the threshold of her bedroom creaked. She stared ahead at the void, her eyes stinging from keeping them still; she dared not even blink.

Her room filled with the familiar smell of cigarette smoke, seeping into her bed clothes, underneath her wardrobe door, into her hair, into her nostrils. Through the silence, came the soft crackle of a cigarette being dragged on. She watched the tiny orange circle of fire glowing intensely and then ebbing away to a dull glow. Then the circle moved off with a creak of the floorboards again and a scuffing of slippers.

Beth's body unwound like a snake uncoiling, her muscles sinking luxuriously back into a relaxing pose for sleep, followed by the sensation of hot liquid flowing between her legs and spreading behind her back. She enjoyed the feeling of warmth for a moment, wondering when she had last felt so warm in bed, until the smell of urine met her nostrils with the terrible realisation that she would be punished for this crime.

"Ohhh!" she called out, jumping up, wondering how to hide the accident. And then she clasped her hand over her mouth and stopped breathing again.

Sure enough, there came the sound of scuffing slippers approaching along the hallway and once again there in the doorway was the orange circle.

Beth began to shiver, her wet nightie clinging to the backs of her legs. "What you doing awake, Princess, eh?"

The light snapped on. Beth winced underneath the yellow glare of the unshaded light bulb. "Looking for your mummy? Pammy's here now, Princess, and Pammy loves you."

Pammy held out her hands – hands that were gnarled and warped with arthritis, as twisted as the damaged bark on the tree that stood outside Beth's window. The tree had been struck by lightning, one of the neighbours had told Beth. She didn't know whether the tree was dead or alive. In all the seasons that she had lived here, she hadn't seen it shed a leaf nor grow one, but still she liked to sit with her back against it in the summer with her legs in the long grass, hoping that one day she and the tree would be happier.

"You want to give me a hug, Princess?" Pammy was still holding out her hands, squinting as she held the cigarette between her lips. There were so many lines across her mouth from having used it so often as a third hand to hold cigarettes, that Beth reckoned water could be stored there, running along the cracks like tiny streams.

"I'm wet," said Beth.

"You what?" said Pammy, plucking the cigarette from her mouth to drag on it fully. She exhaled the smoke between her teeth.

"I wet the bed." Beth stood still, clutching the back of her nightie.

There was a silence. Another inhalation and exhalation. "What d'you do that for?"

"I didn't mean to. I was scared."

"Scared?" Pammy laughed a crackly laugh that sounded as though it was catching alight – maybe it was. Last summer holiday, Beth had counted how many cigarettes Pammy smoked and had reached twenty-eight by lunch time.

"Well, get up then," said Pammy. Beth stayed where she was. "Get up!"

Beth moved stiffly, holding her nightie out behind her

away from her legs. Her feet and hands felt icy. It was winter. Beth blew her breath out in front of her.

"You trying to tell me something?" said Pammy. "We can't afford central heating. Not if you want me to give you food to eat. Have you any idea how hard I have to work? You kids these days – you want it all. Isn't this enough for you – a roof over your head?" Pammy pulled the wet sheet off the bed. "Take them wet clothes off."

Beth didn't move. "Get them off, I said!"

Beth turned away and then eased her nightie over her head, grateful that she had remembered to wear pants in bed, before remembering that she would have to take them off too.

"Give them here," said Pammy, putting her cigarette back in its holder between her lips and taking the wet clothes down the hallway to the bathroom. Beth perched on the edge of the bed, listening to the sound of running water as Pammy rinsed the clothes and sheet out.

"Here," said Pammy standing in the doorway, holding the dripping laundry out to Beth. "Put them all back on."

Beth opened her mouth to speak, but didn't know what to say.

"Get on with it!" Pammy threw the clothes and sheet at Beth. Beth began to cry. She looked about her for something else to put on. Her body was starting to look a purple colour and her legs were bumpy and spiky-haired. "No, not the tears. I can't stand it. Do you know what time it is?"

"I'm cold," said Beth, crying more heavily. "If I put those clothes on, I'll freeze to death."

"At least you'll be clean, you ungrateful bitch," said Pammy. "Now get dressed and I don't wanna hear another word out of you."

"No," said Beth, stopping crying and stiffening her legs. When she stood up as straight as she could, she wasn't that much smaller than Pammy.

"What d'you say?" said Pammy, jerking her head back ever so slightly in surprise.

"No," said Beth.

"You cheeky little vermin," said Pammy, half-smiling, half-glaring. It wasn't an expression that Beth had seen before or since. Pammy was the master at being nice and horrible at the same time.

Slowly, Pammy approached, rolling up her sleeves until she was parallel with Beth. Her cigarette had burnt low so she dropped it onto the floor and ground it with her slipper heel. Keeping her eyes on Beth, she reached into her dressing gown pocket for her cigarette packet. Beth watched the entire ritual: the tapping of the cigarette on the side of the packet, the hesitant flick of the lighter, the burst of the flame, the crackle of the ignited end, the satisfaction filling the eyes upon inhalation.

Beth eyed the open door and then darted towards it, but Pammy was fast. She grabbed Beth's wrist and led her to the bed. "You little shit," said Pammy, gritting her teeth. "I've bent over backwards for you, but this is the last time I'm letting you off. Think you're something special, don't you? I'll show you how special you are."

Beth had no idea what being something special meant, but at that moment she knew that it was a description that didn't apply to her. It applied to the girls with hair in ribbons wearing velvet dresses who walked along the path at the bottom of her garden to Sunday school at Pengilly Methodist opposite the quay. And to the boys whose dads stood in the drizzle with their hands thrust in their anorak pockets, heads bent against the sea gale, cheering their sons on at football on Saturday mornings when Beth passed on her way back from running grocery errands for Pammy.

"Please, don't," said Beth. *"Please,"* she said. She looked into Pammy's eyes – opening her own eyes as wide and imploringly as she could. "As one human being to…" It was a phrase she had heard on the television.

"…To another?" said Pammy. "You think we're equal and you're only eight years old?" She laughed. "Don't forget, Princess, that I'm the boss. Maybe this will help remind you."

As the cigarette fizzled against her shoulder and Beth smelt herself burning and felt the searing sting of her flesh weeping, she closed her eyes and vowed that she would never appeal as one human being to another ever again.

A week later, Beth ran away. She took Pammy's stash of cigarettes with her and threw them into the sea, watching the cardboard case bobbing on the inky water until it drifted from sight. The bus drove her from Pengilly to the city of Treale, where she caught the train all the way to London, changing at Bath.

In the hour that she waited at Bath, a stray dog sat on her feet to keep them warm and a lady eating an orange said hello and asked Beth if she would like one too. Beth decided that if she ever needed to run away at a later date, she would come back to this neck of the woods.

"Mum?" Danny listened. "Mum?" Lee went to move forwards. Danny held his hand out to stop her. "Wait here," he said.

A letter was lying on the dresser. It was his mum's court summons. The date was next week. They had been warned that it would be rushed through because Brett wouldn't be able to legally remain with Rosie for long, but seeing it in writing was chilling.

He pictured his mum reading the letter on her own, her head spinning with frightened conjectures of what was to come.

There was the sound of the key in the front door behind him. Danny tensed himself in anticipation, expecting his mum to come in saying she'd been to the shop for milk, welcoming the relief that the sight of her would bring him, but it was Erland.

"Where've you been?" said Danny. As usual, Danny was barely able to calm his heart enough to make it remain in his rib cage and here was Erland strolling in listening to Pink Floyd on his Ipod as though the entire world was made of marshmallow and he didn't have a care. Erland kicked off his heavy trainers without bending down to untie them and made his way for the lounge, ignoring Danny.

Danny followed him into the lounge. "Where's Mum?" Lee had taken his instruction seriously and was still hovering by the front door, awaiting his next command.

"Upstairs somewhere," said Erland, sitting down on the sofa with his legs outstretched, hanging over the edge. He pulled his chess magazine from his rucksack, bent the cover back and began to read.

"What did she say about the letter?"

"Ask her yourself," said Erland, scowling.

"I'm asking you."

Erland lowered his magazine. "She said she didn't think anyone was going to believe her."

"So what did you say?"

"Nor did I."

"Nor did you what?" said Danny.

"Nor did I think that anyone would believe her."

Danny grabbed at the magazine, ripping it from Erland's hands. "Why would you say that, you moron?"

"Give me that back!" shouted Erland, jumping up, trying to snatch the magazine back from Danny with wild movements of his long arms, like seaweed moving in the ocean.

Danny stared at his brother briefly, at his eyes set so deeply and remotely that they may as well be made of clay, and then hurled the magazine at his face. In that second, he hated Erland more than he could remember having hated anyone, with the exception of Jacko.

"I just said the truth!" said Erland, his face flushing with anger. "I don't believe her and nor do you, so no one else will! It's obvious!"

Danny clenched his fists and stepped forward, hopping from foot to foot like a boxer. Then he held his hands to his head and pressed hard in frustration, not wanting to give his younger brother the bloody nose he deserved.

"Danny?" It was Lee. She stood in the doorway, her face pinched and anxious. Things like this didn't happen in the Paris household. She had once thrown a cushion on the floor because her brother had eaten the last homemade cookie and they all talked about it still at her house as *The Day that Lee Threw the Cushion.*

Danny dropped his hands to his side, deflated. It was hopeless. He and Erland would never understand each other, not even when their mother needed them to most.

"When did you last see Mum?" said Danny, quietly, hanging his head.

Erland shrugged. "Lunch time."

Danny turned to leave the room and then turned back to his brother. "For your information, I do believe her. I always have and I always will."

Erland picked up his magazine and sat back down on the sofa. "Whatever."

Danny was about to retaliate by telling Erland what a loser he was, when Lee led him by the arm back out into the hallway.

"Her bag," she said, pointing underneath the stairs to where Danny's Muddyfox used to reside. His mum's handbag was lying there, its insides hanging out – very untypical of her. She had been in a rush. He picked it up and hung it up on the coat peg where it normally nestled amongst their school duffels.

"I'm going upstairs," he said, motioning for Lee to go back into the lounge. She stood frowning at him, her mouth open, and then nodded.

As Danny climbed the stairs, he remembered feeling the same way as he had when he came home to find Brett unconscious. With each stair that he stepped onto, he tried to think of an appropriate magic spell to work, but all that he could come up with through his mental fogginess was that an even number of steps would bring a positive outcome and an uneven number a negative. Chelsea was playing Aston Villa tonight for their place in the Carling Cup so it was doubly important for him to hit positive.

As he counted seventeen, his heart sank.

He stood on the landing between his mother's bedroom and Brett's, before instinctively choosing to enter Brett's room.

The door was shut. It was dark inside. He sniffed the air. It smelt funny – of smoke. He wanted to snap the light on but didn't want to out of respect for his mum; she might be asleep on the futon. She sometimes slept here when she was missing Brett.

He waited for his eyes to adjust. "Mum?" He moved towards the window to open the curtains and release the shut-out blind. As he crossed the room, he stumbled forward. "What?" He jumped up and raced for the light.

There on the floor lying on her back was his mum, her eyes staring straight at him, unseeing.

"Oh, no, oh, no," he said, dropping to his knees to feel her hand. Her skin was still warm. He felt for a pulse – there was one.

"Lee! Erland!" He ran to the door and shouted as loudly as he could. "Call an ambulance! Now!"

He moved back to his mother, standing over her, glancing around the room for signs of an overdose or a note, but there was nothing.

He hadn't often seen her asleep before or unconscious or anything other than awake. Children didn't see their parents asleep, but parents saw their children asleep every night. To feel a parent's eyes upon you – looking without noticing – was the eeriest thing. Until he realised that she had been looking at him without seeing him for quite some time now.

"Please, Mum," he whispered. "Please don't die." He hugged his arms around him to stop himself from crying.

Something caught his eye, lying underneath his mother's hand. She had been holding something, until her grasp had softened. He moved forward expectantly to retrieve a note, but to his surprise it was the most unlikely of objects: a packet of cigarettes.

"Danny?" It was Lee, calling from the bottom of the stairs. "The ambulance is on its way."

Danny sat backwards, holding the cigarettes in his hand, staring at them, uncomprehending. And then he dropped the packet as though it were on fire.

There, on his mother's arm, was a trail of burn marks – a multitude of fresh whelks etched into her skin.

"Mum?" Erland was stood in the doorway, gazing at their mother and Danny in turn. "*Mum!*" he screamed.

The three of them – Danny, Erland and Lee – were sat in line on the pavement outside the house when Mrs Paris pulled up in her four by four. She was one of those mothers who drove around the city in a big car that said *I am running a business here, you know*, the business being having a family. From the looks of it, Lee's brother had been in the middle of tea because he was sat on the back seat eating a sausage and looking disgruntled.

Mrs Paris smiled as she turned off the engine, but her eyes were alarmed as she homed in on Lee. Lee looked down to the pavement and kicked a stone with her pink plimsolls. She hadn't said anything the whole time they were waiting for her mum. It had been Lee's idea to call her and the boys hadn't disagreed because who else were they supposed to call? But then once Lee had made the call and they sat and waited, she went all quiet as though she was beginning to think it was a really bad idea.

Or maybe she thought Danny was a really bad idea. She

had looked pretty freaked out as they stretchered his mum out to the ambulance. Lee's skin was green-ish and her top teeth were biting down on her lower lip in the expression that people normally adopted when something had gone wrong, like a tyre was flat or a cat had gone missing.

"Is that all you are bringing?" said Mrs Paris, looking at Danny's school rucksack.

"We're not planning on staying long," said Erland, standing up. As Erland moved, Danny smelt a whiff of urine and eyed his brother's trousers. Erland had wet himself; he was trying to pretend that it hadn't happened by just ignoring it – the old leave it to dry technique that tramps used in the summer.

"Erland's right," said Danny, joining his brother and putting a protective hand lightly on his shoulder. "We'll leave first thing in the morning to go and see Mum. I'm sure she'll be out by lunch time."

"Quite," said Mrs Paris. She crouched down in front of Lee, holding onto both her arms. "How are you, darling?" she said, her voice lowered as though to emphasise that the boys weren't subject to this show of motherly love.

Lee shrugged her reply. Danny squinted into the sunshine, annoyed. Whilst waiting for Mrs Paris to arrive, he had pictured how jealous and upset he would feel upon seeing her: her perfect car, her perfect clothes, her perfect everything. Whilst their imperfect mum was being rushed unconscious to hospital covered in weeping cigarette burns, her life in the paramedics' hands. But now that Mrs Paris was stood here in front of him, comforting her daughter and not seeing to Erland who clearly could have used a hug from someone older and female, he realised that there was nothing perfect about her at all.

"I'll see to Erland then," Danny found himself saying aggressively, heading indoors. He grabbed a pair of boxer shorts and a pair of combats for Erland from the airer, considering whilst doing so that his mother had hung all the clothes here. What if she never did this again – never came home again? He held his head in his hands for a moment and told himself to get a grip. He couldn't break down now. Not with the Parises outside.

As Mrs Paris loaded them into the car, the doors chimed politely in the way that posh cars did when the doors were opened or a seat belt was undone. Danny and Erland were going to be like those children that he saw driving around town in the back of big cars, looking glum, static, restricted, whilst their mothers ignored traffic lights and cut other drivers up.

He felt bad that he had wanted to be Mrs Paris's son, rather than his mum's son. So many times he had held his mum up against Mrs Paris and found his mum inferior in every way. He felt like a traitor. His mum didn't give a toss about the sort of car she drove; she was more interested in the type of programme they listened to as they drove along, the exhaust pipe hanging off.

If his mum died, he would never have told her that he was sorry. That he was sorry not only for being a traitor, but for what she had gone through as a little girl. He thought again of her lying on the stretcher, of her pale near dead countenance, of the wounds on her arms, and he hung his head in shame, rocking to the movement of the car.

The real people in this world were the people with the scars. He knew that now. Then he noticed that Mrs Paris was watching him through the rear view mirror. So he asked cheerily, "What's for dinner, Mrs P?"

CHAPTER SIX

Jacko was having sex with Natasha when Charles Langley phoned. It used to be making love, but now it was sex. He thrashed at her angrily – angry that she was a competitive bitch whose ego had soared to new heights – or lows – of arrogance since her perceived triumph over his wife.

The sad thing was that Natasha didn't seem to notice or mind. The harder he thrusted, the more she seemed to enjoy it, saying things like *yeah give it to me, that's it big boy.* When did love sour into hate and how come it had soured anyway, since he hadn't even loved her in the first place?

He was just thinking this as he kissed her nipple, when the phone rang. He rolled off Natasha and answered his mobile, lighting a cigarette. Natasha lit up also and lay back down, stroppily. He could tell when she was stroppy. Her mouth turned down like wilting grass.

When he hung up, Natasha sat up behind him, her arms draped around his neck, her cigarette held between her teeth. He shrugged her off and got dressed. "I've gotta go," he said.

"But we haven't finished."

"Yes we have."

The plan was to treat her like a commodity, because that was what she had always said that she hated. And yet…he glanced back at her as he left. She looked quite content. Lying on her back with one arm behind her head, dragging on her cigarette.

On the way to the hospital, he bought lilies. He didn't know if that was the right thing to do. Lilies seemed a bit death-like, but the florist said that pink lilies represented prosperity.

Beth had been in for twenty-four hours. She had been critical, according to Langley, but was stable now and recovering nicely. Jacko resented this bit more than anything else: the fact that children's services had been the ones to tell him. It was like they owned his life now. They knew who his mistress was; they knew what his son liked for breakfast. They had mapped his wife's day out with an intense schedule of therapy, parenting classes, support groups – no wonder she had tried to top herself.

She wasn't the only one that was depressed. His life stank too. His clothes were still in bin liners on Natasha's kitchen floor – she spiked them with her heels in the morning as she tottered around looking for coffee filters. He hated Natasha more than was necessary, given that she was offering him a home and lots of sex. And he missed Beth more than he would ever have thought possible.

He was upset at the news, but not entirely shocked. He had known about Beth's childhood from the start; she had told him casually on their third date as though she were reeling off how many GCSEs she had, and then never mentioned it again. He hadn't really cared about all that. Everyone had their problems and it wasn't as if Beth was a screwball. He knew how to spot nutters from a mile off, having dated quite a few of them. Beth seemed not only to have dealt with her past, but to have put it in a place where she didn't need to go.

Or so he had thought. Yet now Beth had proved to him what he had always suspected, but hadn't wanted to admit because he had wanted her so badly: that damaged goods were damaged goods no matter how much you tried to repackage them.

Beth looked worse than he had anticipated, having pictured her sat up in bed wearing lipstick like they did in hospital dramas on T.V. Instead, she was lying motionless underneath a yellow waffle blanket with her head turned towards the window.

The whisky and painkillers cocktail that she had taken had been pumped from her stomach. Beth hated whisky, he told the nurse. Oh, really? the nurse replied dryly. He supposed it was a bit stupid to say so. Killing oneself wasn't supposed to be in any way pleasurable.

The nurse left him alone with Beth when he said he was Beth's husband, although she was rather frosty with him, he felt. Probably because a decent husband wouldn't have a suicidal wife.

He perched on the corner of the bed, staring at Beth's arched frame. She was breathing faintly. "Beth," he said, reaching forward to touch her shoulder.

"What do you want?"

"I've brought you these," he said, standing up to put the lilies on the window sill where she might see them.

"I hate lilies," she said.

"I didn't know what your favourite flower was," he replied, "so I took a gamble."

"I'm only your wife. I wouldn't expect you to know."

He put his head in his hands. "Beth, please…I've come in peace."

"And I nearly went in peace," she said. "Don't think this was a cry for help or anything. The doctor said only another half hour and I would have pulled it off…"

"Sure," he said. He didn't believe a word she was saying. "So why the cock up with the timing?"

She paused. Her face was still turned away. When she spoke, her voice sounded small. "I was supposed to be giving Danny a lift somewhere. When I didn't show up, I thought he and Lee would make their own way."

"Lee?"

"His girlfriend."

"Oh, oh, this is too good!" Jacko threw back his head and laughed. "Danny has a woman in his life? I love it!... So how do you feel about that?"

The blankets rose and dropped as Beth shrugged. "He's old enough. I couldn't keep him a little boy forever."

This couldn't be sitting as lightly with her as she was making out, Jacko thought. It had to be eating her up inside. Danny was her precious boy. The idea of him with some girl? She would hate it.

"When did you last see Brett?" said Jacko, thinking suddenly of his own little boy.

"I see him every other day," she said.

"Did you stop to think what this might do to him?"

She sat up, turning to look at him. Her face was pallid; the rims of her eyes were scarlet. Her hair was unbrushed and...he set his eyes upon the burns on her forearm. "What the hell?" he said.

She quickly put her arms under the blanket.

"Beth, honey...please tell me you didn't hurt yourself? Beth..." To his astonishment, he wanted to cry. A tear even had the nerve to try to put one over on him – sneaking out the door without him noticing. He flicked it away and stared down at the blanket, hoping that his wife hadn't noticed.

Beth reached for his hand. It was the single best thing that had ever happened to him. Then she reached out to his face and held her hand there. He tried not to smile for joy, knowing that she was trying to comfort him in his misery so it wouldn't be right for him to be chuffed.

"I wanted everything to be perfect, Jacko," she said.

"That's why my life was so hard work. I was striving for perfection because I didn't want to be like them." She widened her eyes. "And you know what? I was so hell bent on *not* being like them, that I was this close to becoming them." She formed the distance of about five millimetres with her thumb and forefinger.

He nodded, but didn't understand. She wasn't going to have that though. She knew when he was faking. She needed him to get this. She lent forward and touched his hand again, keen as freshly baked pie.

"It's a circle, Jacko," she said. "You keep running but you always end up at the start again. It's a *circle.*"

As Danny entered the hospital ward at Bath Central, he remembered a mirror maze that he and Erland had gone into with their mum several years ago for a birthday treat. The mirrors had been so well polished that he and Erland kept running straight into their own reflections.

Life felt like that mirror now – mirrors everywhere, throwing him off track, the same thing happening over and over. For instance, there was the one where he came home and climbed the stairs to find someone unconscious, and the one where he unexpectedly found his mum and Jacko sat with their arms around each other as though nothing bad had happened at all, which was the one that he was being blinded with right now.

His mum had a hospital gown on and looked small and pale, alongside Jacko who was wearing a polo shirt revealing his bulbous biceps and a pair of designer jeans that seemed to clutch at all the right places, or wrong ones.

Danny disliked magic that employed mirrors, smoke screens, deception. Magic was something tangible that you harnessed, not something seedy and deceitful. His mother and Jacko appeared to be using smoke screens. They had been pretending to be separated these past seven days or so, but were in fact as close a couple as ever.

Danny felt Erland's disgust ripple through his brother's skinny body and so put his hand on Erland's arm to stop him from retreating.

Erland had taken the past twenty-four hours really badly. The entire time at the Parises, Erland had sat on the sofa with his face covered by a cushion and his knees drawn up around him. As *Hollyoaks* merged into *EastEnders* and *Coronation Street* on the television, Danny realised that in the absence of their mum, he and Erland only had each other. In the Paris household, they were the outsiders and suddenly their Trelawney blood seemed a lot thicker. Danny had stood protectively by his brother as Mrs Paris asked where he wanted to sleep, what he wanted to eat, whether he was warm enough. Erland didn't seem able to answer even the simplest of questions.

And now this. Perhaps more shocking than the notion that their mum had wanted to take her own life was the notion that Jacko might be coming back into it.

Jacko departed from the ward within moments of their arrival. They hadn't told their mum they were coming. The nurses said it didn't matter because she was sleeping a lot. After failed suicide attempts, the person tended to feel chronically fatigued, they said. They would be lucky to catch their mum awake.

Or with Jacko.

Jacko pushed past them, pretending to look respectful and sombre but Danny had no trouble mistaking the look of triumph in his eyes.

"Come here, boys," said their mum, patting the space on the bed next to her where Jacko had just been sat. Danny and Erland moved forward mechanically and stood next to the bed.

"Who's been looking after you?" she said, wincing as though her throat was sore. She lowered herself down, laying her head on the pillow and her body so far under the sheets that only her face was visible.

"Lee's mum," Danny replied.

"Oh?" she said. Danny had known that would rile her. She didn't know Lee, didn't know Lee's mother, didn't even know where the Parises lived. "Was she nice to you?"

"Yep," said Danny, lying. "Really really nice."

On the way to the hospital, he had been thinking of a completely different plan – of how he was going to tell his mum he was sorry about the traitor thing, about how Mrs P was a bullshit mum, about how much better it was to have… well, sores and scars and things… but Jacko changed everything as dramatically as water to a pot noodle. As soon as Danny had spotted Jacko, he hated his mum.

"I'm coming home tomorrow," she said.

"No rush," Erland muttered, walking away to look out the window, his sweater hood up, his hands shoved deep into his pockets. If he could have climbed into his clothes and disappeared entirely, Danny suspected that he would have.

Luckily, their mum hadn't heard the comment. She was talking about the safety plan that the hospital psychotherapist had devised and about how she had to have an ally and a support network.

Danny couldn't help but think that this was merely another plan. She had only experienced a couple days of the first one in action and she had tried to kill herself. What was the point of yet another plan?

He gazed at his brother's back, at his rigid shoulders, at the anxiety that his demeanour was suggesting. It was his birthday tomorrow. Erland would be wondering whether there would be any cards, any presents – even a 'happy birthday' from someone who loved him. Their mum wouldn't register the date in her current state. And for once, Danny didn't feel like covering for her.

"I'm sorry, Dan," she said, reaching for his hand. He took a step back and shook his head. "Danny?" She looked up at him, confused. She looked terrible, like she'd been left out in the rain all night.

"Well, what do you expect, Mum?" Danny said. "Jesus. You tried to kill yourself!" He was shouting.

A nurse entered the room. She frowned at Danny and then picked up a clipboard and started writing on it, glancing at the watch on her uniform.

"What about us?" Danny whispered. "Did you think about us?"

Erland had moved away from the window and was hovering behind Danny, evidently wanting to hear this too.

"All the time," their mum said. "I thought I was doing this for you."

"Oh, that's great," said Danny, laughing bitterly and turning to Erland. "Isn't that great? She was thinking of us."

"Peachy," said Erland, nodding.

"Boys, please..." She turned her face away and wrinkled her eyes tightly shut. Danny hesitated. Maybe they shouldn't have provoked her. The nurse seemed to agree. She was holding the door open for them with a look of annoyance on her face.

Danny didn't want to leave like this. He could feel the turmoil rotating in his stomach. They would have to kip at the Parises again. He knew he wouldn't be able to get to sleep, that he would feel guilty and repentant again, that there was a possibility that Erland could wet the bed, or set fire to the tablecloth at breakfast. But the alternative – to tell his mum that it was all okay and that he forgave her – was something that he wasn't old enough to do now. At least, he assumed and hoped that it was his age. When he was twenty, he was going to be this peaceful guy with a beard who forgave people. But right now he was a thirteen-year-old boy with a sweaty T-shirt and a hunger that needed sorting.

So he pushed past the nurse and walked with Erland out

of the hospital and into the night, both of them wondering whether Mrs P would ever find out that they popped into Burger King.

"Left here, please," said Beth. The sun was streaming into the car window, warming her arms and legs.

As the taxi pulled up outside her house, she felt overcome with emotion. She paid the driver and turned to look at the view, breathing in deeply. When was the last time she had taken the time to really breathe, to notice that she permanently clenched her jaw, her fists, her knees, her shoulders? She concentrated on where she was tensing and she let the tension go, feeling as though she might flop to the floor. Then she turned to the house and slowly climbed the steps, feeling void of ample energy to do so.

She let herself in quietly, slipping her arm into the hallway cupboard to retrieve the dresser key that dangled on a piece of ribbon. Within the dresser were four presents wrapped in silver and blue star paper, and a card. She went into the lounge and arranged the gifts on the coffee table and then sat down on the sofa, her hands resting in her lap, her head feeling heavy and muzzy.

She could hear voices in the garden. The boys would be playing out there. She had arranged for them to come home this afternoon from the Parises, in order that they might all be together for Erland's birthday. She didn't like the idea of the boys staying somewhere that she didn't know, with people whom she had no idea about. It was essential, she told the hospital staff, that she return home to look after her boys in an environment that was known to them after everything they had been through. The best thing right now was for her to feel needed.

She knew that the boys didn't need her at the moment – didn't want her, or like her. And why should they? Mrs Paris sounded perfect. The longer the boys looked at Mrs Paris, the uglier she herself would seem. She remembered sitting by Brett's cot in hospital that first night waiting for him to wake up, worrying that he would never look at her in the same way again. It hadn't occurred to her that further down the line it would be Danny and Erland too – that they might look at her with hatred. She had to fix that.

There had to be something good here to concentrate upon. Erland's birthday: that was a good thing. She was home for his birthday. She was alive for his birthday. There might even be time for a cake – she could make Erland's favourite devil's food cake.

She glanced down at her arms. She would run upstairs and put a long sleeve top on. The thing was, she thought, touching one of the wounds with detachment like tapping paint to see if it were dry, that she couldn't remember how her arms had got like that.

The voices had stopped. She cocked her head to listen. The back door slammed, footsteps were approaching. Danny entered the lounge and jumped at the sight of her.

"Couldn't you have rung the doorbell or something?" he said, scowling, hurling himself down onto the sofa in the way that teenage boys liked to do.

"In my own home?" Beth said. "I don't think so." She smiled shyly, holding her messy arms down by her sides. "Where's Erland?"

"Dunno," said Danny, staring at the arrangement of presents on the table.

"Oh. So who were you talking to in the garden?"

"Cordless phone," said Danny.

Beth jumped up. "Then he must be in his room." She was moving towards the door when Danny stopped her, his hands on his hips in a pose that she hadn't seen him adopt towards her before: defiant, aggressive.

"You might find," he said, "that he's a bit off with you. He's really freaked out by what happened and he…we…thought you'd forgotten what today was."

Beth bit her lip to stop herself from shouting at Danny.

Fighting anger impulses was something that she was working on, but there was only so much she could achieve in a few days. So instead of shouting, she managed to modify herself to a loud volume. "You thought I'd forget? What sort of a mother do you think I am?"

Her son replied by raising an eyebrow.

She started to make for the stairs when she noticed that Erland's trainers were missing from the shoe rack and that his summer jacket was missing from the coat pegs. Her heart fluttered and she turned to look at Danny who was right behind her.

"Where is he?" she said, accusingly, as though Danny had him hidden up his jumper.

"I don't know," said Danny, flushing red and holding his hands out to protest innocence. She pushed past him impatiently and went to the dining room, the kitchen and the garden in turn, calling Erland's name. Then she ran upstairs and entered each of the rooms, even opening the airing cupboard door.

She returned downstairs to find Danny sat on the sofa again, his head in his hands, moaning.

"What?" she said.

He held a small book out towards her. She took it. It was his post office account book. "What?" she repeated.

"My money, Mum," he said, his defiance melting back to the Danny she was familiar with. "It's gone."

PART TWO

CHAPTER SEVEN

On press night, Peter always ended up texting and emailing friends to cancel the plans he had made with them. He hadn't made the plans because he had thought that he would get away from the office before eight o'clock, but because he got a secret kick out of the feeling of usefulness that consumed him when he realised that there was no way that *Travel News* would get published if he didn't put it to bed himself. So with fake – and sometimes real – angst he postponed arrangements and set about editing and sending the final pages to the repro house, cursing under his breath about how employing monkeys on his editorial team would be more fruitful.

Tonight, one of the feature editors had ballsed up an article on New England tours. She had overwritten by 2,500 words and hadn't spell checked. No matter how much he chopped her text, he still had 800 words to reject if he was to squeeze the copy into the remaining column space on page six.

He took his glasses off and rubbed his eyes, glancing at his watch. If he got this finished quickly and off to repro within the next twenty minutes there would still be time to meet Sheeny for a swift one at the Lamb.

Twenty minutes later, he texted Sheeny to say sorry. An hour later, he was rocking backwards and forwards with the motion of the Tube, too tired to read the book about the poets of the First World War that was propped open on his lap.

He got off near the end of the Piccadilly line at Bounds Green. His house was literally two minutes from the Tube – you could see the underground sign out of their bathroom window if you stretched your neck out – which was great for the property's saleability but not so great for kids streaming past their front door at midnight on Saturday nights.

His phone beeped and vibrated in his jeans pocket and he was intent on reading the text message reply from Sheeny that called him a loser and said little else, when he almost stumbled upon a pair of legs sprawling on the step of his front door. Lucky it was summer and still light out, else he might have injured himself.

"What the hell?" he said, pushing his glasses back to the top of his nose and glaring at the owner of the pair of legs. He was about to take the kid to task when he considered that this young person was a hoody and could therefore be stoned or drunk or both and carrying a knife.

"Can I help you?" he said, trying to sound polite but not patronising. A socialist, he liked to think that he could relate to anyone – so long as they weren't about to break his arms.

The hoody didn't reply, unless staring up with huge serious eyes could be considered a response. He looked vaguely familiar. Did he live in the street? "Are you in some kind of trouble?" Peter asked, crouching down to rest on his hind legs.

"Don't you know who I am?" said the kid. He looked forlorn and tired.

Peter realised that the boy was holding a train ticket – turning it round and round between his fingers. Peter reached for the ticket, plucking it from the boy's fingers. As he read the small print of the journey details, he pursed his lips and took in a quick tight breath.

"Danny?" he said.

"No," the boy said, rising. "Erland."

Peter sat back on the path abruptly and whistled. "Does your mum know you're here?"

"Nope."

Peter rubbed his unshaven face and then cleaned his glasses on his shirt sleeve before replacing them.

"You have my eyes," said Erland, a smile attempting to appear on his face. That was why he was familiar, Peter considered: he and the boy had the same angular chin and nose, the same sunken eyes, the same grey look of *the end is nigh* if you caught them in the wrong light and frame of mind.

"I think you'll find that you probably have mine," said Peter, attempting a smile also. "Jeez, I didn't think I'd ever meet you – not all grown up anyway."

"I'm hardly grown up," said Erland, clearing his throat. "I'm just eleven."

"Just eleven?" Peter said. "Now let me think when that was…" He gazed up at the sky, his mind trying to recall data that it had had no reason to peruse for many years. He looked triumphantly at Erland. "You would have turned eleven on the fourth of this month, yesterday, no – today."

The boy turned his face away to the wall. Exactly what Beth would have done.

"You'd better come inside," said Peter. "Is that all you have with you?" He eyed Erland's small grubby duffel bag, the sort of bag that a lad liked to drag everywhere with him.

Inside the house, Peter flicked on the stereo and went straight through to the kitchen for a bottle of beer. He poured Erland a Ribena and found him a straw, without asking whether Erland liked Ribena or wanted a straw. Erland didn't seem to mind. He stood in the centre of the room, still with his hood up, with his hands in his pockets, slowly rotating like a darlek in order to take in everything within his range.

Suddenly, Erland stopped. "You have children," he said, his voice sounding small from within his hood.

"Yes," said Peter, handing Erland the Ribena and a Penguin bar – the only one left in the biscuit barrel. Peter had a habit of eating several Penguins on Saturday nights whilst watching *Match of the Day*. "I'm sorry."

"No worries," said Erland, shrugging. "I expect you're a great dad."

Peter shot Erland a look to decipher whether this comment was supposed to be sarcastic, but there was nothing on Erland's face that revealed an intention to hurt or otherwise.

"Danny…" said Peter, taking a seat in his battered old armchair that had been picked to death during every Chelsea game that it had had the misfortune to have to sit through with Peter. He motioned for Erland to be seated on the sofa opposite. "Is he –?"

"Yeah," said Erland, intuitively. "He's like you." Peter nodded. "You'd like him. I don't. But you might."

"I'm sure I would," said Peter. He took a long drink of beer and his eye fell upon the photograph of his children that Erland hadn't taken his eyes off since arriving. It had always brought Peter joy, that photograph, but now it seemed one of the most insensitive things that he could have in his lounge – so casually, so carelessly, so mindless of the other people out there in the world, no, in the same bloody country, who might have different feelings about this object.

"What are their names?" said Erland, not needing to point out who he was referring to.

"Sasha and Sarah. They're identical twins."

"So I see," said Erland. "Nice. How old?"

"Six."

Erland turned the corners of his mouth down and nodded in a gesture that said *cool, impressive*, but he wasn't fooling anyone. Aged just eleven, he wasn't yet master of the skills that his mother had honed. Yes, he was pretty good already – probably might even be better than Beth eventually – but he hadn't learnt that altering the mouth didn't necessary alter the eyes and that in order to pull off a look of nonchalance when feeling pain you had to look away.

Not that Peter had any idea how to pull off any of these looks. He was the most transparent, over-sharing person possible; it had always been the thing he most despised about himself. He just had to walk into a room and everyone could tell him how he felt and what he had for breakfast. Not only because he always ate the same thing – three shredded wheat with warm semi-skimmed milk – but because he spilled most of it down his front because he was eating whilst reading the sport in the paper and listening to the sport on Radio Five Live, and didn't realise he had spilled until he spotted flecks of dried wheat on his tie during the features meeting at ten o'clock.

"Why are you here?" said Peter. He expected the kid to say something about how he had been longing to meet his father, that half of his life felt missing, that he wanted to create a bond…

"Because Mum's been charged with hurting our two-year-old half-brother," said Erland, fixing his soulful eyes upon Peter.

Peter stopped, holding a mouthful of beer in his mouth, feeling the truth fizz around his gums. He was staring too hard, looking too alarmed, so he relaxed himself back in his chair and attempted a casual stance. But it was no good – he sat forward again, holding both hands to his forehead to force his brain into action. Erland was looking at him for a response.

"I thought you might be able to help." Erland carefully unwrapped his Penguin bar and began to nibble the chocolate biscuit from the top so that he would be left with the soft bed of chocolate flavoured cream underneath. Peter temporarily forgot the context of the situation and smiled broadly. This was exactly the same way that he ate a Penguin himself, or a Mars bar, or Twix – anything that had layers. He liked to deal with each one at a time, isolating the flavours. He bet that Erland wasn't a fan of one-pot dishes such as casseroles, but loved airplane meals and wedding buffets.

"You think it's funny that I'm asking for help?" said Erland. "Who else do you think I could ask?"

"I…uh…I don't know." Peter rose to get another beer. In the kitchen, he wiped his hands on his jeans. He was feeling sweaty and nervous. He glanced in the mirror, his eyes wide and sincere like the boy's in the lounge.

He wished that his wife, Clare, were here, despite the horribly cringey atmosphere that would create. She would know what to do. Instead, she was in Dublin with the twins celebrating her father's birthday. Peter should have been there too, but he was on a deadline so had to decline. They were better off without him anyway. Clare's family were big on blood. At family gatherings, non-blood relatives hung in the corner as far away from view as possible, like dejected bats. Non-blood were all smokers, just so they could skulk outside in the rain. Peter really had to take that up.

And there suddenly in the mirror behind him was blood. His blood. His own eyes looking back at him. "Erland, I think I should call your mum so she knows you're here," he said.

They both knew it was a cop out.

Ten minutes later, Beth had been informed of Erland's whereabouts and reassured that not only would Erland have a bed for the night but that he would be safely installed on the train at Paddington station tomorrow morning. Peter could have offered to drive him personally to Bath. This thought had occurred to him during the very short and awkward telephone conversation with Beth, but he had tossed the annoying thought away before it became spoken.

But as he set Erland up in the futon in the spare room (he couldn't bear the thought of him sleeping in his daughters' room – the thoughts that would spiral round the lad's head all night whilst looking at the luminous solar system on the ceiling, the eight hundred pound Victorian dolls house from Clare's parents, at all the stuffed toys…) he began to feel consumed by a sense of uneasiness. As he cleaned his teeth, the uneasiness grew. As he got into his pyjamas, he was dizzy with it. And then he lay down and in the darkness he finally got the space he required in order to work it all out.

Slowly before him the image of Beth formed – an image that he had stored in his memory bank in a thousand pieces, allowing them all to reassemble infrequently and under strict supervision. He couldn't have the image forming willy-nilly at any given point in the day. The effects could be devastating.

The image was a carefully restored picture of Beth as he had first seen her during Freshers' Week at university – of the moment he had picked her out from a sea of bodies gyrating on the dance floor, from a throng of freshers queuing at the bar, from a line of pretty bar women bopping about wearing tight promotional Blackthorn T-shirts, serving thirsty students.

He homed in on the only bar woman that wasn't jigging to the beat. She was stood still, her head tilted in concentration, her black hair scooped around to one side of her neck, her eyes watching the pint glass that she was filling with Blackthorn. He moved closer towards her, making his way through all the bodies until he was close enough to see that her wrists were sparkling with silver bangles and that her fingernails were painted black. *There She Goes* by the La's was playing on the dance floor.

Then all of a sudden, she looked up at him. Her eyes were so brown that they appeared to be almost dissolving, fuzzy, bottomless. He felt his heart thump a little harder and he smiled at her, but she didn't smile back.

He wasn't the only finalist boy that had spotted her. From all around, men – finalists, freshers, any guy with a pulse – were homing in on this new girl, this new specimen of beauty. They all wanted to smooth her hair, to kiss her lips – to make her lips smile only for them – and to unravel the mystery as to why this woman was so very different from all the other pretty young things around them.

It took forty-two days of hanging around the bar on Tuesdays, Thursdays and Sunday afternoons – Sunday being the best one because it was Acoustic Afternoon so it was quiet enough to talk – for Beth to agree to go out with him. One such dull Sunday, just as a hippy lad began to play *More than Words*, Peter took his cue and asked Beth if she would go to the cinema with him to see *Drop Dead Fred*. To his surprise, she agreed. At least, she didn't say no. She scribbled her phone number down on a till receipt and handed it to him, her jumper pulled down over her hands. Then she looked off into the distance and Peter ran all the way home, too excited to travel at the speed of walking.

He had anticipated showing Beth, the young fresher, the ropes – directing her around campus, taking her to the best bars and student clubs in town, showing her how to blag free extras such as onion and pineapple rings on top of her pizza at the campus cafe, how to smack the chocolate machine outside the union building so hard that you got a free Boost bar. But it turned out that Beth wasn't eighteen, but a twenty-two-year-old mature student who was studying English Literature and hung out with all the bodily-pierced mature students on the grass outside her faculty building to discuss Chaucer and Feminism, or any other subject that he didn't have a hope of joining in with the discussion of. He stood about, blinking in the sunlight, doing up his shoelaces again and again, wondering when these women – and a couple dorky guys – would shut the hell up so he could go and have sex with Beth again.

Sex with Beth was...there was no one word to describe it. It was difficult to think of it now – difficult to imagine being with her again in a way that didn't make him feel as though he were being unfaithful to his wife.

Beth was needy, but never clingy. She was intensely beautiful. She was prone to tears when drunk, which was why she absolutely insisted upon sober sex. For a student such an insistence was almost impossible, but for Beth it was worth it. He abstained from drinking on Friday nights at the union bar; he skipped lectures to make love to her in her cramped bed on campus; they made love first thing in the morning in his relatively spacious bedroom out in town.

And then one night, two and a half years after they had begun dating, they stumbled home after a night out celebrating Beth's birthday and for the first time ever made love whilst drunk. And he forgot to put a condom on.

Beth wanted a termination. She didn't want anything to mess up her finals. He begged her not to terminate the pregnancy so she didn't, but the resentment was there in her eyes when he least expected it – first thing in the morning, last thing at night. She passed her finals with a First Class Honours despite being heavily pregnant, but it still wasn't enough for her to forgive him. So he was shocked when she said she wanted to try for another baby once Danny was a year old. At the time, he had fooled himself into thinking that it was because she was making a commitment to him. Years later, he realised that she had merely wanted another blood sibling for Danny. To an orphan like Beth, family was oxygen – not something she was going to deprive her child of.

Family didn't mean fathers. It meant siblings, apparently. She had no misgivings about depriving the boys of a parent. Parents were totally disposable; she didn't have any, for a start. So when a great job came up at Bath University as a lecturer in the English faculty, she set off with the boys and her minimalist luggage telling him that there was no point him coming too because this was something that she had to do alone.

She literally told him no more, no less. She didn't elaborate about why she was leaving him, whether he had done anything wrong, whether he was going to ever be a part of her life again.

After Beth left, he considered – after months of introspective alcoholism and hermitage – that he had never really known her.

"I can't stand up in court and vouch for your mum," he told Erland the next morning, as the lad gazed at him expectantly at Paddington station in front of the departures board. "I don't think I ever knew her that well and I certainly don't know her now after not having seen her for over ten years."

"And whose fault is that?" said Erland, looking at Peter with condemnation. Erland's bottom lip trembled and Peter thought for a terrible long minute that the boy was going to start crying. Evidently, he was stronger than that – or less open than that. Danny would have cried. Peter knew that without having met him.

Well, he had met Danny when he was little. He was one of those sorts of little boys that hung on your every word, sat by the window waiting for your arrival, stood on the front door step waving until you were just a speck of dust on the horizon. He was the sort of kid who would still believe in Father Christmas way beyond his years, not because he didn't know the truth deep down but because he refused to give up on the sheer wonder of the idea. Peter had been like that too. And in the short precious time that they had spent together before Beth left, Peter had spent an unaccountably large amount of that time whispering stories of magic into his little boy's ear.

"My fault," Peter said, nodding sadly. "The fault's all mine."

The platform number for Erland's train flashed up on the board. They had both been staring at the board, using it as a focal point for this awkward juncture in their lives. Last night had been pleasant enough due to nightfall and bottles of beer, but this morning huge gaps had opened up between them whilst they had been stood in Peter's lounge.

"I can go alone," said Erland, turning away, heading for his train.

Peter grabbed at his arm and pulled him round. "Listen," he said. Erland looked at the floor, scuffing his feet. Peter's mind raced for the right words to explain to this boy who was going to take away whatever garbled message he gave him now and relay it not only to his brother and his mother, but to anyone else of significance in his life now and in years to come. "I…"

He couldn't explain it to him. He opened his mouth again and shut it. Erland pulled away forcibly, walking off without a backward glance. Peter went to run after him, but knew that another opening and closing of Peter's mouth wasn't what the boy wanted.

He watched as Erland queued to put his ticket in the gate. The boy looked a sorry little character: his hood up again, his legs skinny in his tapered jeans. Erland went through the gates and as he walked parallel to the train, Peter noticed that he flung his feet out as he walked, in the same ungainly way that Peter did.

He was surprised to find it hard to swallow, emotion

pricking his throat. He coughed and looked about him, lest someone he knew should spot him seeing off his undeclared son.

He didn't want to go home yet so he headed out the main exit to a pub opposite the station that he had been to a few times before. As he walked, hands shoved hard in pockets, frustration and sadness overwhelming him, he thought about how he wished things hadn't turned out this way – about how hard he had begged Beth to give Danny life, and now it had come to this.

It hadn't always been this way. At first, he had travelled down once a month to see Beth and the boys. He had even interviewed for a job in Bath with a view to moving to the area and trying to get back with her. He was offered the job and just as he was deliberating about the move, he met Clare.

He wasn't really interested in Clare at first because he was still in love with Beth. But Clare was really interested in him and her level of attention and devotion was played out in sharp relief to Beth's literal and metaphorical distance. He was at an age where unrequited love wasn't quite so sexy any more, compared to its appeal during his teens. Clare didn't mind about Beth – didn't mind the idea of her anyhow. Until she met her at a wedding and the whole fragile structure came toppling down.

Clare wasn't as beautiful as Beth. He hadn't mentioned how pretty she was, Clare said, accusingly.

After that, Clare moved in. It turned out that she was reproductively challenged. Beth and the two boys became an ugly, taboo topic of conversation. He understood his wife's pain, particularly after two rounds of IVF. He understood that he couldn't go to visit the boys any more.

By the time Clare gave birth to the twins, Beth's boys were seven and five.

Peter crossed at the lights and headed for the King's Arms. Did men only keep in touch with their children if their partner permitted them to? This question plagued him. It seemed unbelievably weak of his gender and unbelievably fatalistic to allow such a vital relationship to fall into the hands of whatever a bloke's missus thought about it.

He ran his hands through his hair as he entered the pub. There was no one there except two studenty types surrounded by luggage, and an old boy watching the races on television. Peter ordered a pint of Guinness and a double whisky chaser, glancing at his reflection in the smoky mirror behind the bar as he shuddered his whisky down.

"She tried to kill herself."

He jumped. There in the mirror again was his son's face next to him. "Erland! What the hell–?"

"She tried to commit suicide," said Erland.

"Jesus. Why didn't you say this before? Is she all right?" asked Peter.

Erland shrugged, his hood moving up and down around his face. "She's home from hospital," he said.

If he had been putting on an act until now then the lad could no longer put it on. He fell towards Peter, burying his head into his shirt. Peter glanced about the quiet room and then cradled the boy's head, rubbing the top of his hood with detachment and yet with something like affection trying to stir within him. He hadn't ever touched anyone of his own sex this way. Erland didn't feel like his son, but it was becoming apparent that the boy needed a dad, or at least someone in the world to turn to right now that might give a shit.

"Why didn't you care about us?" said Erland, pulling away, his face strewn with upset, his nose running. Peter grabbed a napkin from the bar and pressed it against Erland's face. It was the same clumsy way he would have wiped his girls' noses.

"I wish I could explain," said Peter, shaking his head

and sitting down on a bar stool. He motioned for Erland to do the same. "It's complicated. It's not a case of not caring or not wanting to be in your lives. There was a time when I was consumed with the idea of being your dad. It was all I wanted…"

"Then what happened?"

Peter gazed at Erland, trying to read how much the boy's brain was capable of processing. He looked pretty bright – really bright, in fact. There was some kind of chess magazine sticking out the top of his dingy duffel bag. Peter had never taken the time to become good at chess. This lad was smart to be reading that kind of stuff at his age when *Beano* was on offer.

"My wife hated the idea of you – of your brother and your mum."

He kept his eyes on Erland as he spoke and sure enough there came the flicker of incomprehension followed quickly by scorn and disrespect.

"That's the real reason?" said Erland, narrowing his eyes at Peter.

And then a little coincidence occurred – so little that everyone missed it, aside from Peter, who immediately wished that there were someone else who could appreciate the moment with him.

As the two of them sat there fronting each other out, wondering who was going to crack first and confess whatever it was that was in need of confessing, one of the students with all the luggage got up, went over to the jukebox, pushed a coin in, chose a record and it began. It was *There She Goes* by the La's.

The introduction played and as Erland gazed at him and the whisky chaser began to relax his brain, Peter felt a burning sensation of happiness rise in him. The sense of uneasiness that had grown in his bed last night now revealed itself in its full splendour.

There, sat in the King's Arms in Paddington with his

son, Erland, whom he had named after Erland Johnsen, Chelsea's Player of the year 1995, he realised with mutual horror and ecstasy that the reason he hadn't visited Bath over the years was because he was afraid of being married to someone else, and of falling in love with Beth all over again.

"So *that's* why," said Erland, perceptively, taking his hood down and nodding, smiling.

Whilst that song played, Peter was happy. When it ended and the bar fell quiet again, he knew that he had to see this boy whom he barely knew onto the train home, and then go and tidy up his house and remove all traces of the lad in order to prepare for the return of his wife and two daughters.

Klaris was surprised to see that the spider's web was still there on the streetlamp outside. She had supposed that spider's webs were temporary things that they set up at dawn and removed at dusk, like street vendors dismantling their market stands. This cobweb had been there for at least two months, she reckoned.

She yawned and rubbed her face. It was four forty in the morning. Her sleep patterns had deteriorated since the phone call from Demon Man. She couldn't get to sleep, and when she did sleep she woke up and couldn't drift off again, nor could she summon the energy to lift her head off the pillow sufficiently to see what time it was. So she lay in the dark, wondering how long she had been doing so and how much longer she had to do it for.

This morning, she had given up. Normally, she didn't know what was causing her insomnia. Today, it was clear. Anger was gnawing at her breast bone, rattling her chest until she didn't know what to do with herself.

She poured a strong coffee and watched the spider's web flapping in the spitting rain. She was like that web. She looked frail, benign, but she could withstand the strongest storms. He had all but destroyed her four years ago, but she was still here, living in this house, proof that she was tougher than whatever he could throw at her. Wasn't she?

She had a meeting in five hours with Charles Langley. He had been holding mini case conferences with the key members of the team during the past week. Beth Trelawney's suicide attempt had complicated matters terribly, throwing her testimony of innocence right up in to the air and leaving a trail of paperwork floating down in its wake. Bath Central's psychologist's report stated that Beth had entered a fatalistic stage, convincing herself that her past couldn't be undone and that she was less of a risk to her children by being dead. It was practically a confession.

Still, the meeting request today from Charles Langley was unexpected. It wasn't the whole team, or even part of it. It was just Klaris. Part of her was flattered and thrilled because Charles had several times alluded to Klaris's role in bringing the Trelawney case to light and thus aiding the protection of a child. If there were more health visitors like her working in communities…Charles had said.

But she was also anxious. The meeting had been scheduled the morning after the call from Demon Man. Did Charles know who Klaris was?

How dare her ex-husband infiltrate her life here? She had worked so hard to start afresh, to begin over after what he had done to her. He wasn't going to get away with this.

She went to find her mobile before realising that she couldn't contact him. She no longer had a mobile and therefore had no phone number for him. No, that wasn't true. She had it written in her address book – pencilled in on the last page at the back. She hurried to the desk drawer and ransacked it, emptying its contents on the floor. There was the book and there was the number. She dialled it.

"Klaris?" It was five o'clock. She had woken him up. He would be blinking rapidly, dry-mouthed, stiff-limbed.

"You bastard," she said. "Stay away from my world."

"Your world?" he said, clearing his throat.

"Yes."

He laughed. "When are you going to realise that it's not *your* world?"

"Who is it, hun?"

The voice of a female in the background stunned Klaris. She stared motionless at the phone and then closed her eyes and screamed.

When she opened her eyes, she heard the dialling tone and he was gone.

Danny picked at the rubber on the sole of his trainer. It was hanging loose like a long elastic band. He pulled it and let it snap back onto his foot. It caught his finger. He scowled and folded his arms.

His mum was next to him. She was wearing make-up and her perfume was filling the car. She only ever needed a squirt of scent because she was one of those people who soaked up the scent and became it for the rest of the day. He knew that because he was like that too. Lee had told him this. It was to do with hormones and salt content in the skin. Or something like that. It was the reason why Danny should only wear the slightest splash of aftershave, Lee said. Which was good because Danny hated it anyway. He only wore it when he was off to see Lee and that was because she had given him an expensive scent for his birthday, one which Mr Paris had brought back especially from the States.

His mind was racing. It was because he was livid with Erland, but had been given the strictest instructions not to be so he was trying to distract himself. He thumbed the button on the radio to change channel, but his mum tutted and changed it back. She was listening to *Woman's Hour*. It was about female poets. He should have known better.

He was also angry at his mum. It had always felt like

him and her versus the world. Even him, her and Erland versus the world sometimes. But Erland had really messed that one up by stealing Danny's post office money and taking off to find their dad without telling him. And his mum had really messed it up by trying to top herself. So now it was just him versus the world on his own. And he hated doing things on his own.

His mum had said she would give him the money for his Silverfox Demon 26 inch dual suspension bike, but it wasn't the same. He had saved up that money bit by bit, and now he was being given the money instead. *What the hell does it matter?* his mum had yelled at him. She was pretty stressed out about Erland disappearing. The police had been searching for him. Overnight, they had gone from a fairly screwed up family with a missing sibling, to a totally screwed up family with two missing siblings.

Lee was going to dump him. He could feel it. Either that or he was going to dump her. Which way round was it?

And right then his mum put her hand on his knee and just kept it there. The radio programme was kind of soothing. A woman with an Irish accent was talking about how she felt that her poetry had given her a great sense of freedom. His mum listened to nice things, he noticed. Happy things about people being free, expressing themselves, fulfilling themselves. She was a soothing, optimistic person, his mum, when she wasn't yelling at them or trying to top herself.

"It's a mess, isn't it, Dan?" she said. "Don't be too hard on Erland. This is a really tough time for us all. Toffee?" She pulled out a bag of sweets from the side compartment.

He took a toffee, unpeeling the wrapper slowly, enjoying the sound of it crackling. These were his mum's favourite sweets. He couldn't pass through a M&S check-out without buying her a bag, not that he went there very often, if ever.

The Parises did all their shopping there. That was the problem between himself and Lee. Their experiences were so different. Was it possible to be happy with someone whose biggest dilemma was whether to wear polka dot socks or striped?

He didn't mean to be nasty about Lee. He loved her. It was just that the harder his life had become this past month, the fluffier her life had become in comparison. It was so fluffy that he was surprised it had enough weight to hold itself down to earth.

"How's Lee?" his mum asked. His mum and Erland had this way of knowing what was on your mind, particularly when it was something that you didn't want to talk about. Danny shrugged. What was there to say?

He glanced sideways at his mum. She was sucking her toffee, listening to the programme. He didn't trust her any more. He didn't know what she was going to do next, what was going to happen to any of them. The court case was coming up and she had barely mentioned it. Things would go against her now that she had proven herself to be mentally unstable. He didn't know if Erland and himself would be able to stay with her any more, let alone Brett.

It was unforgivable. Yet he wanted to place his hand on top of her hand on his knee and hold it there. But he couldn't.

And just as he was deliberating upon this, the train arrived.

His mum jumped into action, locking the car and leading Danny along the platform in search of Erland. They didn't know what he was wearing so they could look out for him, or whether he had even made it onto this train. Peter had called to say that Erland was on it, but knowing Erland he could have got off at Swindon.

"No," said Danny's mum, shaking her head. "He's not here."

Danny felt slightly sick. He had no idea what to do if Erland didn't show up. Things couldn't get much worse.

"Mum." Danny tugged at his mum's sleeve. At the very last second, when everyone else had embarked and left the platform, a carriage door slowly swung open and down the steps came Erland's skinny legs.

The train pulled away. Erland stood still, his hood up, his duffel bag hanging from his hand. Danny and his mum hurried towards him. As they drew closer, Danny's heart lurched at the sight before them, and tears welled up impulsively.

Erland was crying without control. His face was screwed up. His nose was running. He was crying like the time he had smashed his two front teeth on the swing in the back garden. "He's not coming back," he was saying, trails of saliva hanging between his teeth as he spoke. "He's not going to help us."

"Oh, my baby," said their mum, pulling Erland to her and cradling his head, smoothing his hair. "It's okay, it's okay. Get his bag for us, Dan," she said, over Erland's head.

Danny picked up Erland's bag and was amazed at its lightness. Somehow the pathetic grubby bag seemed to represent Erland, like seeing someone's old used slippers after they had died. He wanted to hug his brother too, but couldn't allow himself to do so after everything that had happened. The old Danny wouldn't have cared about his pride, but the new Danny cared about pride more than anything else because he felt it was the only thing he had left.

They went back home and Erland had a bath and then sat under a blanket in the lounge, cradling a hot chocolate. He was rocking himself gently. Danny was listening to the football results on the radio. Their mum was making the tea. For a moment, everything felt like before.

Then their mum came into the room holding an egg

whisk in one hand, her other hand cupped to catch the drips. "It ends here, boys," she said.

"What does?" said Danny.

"All of this. It's all ending here. Everything. I'm going to get myself together and fight these charges against me. Don't you see? We've been allowing ourselves to be controlled by everybody else. We've been sitting around waiting for them to tell us the way it's going to be. Well, it's time for us to take the control back and run our lives again."

"Lovely," said Danny. "And just how are you going to do that, Mum?"

She sniffed defensively. "I've got a plan."

"Yeah, right." He turned up the volume on the radio.

"I'm serious," she said, standing over him and tapping the radio off. "I just called Professor Moss. His wife's a childcare solicitor. Or was. She's retired now, but she's going to give me some advice. I've come to realise that not asking for help is a dead man's game. And…" She hesitated, glancing at Erland. "…You're going to stay with Professor Moss for two days."

"What?" Erland leaped up, dropping his blanket and spilling his drink. "I can't go," he said, looking as though he was about to cry again.

"I know, sweetheart." She reached for Brett's wet wipes that were gathering dust on the bookshelf and wiped hot chocolate from Erland's blanket. She settled him back under the blanket and kissed his cheek, like soothing a baby.

Maybe Erland *was* her baby, Danny thought, now that Brett wasn't. He hadn't thought until now what effect it had upon Erland, suddenly going from baby boy to middle-child when Brett was born. Maybe that was why he was such a geek.

"You want things simple and back to normal," their mum was saying, stroking Erland's hair and talking in a sing-song way. "And so do I. More than anything. It's only for two days and one night. You've been to the professor's before. I don't have anyone else to ask right now, although that's something I'm working on. We're not going to be this vulnerable ever again."

"Where are you going?" Erland said.

"Away," she replied.

"Let me come with you," said Danny, standing up, the blood rushing to his head.

"No," she said. "This is something that I've got to do alone."

"You're not Indiana Jones, Mum."

"Aren't I?" she said, smiling.

Things were really awkward at work. Ned hadn't forgiven Zoe for walking out on him in the middle of the night and Zoe hadn't forgiven herself for being there in the first place. They were just about managing to get through the day without anyone noticing how badly their relationship had deteriorated. It was such a shame, Zoe thought, and it was entirely her fault.

Lately, she had taken to wearing less anarchistic clothes and had even gone as far as to buy a pair of Birkenstock sandals, albeit black ones. And her tooth brace had gone. This was a big deal, as though a considerable source of ugliness had been removed from her body like lancing a boil. But Ned hadn't even noticed. So much for being into her. Her orthodontist had told her that she could smile more now. She had told him that it wasn't likely.

"Nice sandals," Ned grunted, as they walked out to the car park.

"Don't take the mick," she replied, pulling her braids around her face to disguise her embarrassment. She wasn't sure why she had decided to make changes to her appearance. If she were lying, she would say it was because she liked to think about change during the summer holidays with a new school year looming. If she were telling the truth, she would say it was because of that night with Ned.

Luckily, no one was asking.

"I wasn't," replied Ned, typically belatedly, and tutting. He seemed as irritated by her now as he had always been – if not more so post-sex. He was irritated by her inability to see the best in everyone, to recognise affection and warmth. He was irritated by her bitterness and scepticism.

She wanted to cry into her hair. Sat there in the car, she wanted to wrap her braids so close to her face that she could no longer breathe.

As Ned started the engine and drove in silence, she thought of Beth Trelawney. They were on their way to see her as part of her daily programme. It was a form-filling box-ticking exercise. They couldn't hope to achieve anything until the hearing at the end of the week. After that, things would change dramatically. She was going to lose the court case. Attempted suicide had pretty much sealed her fate.

Beth Trelawney, unlike Zoe, seemed to be under the naïve impression that she was going to win everybody over with her intelligence and beauty. She was one of those women who got by by fixing her beguiling eyes on the ticket warden and holding his gaze a little longer than usual. It worked for the occasional ticket warden and definitely for most blokes on a Saturday night in town, but it didn't generally work for the judge at the magistrates' court faced with a perpetrator of child abuse.

Ned suddenly stopped the car, pulling over into a slip road on the hill that led up to Beth's road. He turned off the engine and sat still. Zoe gazed at the view of the city facing them in the valley below. She could pick out the Royal Crescent, the park, the football ground, the church that wasn't the abbey but was striking nonetheless and she should really know the name of but hadn't a clue.

"Zoe." Ned turned in his seat to look at her. She realised that he had grown his goatee back. When had he done that? How come she hadn't noticed? Probably because she had been staring at her feet for the past couple of days. Like she was now. She liked her sandals, but wished she had gone for that pearly pink colour. Her feet would have looked prettier. As it was, they looked pale and clumpy against the black.

She wanted to keep thinking – thinking about her feet. Not thinking about what Ned was going to say. Or wasn't going to say. About whether he had enjoyed being with her that night. About whether he kept having as many flash backs as she did.

"Look, I'm sorry I left," she said. "I do that all the time. I never stay till morning. I'm not a stay till morning kind of girl. Okay?"

He looked into her eyes, as though trying to determine whether she was telling him the truth. The fact that he had accepted her words as being based upon some kind of reality was damage enough. "Just drive," she said, angrily. "We're late."

"Fine," he said. He started the engine.

By the time they had queued to get back up the hill in the traffic and had arrived at Bloomsdale Rise, Beth Trelawney's street, the tension was so bad that Zoe wanted to jump out the car whilst it was still moving and escape into the Trelawney's where the atmosphere would no doubt be more congenial, even given all their problems. Because other people's problems were always more congenial than one's own.

Inside number eight, Zoe was surprised to find Beth stood doing her make-up in the hallway mirror, a rucksack at her feet. Zoe and Ned exchanged puzzled glances, temporarily forgetting their hostility.

The two boys were stood in the lounge, a small suitcase between them. Zoe perched on the edge of the sofa. "Going somewhere?" she called out to Beth.

"I'm taking a two day trip," Beth called back. "Jacko is

going to visit Brett in my absence. Brett's used to seeing me most days, so someone needs to go." There was an air of defensiveness in Beth's voice, lest anyone should judge her more than they had already.

"And the boys?"

"They're going to friends of mine for the night."

Zoe nearly said that she thought that Beth didn't have any friends, but checked herself. "Were you intending to let us or Charles know?" Zoe said, stepping back into the hallway.

Beth stopped applying her mascara, waving the wand mid-air. "Are you my keepers?"

"Uh….kind of!" said Zoe.

Beth was looking exceptionally chic and slim in a white polo neck and white jeans. Zoe glanced down at her own clumpy gypsy skirt, at the charm bracelets and silver bangles on her wrist – so many of which that they defeated the object and looked ugly and clumsy – and at her ratty vest top that had been worn so often that the straps were baggy and the material was covered in bobbles. She was an ugly, clumsy person. And it had never been so apparent as now.

She moved towards Beth and stood in her shadow, watching her applying her lipstick. Beth didn't need much make-up. It was a token effort, like putting one too many dollops of paint on a Renoir. "I'm coming with you," Zoe said, in a low voice.

"What?" said Beth.

"Shush!" Zoe glanced over her shoulder. Ned was still in the lounge talking to the boys. He really liked Danny. They were talking about Drogba and Anelka again, whoever the hell they were. "Listen, I know this is weird, but I want to help you. Wherever it is you're going, whatever you're doing. I can help."

"I'm not a charity case," said Beth, snapping her cosmetics purse shut and pursing her lips to seal her lipstick. "And I don't need a suicide watch."

187

"It's not a suicide watch. I've not taken any holiday yet this year. And I'd…" Zoe stopped.

Ned was behind her in the hallway, as were Beth's boys. Everyone was looking at her.

What was she doing? She couldn't take off with this woman. She barely knew her, didn't even know where she was going. She could be headed to the Highlands by coach to visit a dying aunt.

"Okay," said Beth.

"Okay what?" said Ned, frowning.

"She's coming with me," said Beth, casually, picking up her rucksack. "I don't mind."

"Going where?" said Ned.

"I thought you said you had to do this alone, Mum?" said Danny.

Now everyone was looking at Beth. "Well, like you said, Dan – I'm not Indiana."

"Eh?" said Ned. He was so confused he was swivelling around, looking from one person to another for enlightenment.

"Can you let the team know I'll be back Wednesday," Zoe said, pressing Ned's stomach with her fingernail lightly to make him take in what she was saying. "And can you get someone to cover my two o'clock and four o'clock. And the same for tomorrow."

"Someone? Like who?" said Ned. "You know how busy and stressed–"

"You know we don't talk about that!" snapped Zoe. Ned closed his mouth obediently. She turned to Beth. "If you could swing past mine so I can get some stuff?"

"Sure," said Beth. "Come on boys."

They all left the house and went outside, leaving Ned stood on the doorstep, scratching his goatee.

As the car pulled away, Zoe looked back at Ned. He was leaning on the side of his car, talking on his mobile phone. He was either letting work know about Zoe's annual leave – he was pedantic like that – or was cancelling his next appointment to visit the coke head on the council estate because he hated going there alone. He found drugs disturbing, which was a bit silly for a social worker.

For a brief moment, she allowed herself to think again of pressing herself down onto Ned, of how it felt to be so close to him, so wrapped in his unwavering attention. She had felt more secure with Ned against her than she had thought possible in such a vulnerable state. He kept saying her name, had held her face between his hands as though it was the only face he had ever beheld.

She closed her eyes fleetingly in memory and then sighed away the thought. It was an hour or so that she would remember always. An hour that hadn't deserved to be born.

The boys were quiet in the back of the car. Beth was singing quietly to herself.

Her eyes were as blue as the holes in the clouds
Her voice was as gentle as a fairy child
I loved her so that my heart beat out loud
But I never could wed her 'cos her soul was wild.

Zoe sat back in the seat of the car and found that she was no longer pulling her hair over her face and wanting to stop breathing. Rather, she wanted to breathe in as much of this feeling as she could. She was doing something totally un-Zoe-like. She was changing the course of her day. She was going out of her way for someone else. And she hadn't phoned home to tell her son where she was going.

Why should she? No one had bothered to tell her anything her whole life, like how her braided hair made her look as though she didn't know what shampoo was. Like how her parents hadn't bothered to tell her to be home by a certain time. And how when she was seventeen that guy hadn't bothered to tell her that he didn't like using condoms so he wasn't going to use one.

Was that when she became bitter, she thought? Had he literally impregnated her with self-loathing?

Yep, she thought, blinking at the sudden downpour of sunshine through the windscreen, she was going so far out of her way today that she didn't have a clue where the hell she was heading for.

CHAPTER EIGHT

It was a tough call as to where to go first, but Beth decided that chronological order would be best. She stood on the balcony of the council flat in Pentruthen, gazing at a rotting sofa next to her as she knocked on the door, feeling self-conscious in her all-white ensemble. Why the need to dress up? She glanced down at the car below, at Zoe's face peering up at her. Odd decision – Zoe's decision to tag along.

In truth, Beth was glad of the company. There was no one else that she could have asked to come along. It wouldn't have been fair to ask either of the boys to make the trip with her. Danny had seemed put out though. He hardly said goodbye at Professor Moss's and watched her leaving with his face pressed against the lounge window like a child. She was determined to be more of a parent from henceforth. So here she was, being the adult – sorting things out.

Zoe hadn't said a lot. Between the two of them, about fifty words had been exchanged from Bath to Exeter. From Exeter to Treale about another hundred because Zoe became bored and started asking Beth about the impending court hearing. Beth didn't want to talk about the court hearing, so it was mostly Zoe who notched up the hundred words, telling Beth what to expect and to brace herself for the worst case scenario.

Worst case scenario. Wasn't Beth already living that?

Zoe liked coffee – lots of strong coffee and gummy bears, and cheese and onion crisps, and lots of toilet trips. She was a funny girl, Beth thought, glancing at her occasionally when Zoe wasn't looking. She was almost child-like – a child that knew way too much for its years and had been dragged up the rough way.

A seagull was crying above Beth's head, before swooping down to scavenge the bins that were full to the brim in the communal refuse area. A bin liner had spilled open, rotten food spewing out. It was a warm day and the smell of rubbish was potent. The bin men were evidently on strike. Aside from the gull, there was no movement in the courtyard below – not a sign of life. Where was everyone?

Number forty-five's door finally opened. Beth held her breath. A teenage girl bounced a baby on her knee. "What?" she said, argumentatively.

"Oh," Beth said, looking beyond the girl to the room within in the hope of recognising something. Nothing was familiar. The brown chess board carpet would have been pulled up by now, the stained kitchen lino replaced, the nasty spiky mattress upstairs thrown onto a tip, the rank refrigerator replaced. "Would it be possible for me to come in?"

"Eh?" The girl wrinkled her nose and looked Beth up and down, resting her eyes upon Beth's heeled ankle boots. "Why?"

"I…I used to live here. I'm looking for someone."

"Who?"

Beth hesitated. It had been a long time since she had said these two words. "My mother."

"Well, there's no one living here that would be your mother, unless it's me," said the girl, laughing.

"Sorry to have troubled you." Beth turned away. The door closed behind her, and that was that. She looked down to Zoe and held her hands out in a despondent shrug.

She was making for the stairwell when the door of number forty-six eased open. A woman aged about seventy with blackcurrant-coloured hair held the door open just enough to peer out. "What did you say your name was?" she said.

"I didn't say," said Beth. "It's Beth Trelawney."

"Trelawney, you say? Vivien's girl?"

Beth felt her face flush red. "I believe that was my mother's name, yes. I don't remember – "

"You don't remember me? Mrs Gray?" the woman said, stepping outside and squinting at the sunshine as though she hadn't left the house all week. She was wearing a woollen jumper, stained baggy trousers and washing up gloves, soap bubbles still attached. "Well, come on in!"

Beth glanced down at Zoe again, before following Mrs Gray into the house. Inside it smelt of chicken soup and as Beth made her way across the yellow and blue spiral carpet she felt her memory prickle to life. She had trodden this carpet before, had smelt soup cooking here, had seen the line of milk saucers for the cats and the hundreds of china figurines displayed on the dresser.

"You'll have to excuse me," said Mrs Gray, moving a pile of Tupperware boxes off the sofa so Beth could sit down. "I run a business of sorts. Wasn't expecting visitors." She touched her hair as though checking whether she had rollers in. "Cuppa?"

Whilst Mrs Gray made the tea, Beth looked around uneasily. The model of the house would be the same as next door's. She knew where each of the doors led – that the toilet was under the stairs, that the kitchen led off from the lounge, that there was no dining room, that upstairs there were two bedrooms and a large airing cupboard where the boiler lived.

Mrs Gray returned carrying a tray, cocking her head to one side to survey Beth. "It seems obvious now that you're Vivien's girl. You haven't changed. You always were pretty." She sat down in her armchair and sipped her tea thoughtfully, nodding in memory. "You used to help me batch the soups up, you know, and I'd give you a bowl for supper in return. Pumpkin was your favourite."

Beth smiled. "It still is... Did I come here often?"

"Every day," said Mrs Gray. "Your mum wasn't fit to look after you. In those days, people on the estate used to muck in. Vivien needed more help than most. We thought that by helping her we were helping you, but we were just keeping her habit afloat. To be honest, we didn't know how bad it was. Not till you started having the accidents. Course, the school got involved then and you were removed."

Removed. It sounded so disposable, so clinical, like wiping a smear from a sink. "Do you know how I might find her now?"

Mrs Gray lowered her cup and narrowed her eyes at Beth. "She died, poppet."

"Oh." Beth put her cup down with a clump and placed her head in her hands. "Oh," she said again, trying to work out whether this news changed anything.

She could barely remember her mother's face. "Was...was she auburn, freckly, different to me?" she asked, spreading her fingers across her face and peeking at Mrs Gray.

"That's right," said Mrs Gray, smiling sadly. "She had a little birth mark on her right cheek that you might remember."

Beth nodded. She did. She could see her mother's face, could imagine her sat here in this flat, telling Mrs Gray how she was going to go clean, making promises that were as vaporous as the soup smells that Mrs Gray shooed away every evening when she aired the house.

"How did she die?" said Beth, fixing her eyes upon a china figurine that she recognised – a little girl with ill-sized goggly blue eyes that Beth used to pick up and fondle as soon as Mrs Gray left the room. Beth remembered wanting to befriend the china girl, wishing for a smooth, serene porcelain world like her.

"She overdosed and went into a coma. They said she died of respiratory failure. It was about six years after you left. Damn shame because she always said she was going to sort herself out and get you back."

Mrs Gray reached into a drawer for a box of tissues, which she passed to Beth. Beth took it obligingly, but did not feel tearful. Mrs Gray cocked her head again, assessing Beth curiously, waiting for tears.

They wouldn't come, Beth thought. Had her own life turned out differently, she might have cried for her doomed mother. As it was, she was on death row herself and had very little sympathy to spare for anyone that may have helped her get there. She stared at the wall, considering how many times she had fallen against it on the other side.

"Did she use to mention me after I left?" she asked.

"Never," said Mrs Gray. "It was as though you were dead. She only ever had one photo up of you and I noticed she took it down about a year after you were gone."

"Nice," said Beth, reaching for her tea.

"I think she always knew that you weren't going to come back."

"But I did," said Beth, quietly.

The two women finished their tea in silence. It wasn't an uncomfortable silence. They had done this many times, many years before.

Mrs Gray insisted that Beth took some soup for the road, that Beth might help her batch it up one last time.

Beth held the Tupperware box open with a childlike

pose, her arms outstretched, her face averted from splashes as Mrs Gray ladled the soup with her tongue between her teeth in concentration. Everything from the dry skin on Mrs Gray's knuckles to the freckles on her ruddy cheeks was exquisitely familiar.

They said goodbye outside on the terrace, Beth clutching two chicken soups and a plastic bag of buttered granary rolls for dipping.

"Do you have children?" Beth asked.

"No," said Mrs Gray. "We tried and failed. We didn't know why. In those days, you didn't ask questions in case you didn't like the answer. You know what I mean?"

"Yes," said Beth. "I think I do." She turned to go and then turned back again. "Can I write to you?"

"I'd like that," said Mrs Gray. "You've got the address. It's on the sticker on my Tupperware box. Goodbye, poppet," and she closed the door.

Zoe and Beth ate the soup in the car overlooking the bay of Pentruthen, windows up lest the oversized gulls should poke their heads in to steal a bap. The soup was sublime. Whether it was because it was Mrs Gray's or whether a stranger's soup would have tasted the same in the circumstances Beth didn't know, but each mouthful soothed her, provided her with the sustenance to move on.

She surveyed the scene before her. The palm trees were bending their heads, shaking their leaves like carnival pompoms and the Atlantic was gaining the strength to turn its tide.

It was an unforgiving sea, a shifting cauldron of dark seaweeds and slimy creatures. Beth couldn't swim when she had lived here, but used to crouch down barefoot amongst the limpet-clad rocks and press her face into the freezing water, watching the contents below. She had seen a shy octopus once and had reached out to touch it, toppling into the sea. Someone had rescued her. She had no idea who. She wondered now whether she might not have been better off slipping away to the bottom of the bed to join the ugliness there. As it was, she had followed a different swirl – the one that had taken her to Pengilly.

Pengilly was always going to be much harder than Pentruthen. She remembered far more about it, for a start. She packed the soup away and they drove in silence along the cliffside road to Pengilly.

Zoe was picking at her nose stud. "Do you think this is unattractive?" she said, referring to the stud.

"Yes," said Beth. "But each to their own. Didn't you have a tooth brace too?"

"Gone," replied Zoe.

They didn't say anything else until they reached the town sign for Pengilly and then Beth began to quietly curse – just loud enough that Zoe turned in her seat to stare at her.

"Are you sure you want to do this?" Zoe said. "We could drive on home or stay the night at a hotel somewhere or..."

"I'm fine."

She wasn't. From the moment they passed the sign and the yellow gorse hedges grew thick either side of the road and the hill began to climb down, twisting into the centre of Pengilly, Beth began to feel frightened. The sensation escalated as she drove along the sea road and parked opposite the Methodist church across from the quay.

"Is this it?" said Zoe, looking about her. The sun had sloped off. The sea had turned murky. Pengilly, not noted for its picturesque fishing boats or cream tea cafes but for the grubby clay mine that stood over it, could not have conjured a less picturesque scene.

Beth craned her neck to look across the playing field to the wall that did a poor job of sheltering the garden from the gales, beyond which stood the grey cottage.

There, outside her old bedroom window, was the tree that had been struck by lightning. She held her breath, her heart quickening and then she put both hands on the wheel and started the engine.

"Wait," said Zoe, placing her hand upon Beth's. "If this is it then don't run. Face it."

"But you said we could drive on back home," said Beth.

"I wanted to give you a last minute get-out clause, but we're here now...That's where you lived, isn't it?"

It took some time for Beth to nod. Zoe turned the key in the engine, switching it off. "Then we're going in. I'm experienced with people like this. It'll be a cinch."

"A cinch? You don't even know what I want to do," said Beth.

"Yes, I do. You want answers. You want to meet your maker – not the ultimate one, but the one who made you this way."

"What way?" said Beth. Zoe shrugged. "You still think I'm an abuser, don't you?"

Zoe sighed, flicking her braids over her shoulder. "Look, let's just go in. She probably isn't even there any more. We can sniff about and then leave."

"How do you know it's a she?" said Beth.

"I just figured," replied Zoe.

Beth unbuckled her seat belt and pulled the ceiling flap down so that she could look at herself in the mirror. She tidied her eye make-up with her little finger and applied fresh lipstick. She surveyed her outfit, reaching for her blazer from the back seat.

"I'm going alone," she said.

"I don't think so," said Zoe, matter-of-factly, getting out the car. "When are you gonna learn to take help when it's offered? I didn't come all this way with you to sit in the bloody car the entire time."

Beth attempted a smile. The air smelt intensely familiar – not fishy, nor salty, just damp and chilly, even in July.

She looked down at herself and saw the stunted legs of an eight-year-old, the pleated school skirt, the white socks rolled down, the dusty shoes. Her heart lurched at the thought of going home and she stared assertively at the sea willing it to magic a ship with a golden sail that would send a rowing boat to shore for her. She didn't care where the ship was sailing or what ghastly sort of pirates were aboard. She would go with them.

Beth was still imagining herself in her pleated skirt as they were approaching the iron gate, approaching the front door, standing in front of the brass wolf knocker and now reaching out for its mouth to rattle it. The door was still pea-green and paint chipped. Just how many years did it take paint to peel? Lots according to Yew Tree cottage. Yes, thought Beth – the lightning tree was a yew. Of course.

She was turning to look at the tree from habit, knowing that she could just see its branches from this angle where she used to stand after school waiting to be let in, with one eye also on the horizon keeping look out for that golden sailed ship, when the door opened.

It was Pammy.

Beth stared at her former foster mother's mouth, at the wrinkles closing together into their familiar deep tracks as Pammy puffed a cigarette. The wrinkles had already been there thirty years ago. Even if it weren't for their distinctiveness, Beth would have recognised Pammy's eyes. They were like goats' eyes: green with tiny pupils, pupils that had nothing pleasurable to dilate about.

"You from the agency?" said Pammy, hitching up her trousers. Now that she was sixty-five, seventy even, she was wearing elasticated trousers. Her jumper was patched on the elbows and wash-weary.

"That's right. Can we come in?" said Zoe, flashing her social worker identification pass.

Pammy held the door open begrudgingly, glancing about her to check that everything was in order.

Beth stood swaying in the middle of the front room, queasy from the smell inside the cottage, from the familiarity of everything. Hardly anything had changed. How was that possible? For a second, her mind tricked her into thinking that she was back here again as a child, living here, imprisoned by Pammy.

"Go get some fresh air, Beth," said Zoe.

"Beth?" said Pammy, narrowing her eyes.

"That's right," said Zoe, smiling. "Beth Trelawney."

Pammy cursed and dropped her cigarette. Beth gazed at the glowing stub, willing it to set alight to the carpet, to send the whole place up in blazes, to burn Pammy and her cottage to ash. But Pammy, surprisingly agile for her age, dropped to her feet to retrieve her precious cigarette.

Zoe motioned for Beth to quickly go to the car, and then turned to Pammy. "Do you mind if I take a look around and conduct a formal assessment?" she said.

Outside in the garden, underneath the lightning tree, Beth tried to remember the deep breathing techniques that a relaxation therapist had been teaching her as part of her programme. In for five seconds, out for five seconds, in for five seconds...

A man appeared around the side of Yew Tree cottage, startling her. Beth stared at the surfers' emblem on his sweater, at his blond hair blowing about, at the familiarity of his face. "I know you," she said.

"Yes," he said, smiling. "Are you Beth?"

"Yes. And you're Shane."

"That's right. You remember." He held his hand out to her to shake hands. "Nice to see you again."

"Do you still live here?" she said, trying not to sound shocked or condescending. She was unable to imagine anyone acting out their life in this paltry village.

"No, but my parents still live there." He nodded at the row of terraced houses overlooking Yew Tree cottage. He gazed at her. "You haven't changed."

"So I'm told."

He plucked up a long straw-like blade of grass and

chewed it. "Life been good to you?"

She hesitated. "No," she said. "Not really."

She turned away to look at the sea. Even as a little girl, before she had been aware of how different her life was compared to other children's, she had disliked the sea that formed the frame to wherever she went. She would go from one town to the next and there it was, stopping her from running, like a shape-shifting sorcerer. It had been a part of her imprisonment. She had tried to escape it, but all that she had really done was move inland. It had still been there – the past, lapping at the corners of her life.

"Can I ask you something?" she said, turning back to Shane.

"Be my guest," he said.

"Didn't the village think it was odd that I ran away?"

Shane shrugged. He wasn't a quick thinker, she could tell. Not because he was stupid, but because he was considerate; he liked to think about the effect that his words might have. He frowned a lot, opened his mouth to speak and closed it again slowly and heavily with the stiff mechanism of a ventriloquist's dummy. She could remember this mannerism from over thirty years ago – as he sat on the back wall of her garden, squinting in the sun, wearing a cheesecloth shirt and denim shorts. He had thick blonde hair over his legs and arms even then.

He had always been old for his age, which was why she had remembered him as a man, she suddenly realised – as the man who was kind to her in her childhood; the one she had tried to tell the psychologist about.

"When you left there were a few rumours, but Pammy told everyone that you were disturbed. Nobody really knew you, so they couldn't argue."

"So no one did anything."

"I...I don't think anyone knew about the cigarettes."

"But *you* did," said Beth, quietly.

A dog appeared running along the sea front. Its tail was

missing and it ran slightly sideways like a crab. It sniffed at the tyres on Beth's car before running off. It was a stray. Pengilly was that sort of a place. There were stray cats and dogs abound, as though you had stumbled upon a remote Greek island in a corner of England where animal rights weren't in effect. Children's rights weren't in effect here either, so dogs didn't stand a chance.

"I did confront Pammy," he replied, "but she said you were doing it to yourself, that you weren't right in the head."

"Did you think that?" Suddenly, stood there on the seafront of dirty Pengilly, what this man thought of her was the most important thing in the world.

He seemed to realise this too and he opened his mouth and closed it many times before finally shaking his head and saying, "I didn't know what to think. You never said very much. But I liked you. And for a while you and I were the only friends we had in this place."

He smiled down at her, his lips dry from the outdoors. She noticed that his skin was weather-beaten – he worked outdoors. A fisherman? No, he didn't smell enough. Maybe a rescue serviceman or life guard; something heroic and noble.

"So no one can tell me anything?" said Beth.

"No. Did you think the past is here? It's not. It's with you, Beth. It's been with you all along. Only *you* know what really happened between you and Pammy."

Beth looked down at her feet. They seemed a long way away from her, disconnected, as though she was looking at someone else.

How could she have been so misguided? To seek Pammy out was only to seek a miss-mashed version of the truth, like playing a record that had been left outside to warp in the heat. The truth as it stood now was pure – it was her version. If she listened to Pammy's version, she could become confused and lose her own truth. There was no way that Pammy, seventy, in her elasticated trousers and patched jumper, was going to admit to something she had done thirty years ago and stuff up her own life in the process.

She would go into the cottage and get Zoe and head back home. Screw this.

"Do you remember the mood ring?" Shane said.

"The what?" She wrinkled her eyes up to look at the sky. The sun had reappeared. There were no clouds. She thought briefly of lying in the grass at Yew Tree cottage with Shane, looking up at this same patch of sky, unable to believe at the time that this sky stretched on for miles and miles and that other people could see it too.

"The mood ring." He laughed and motioned to the lightning tree. "It was Pammy's favourite thing. She went nuts when she couldn't find it. You stole it from her, put it in a cake tin and buried it under the tree."

"I did?" Beth smiled. She must have been a strange little girl – her hair wild, her eyes so dark that no one could quite make her out. "Why would I do that?"

"You thought the ring had powers, that it told Pammy when to…you know…hurt you. You said it went red when she had to get angry."

Beth laughed. "What an idiot!"

"Want to dig it up?" said Shane, nudging her.

Beth thought for a moment. It was quiet over at the cottage. Whatever was going on, Zoe would be handling it fine because it was what she did every day. "Why not?"

Using a shovel from Pammy's vegetable patch, Shane dug up the hard ground underneath the lightning tree. It was thick with roots. Beth kept her eye on the job in hand, not wanting to glance up at the window beyond, at the room where she was certain demons would still be crouching, throwing themselves against the pane to try to escape, still acting out the desperate thoughts that had plagued her infancy.

It was the most bizarre thing, watching this man dig, keeping an eye out for anyone noticing, hoping evil Pammy wouldn't charge out of the front door and torture them both to infinity. Because there under the tree together, Beth and Shane weren't adults anymore but children clad in hand-me-down clothes, with abominable Seventies haircuts and a die-hard belief in magic – in their ability to control the universe.

As he dug, she knew that he had been the one to dig before, that she had watched over him in the same way, keeping guard of the front door and gate, that he had even used the same spade.

He struck metal and looked up at Beth with glee, wiping sweat from his forehead and peeling off his sweater. "There she goes." He eased the tin up, swept the mud from its surface and handed it to her.

Beth sat down on the grass. The tin was stiff. They used a stone to force the lid open.

"You look," said Beth, handing the tin back to Shane.

Inside were hundreds of seagull feathers. Beth stared in amazement. She must have spent hours collecting feathers that had swept along the beach, got caught in cobwebs on gates, trapped themselves in gorse hedges. It would have taken weeks, months, to collect this many.

She foraged through the feathers and then pulled out the ring. She held it before her, memory rushing through its metal, through her fingertips, up her arteries to her brain.

Then she cried out in horror and flung it down into the grass. "I don't want it!" she cried. "It's hers!"

"Take it," said Shane, retrieving it and pressing it into her hand. "If you keep it then you own its powers. You own the memory. You own what happened. You understand?"

Beth considered it. Maybe he was right.

"Put it somewhere out the way," he said. "Somewhere where you know where it is, but you don't ever have to look at it."

When had Shane become so clever? She turned to thank him, but he wasn't there. There was no sweater, just the spade leaning against the cottage wall.

She turned about her, confused. And then heard the sound of police sirens approaching. She looked up the hill and there weaving their way down into the dumps of Pengilly were two police cars.

The front door of the cottage opened and out stepped Zoe, looking over to the car for Beth.

"Hey!" hissed Beth, moving forward slightly crouched, still mindful of the threat of Pammy. "Are you okay? Sorry to leave you so long, but I –"

"No sweat," said Zoe. "This one was a no-brainer. She's got rats in her kitchen, the place stinks of gas and the kid's mattress has got springs sticking out of it and smells of urine. I'm going to try to get her charged with physical and emotional neglect. If they uncover physical abuse too then so be it."

The police arrived and spoke briefly with Zoe before entering Yew Tree cottage, their radios chattering and crackling. Beth gazed at the siren lights whirling around soundlessly. Where was Shane? What was happening?

Moments later, the police appeared with Pammy.

Beth felt a white streak of fear run through her at the sight of Pammy and stiffened herself against the anger that was sure to be directed at her. But Pammy didn't say anything. If she saw Beth, she didn't acknowledge it. She just moved limply forward under the policeman's guidance, looking old and disoriented.

Beth hadn't expected to feel wrenched with pity and doubt, but she did – overwhelmingly so. She watched the cars pull away with their sirens subdued and still, and found herself alone with Zoe underneath the lightning tree.

"Job done," said Zoe, clapping her hands together. "You pleased? Ding dong the witch is dead. What the hell were you doing out here digging anyway?"

Beth blinked with bewilderment. "With Shane?" she said. "Shane was digging?"

"Shane who?" said Zoe.

"The guy who was here with me? He was my friend. He just helped me..." Beth trailed off, staring about her. "Where is he?"

"I've seen this sort of thing before, Beth. It's a kind of post-traumatic stress disorder. It's 'cos you're at the site of the abuse."

"There's no Shane?" said Beth.

"No Shane," said Zoe, taking her arm. "Come on."

"Wait," said Beth. She stared over at the house where she knew that Shane had once lived. She knew that he had been here once upon a time, that he used to open his mouth and close it slowly, that he had blond hair on his arms and legs, that he wore cheesecloth shirts and that he had been the one to help her bury the ring, and most of all that he had been the one that was kind to her.

She couldn't believe that he hadn't been here with her now, helping her, talking to her with the years showing upon his face. She must have wanted it so badly – for someone from her past to guide her.

There was no Shane.

But she had the ring, which she eased onto her finger for want of somewhere safe to put it. And as she took one last look at Yew Tree cottage, at the dark window beyond which she had been imprisoned, at the lightning tree, she noticed with utter wonder that there was one small green leaf on one of the black twisted branches of the dead tree.

Zoe stared out of the window. Just as they got on the motorway at Exeter, the rain had started to tip down. It was early evening. The windscreen wipers scraped mournfully against the glass. Zoe had offered to drive even though she loathed driving, but Beth wanted to do it. She wanted to get back before nightfall, she said, so that the boys didn't have to spend the night at the professor's after all. She was gripping the wheel with white knuckles, bending forward, trying to see through the rain.

Zoe wasn't sure whether the trip was a success because Beth was the only one that could form such a conclusion and Beth wasn't going to share it with her.

She yawned and glanced at her watch, trying to work out what Ned would be doing now. She had been tempted to call him earlier to find out if he was managing the case load okay, but he would just say that he wasn't and then she would feel guilty and twitchy the whole way back.

She had just drunk a slush puppy so her tongue was blue and her bladder was full. They had stopped off once already to buy the drink, so Zoe crossed her legs and tried not to look at the sheets of water cascading down the windscreen.

When they got off the motorway, things were mellower. Beth put the radio on and visibly relaxed. Spanish guitar music was playing. It wasn't Zoe's bag, but it was better than the hum of the motor. Zoe kicked her sandals off, crossing her legs underneath her on the car seat.

They passed the welcome sign for Glastonbury and Beth suddenly said, "Let's get drunk."

"What?" said Zoe, dropping her legs down to sit upright. "You said you wanted to get back for –"

"Forget the boys. I mean…" Beth checked herself, ever mindful of her shaky parental status. "Look…I don't want to go home yet. I want to take some time out – just one night. They're not expecting me back. Please?"

"Oh, you don't have to plead with me to get drunk," Zoe replied, laughing.

Beth seemed to know her way around Glastonbury pretty well. She navigated the bypass roundabouts, went down a few narrow roads before pulling up into a car park and leading Zoe up a hill by foot to the high street.

"One of my favourite pubs in the West Country," said Beth. "It's the whole mystical thing, you know?"

Zoe nodded, but didn't know. She hated the whole mystical thing and the people who were attracted to it – the whole incense-burning crystal-donning Tarot-reading lot of them. And she was surprised that the apparently cool and serious Beth Trelawney had any time for it either.

To Zoe's further surprise, Beth, in her all-white ensemble, ordered a scrumpy cider – the real sort complete with maggots and crap, not a fake one from Slough.

"I'll have whatever she's having," said Zoe, having always wanted to say that.

They managed four scrumpys each. That was pretty good. Zoe was impressed anyway. She had never managed one pint of it until now. But there was something in the air and it wasn't mysticism. It was…optimism.

"You wanna know why I came with you?" said Zoe, slurring her speech.

"Enlighten me," said Beth, propping her head up with both hands.

"That cracks me up," said Zoe, pointing and laughing. "You can tell you were a lecturer. You use formal words even when ratted."

They were the only customers left in the pub. The barman was stood reading a newspaper with his leg up on a stool.

"*Were* being the operative word," said Beth.

"Ha! There you go again," said Zoe, clutching her ribs. "Hey…" She looked serious. "Why don't you lecture again, when all this is over?"

"It'll never be over," said Beth, shaking her head, her dark hair falling around her face. "I haven't even got through the hearing yet."

Zoe pulled a handful of Beth's hair upwards and peeped inside at her face. "It might be over one day," she said.

"So why did you come?" said Beth, changing the

subject. Beth had this habit of looking right at you, or through you, as though she could predict what you were going to say next.

"'Cos of Ned."

"Ned?" said Beth, almost tottering backwards off her stool. "What's that gargoyle got to do with it?"

Zoe cast her eyes downwards, hurt burning her face. Ned wasn't so bad. He was pretty good-looking. It was Zoe that was the rough one. She could never look like Beth. She knew that ugly people had to exist, but she didn't have to be *this* ugly. She was going to lose the braids and the nose ring and the baggy clothes.

She imagined the new, improved version of herself stood before Ned in their office. He would ask her what the hell she had done, why she had changed herself? And she would say that she wanted to be like someone he could love.

There was no point telling Beth this. She wouldn't get it. She had never had to change herself to love a man. Women like her didn't have to.

"So did you come with me because you wanted to do something kind to impress him?" said Beth, eating the last crisp and then concentrating on folding the packet into one of those tiny origami-type shapes that Zoe always wondered at the neatness of. "It's not too hard to figure out. You're not as complicated as you think you are," said Beth, winking. "People seldom are."

Zoe felt suddenly angry – the old wave of anger that she had felt upon first meeting Beth. Pretty Beth with her intellect, her education. Where had all that come from, because it hadn't come from that condemned cottage in Pengilly or from the rotting council house of Penthruthen?

Damn her.

"So what about you then, Beth?" said Zoe. "Are *you* complicated? Because no one really knows you, do they?"

Yes, Zoe was trying to change herself, but she couldn't –

not just like that. People didn't change overnight. It took years and years and even then she might not pull it off. Which was why she said what she said next before thinking about the effect that it might have upon Pretty Beth.

"You slapped that boy because you wanted someone else to know how it feels, didn't you?" she said, leaning forward to snarl at Beth. "You weren't big enough to break the vicious circle."

Beth stood up, swaying and with a quick jerk of her wrist she splashed the rest of her pint onto Zoe's face and then stood there looking at the empty glass in her hand, staring as though her hand wasn't hers.

Zoe reacted several seconds later, crying out as the cider stung her eyes and made her make-up run. The bar man threw his newspaper in a panic, its pages fluttering over the edge of the bar to the floor. He brought Zoe a fist of green paper towels and ordered Beth to leave.

When Zoe had cleaned herself up in the ladies', she stared at herself in the cloudy mirror, hating what she saw. If the point of the trip had been to show Ned what a magnanimous creature she was, then she had wasted her annual leave.

"He'll never love me," she muttered, hanging her head.

Outside in the street, Zoe found Beth sat down on the doorstep of a crystal shop. In the window display, a huge crystal was turning eternally, catching the street light.

"I didn't mean what I said. I'm really sorry," said Zoe, kicking lightly at Beth's leg. Zoe couldn't do the stroking thing. She was more of a nudge, kick person. She had to work on that too. "Budge up." She sat down on the step next to Beth.

Beth was staring at the pavement, her knees tightly drawn up. She was dainty even when inebriated.

"I hated you when I first met you," Zoe said. "I hated what you represented, whatever that was." Beth was looking at her with her large dark eyes. The poor woman had been through so much and here was Zoe performing her own emotional biopsy on the pavement in Glastonbury. "Then I realised that we're alike. And…I kinda like you. I hate you too, 'cos I hate myself. The thing is…" She hesitated. "When all this is over and at the risk of sounding really naff….well, I'd like us to be friends. You know, good friends."

Beth smiled absent-mindedly. "I'd like that…" And then her expression grew melancholic. "Does everyone think I'm guilty?"

"No," said Zoe, nudging Beth's knee. "Not everyone. *You* don't."

Zoe had managed to persuade the barman to let them take one of the rooms above the pub for the night. She was the last to fall asleep. She lay watching Beth sleeping. Beth was an elegant drunken sleeper – no surprise; her chest rose and fell in her white T-shirt, her mouth slightly ajar. No snores. No dribbling.

Zoe smoothed Beth's hair away from her eyes and pulled the floral eiderdown cover up over her thin shoulders.

Beth was now the child and Zoe the adult. It had been that way since they entered the cottage at Pengilly and Zoe had taken charge.

When Zoe was with Ned, she was the child. Was everyone was like that – accelerating and decelerating in years depending on their company – helpless with one person, feeling invincible with the next?

She had always thought her childishness in the presence of Ned as a highly undesirable thing. Yet she wondered now, sliding underneath the eiderdown next to Beth and trying not to disturb her, whether childishness in itself was such a bad thing? Maybe sometimes being juvenile around another human being simply meant that you felt comforted, able to let go of responsibility, relieved, as though you had

finally arrived home to those marvellous parents whom you
had never known.

CHAPTER NINE

Danny didn't mind too much about staying at Professor Moss's house. They had a television and a massive black Chow Chow dog that was the size of a Shetland pony. And Lee's house was only a seven and a half minute walk away. It should have been an eight minute walk, but he ran the last bit.

Within a few minutes of arriving at the Moss's house, Danny had phoned Lee to arrange to call on her. He was used to leaving messages with anyone in the family regarding his imminent arrival, so he didn't think it odd that Lee didn't come to the phone and that Mrs Paris took the call for her.

He still didn't think it was odd that Mrs Paris came to the door, wiping her hands on her apron and frowning at him. Nor odd that she wasn't smiling, because he knew now that Mrs Paris wasn't perfect and had bad days too.

"Daniel," she said, breathing in sharply through her nose.

"Hi, Mrs Paris. Can I come in?"

"I'm afraid not," Mrs Paris said, fixing her eyes upon him.

Danny laughed. "Ha ha, you got me there. So where's Lee?" He put his foot on the doorstep, about to step up.

Mrs Paris checked behind her, stepped outside and then pulled the front door until it was barely open. She kept her hand on the door, indicating that she wouldn't be staying out here long with him.

"Lee isn't coming out today. Nor any other day."

"What?" said Danny. He noticed now that everything was really quiet in the house. There was no television or stereo on up in Lee's room. There was no sound of footsteps running downstairs to greet him.

"We think it's best that in the circumstances —"

"What circumstances?" said Danny.

"Is there a problem?" Danny knew from the accent, before the front door was pulled wide open, that a big man was about to cross the threshold and take command. Why were all the blokes in his world so damned massive?

It occurred to Danny that all this time he had been going out with Lee, he had never met her dad. But now it all made sense. Lee's idea of manhood had been presented to her by a moustached man wearing chinos.

"Didn't you hear what my wife said, sonny?" said Mr Paris.

"How come *you* did?" said Danny. "Were you hiding behind the door?"

Danny heard a giggle. It was Lee. He tried to see beyond Mr Paris's bulk down the hallway, but he couldn't make very much out other than the floor tiles.

"I want you to stay away from my daughter," said Mr Paris, pointing at Danny. Mr Paris was wearing a cheesy gold sovereign ring and a gold necklace.

"And what does Lee want?" said Danny.

"She wants what I say she wants."

"Ah, a democracy," said Danny, nodding. "Well, I guess I'll just have to see Lee at school then."

"You might wanna wait to hear what the courts say

before you go making plans for where you'll be next term," said Mr Paris.

Danny dropped his mouth open. He looked at Mrs Paris. She looked away.

"I thought you liked me, Mrs Paris?" said Danny. "Are you going to let him do this?

Mrs Paris didn't reply. She shifted uncomfortably on the step before turning away. "Goodbye, Daniel," she murmured.

Danny was about to call out Lee's name, to attempt to rush her father and bowl him over, to pick up stones and hurl them at the living room window – anything to show the intensity of his feelings. And then he realised that they were expecting him to be immature, to explode into a hormone-induced frenzy and try to stab himself or one of them.

So instead he said, "Okay, Mr Paris. See ya," and he turned away and walked down the driveway.

He didn't need to look back to know that Mrs Paris was craning her neck around the door to see what was happening, that Mr Paris was gawping in confusion, that Lee was in the lounge twitching the blinds – each of them wondering whether Lee was really so light as to be that readily disposable.

On the way home, Danny felt numb. He kicked a stone, his hands shoved hard into his jeans pockets. A magpie flew low across his path and landed on a grass verge. He went to salute it to cancel out the bad luck that a solitary magpie brought, and then he considered that he didn't care about any of that stuff anymore – neither superstition nor magic. Somewhere between The Parises house and the Moss's, he had grown up. Which was why he felt numb. The magic was all dead and gone.

Back at the Moss's, Danny rapped on the door. No one arrived so he let himself in. Erland and the Prof were playing chess out in the conservatory, their heads bent low together. It seemed to Danny in that moment that everyone in the entire universe was with someone else except him.

He sat down on the arm of the sofa and waited to see how long it would be before one of the chess players noticed him.

The Prof, Danny thought whilst observing him, was an example of how it was possible to be a geek with social skills, which technically didn't make him a geek any more but perhaps a skeek – a socially skilled geek. Danny had just made the word up and he liked the sound of it. He couldn't think of anyone else that he might be able to apply it to right now because he only knew the one skeek.

He waited twenty-eight minutes. As he waited, he thought of Lee timing the queue at the post office on her new DKNY watch. He thought of his mum going to court in four days time. He thought of Brett never living with them again, of them all never living with their mum again. And then he launched himself as fast as he could into the conservatory and with one quick flick knocked the chess board flying.

"What did you do that to our game for?" said Erland.

Danny turned his face in the direction of his brother's voice. He couldn't see him. The back bedroom at the Moss's had no street lights over-looking it, there was no hallway light on, no nightlight in the room, plus they had a blackout blind and velvet curtains.

Mrs Moss had told them over dinner that she and her husband liked to sleep in total darkness so that their melatonin levels would be increased enough to induce deep sleep, and besides which there was breast cancer in her family and not having sufficiently dark rooms had been linked with cancer.

Mrs Moss was a pretty woman, so far as Danny could tell with someone that old – was she sixty-something? – but she didn't smile much. She told them that they could have more light in their bedroom tonight if they felt insecure, but naturally neither of the boys were about to admit that. Erland had looked as though he might crack, but Danny kicked him under the table.

Danny thought about making a sarcastic or spiteful comment to Erland now, until he considered that there was something liberating as well as suffocating about being in complete darkness. You could either see yourself as being totally encased or totally free, depending on how you viewed the void. Danny saw himself temporarily as faceless, anonymous. He could be honest.

"Lee dumped me. Or her parents did. 'Cos of mum."

He could tell from Erland's quick inhalation that he also was tempted to offer up some heartless retort, until he too reconsidered the invitation before him: to lay bare without being seen.

"Sorry," was all Erland could muster.

Danny smiled to himself. He tossed the blanket off his shoulders and propped himself up on his elbow. "So what was he like?"

"Who?"

"Dad."

Erland didn't reply. Danny cocked his ear. He couldn't hear Erland even breathing. You never could, not even when he fell into a deep sleep. "I'm waiting..."

"There's nothing to say," said Erland, finally.

"Well, what did he look like? Did he still support Chelsea? What was—?"

"He's not our Dad, all right?" Erland snapped. "He doesn't want to know us. He said he was sorry but that he couldn't get to know us. He has his own family now that are more important than us. I *hate* him! So shut up about him!"

Erland had been thinking about these thoughts for some time, Danny could tell. Now and then a thought got trapped in Erland's brain and fluttered about like a moth captured in a jam jar. By the time the thought was set free, it was in such a tangled state that Erland cried with the sheer exhaustion of it all.

Danny listened to his brother's sobs in the darkness.

And then Danny did something that he had never done before, something that he knew they would never speak of in the future. He got out of bed, reaching out in the direction of his brother's bed and found his way across the floorboards to him. He felt for the bed covers and pulling them back he eased himself into Erland's bed. Erland was facing the wall, sobbing silently now, his shoulders rocking, his bed sheet damp, his breath shuddering.

"It's all right," Danny said, laying his hand on Erland's shoulder. "It's all right."

Klaris needn't have worried about the meeting with Charles Langley. He met her at the children's services offices in Bath and promptly took her for coffee at the Pump Rooms. The Pump Room trio were playing – a violinist, cellist and pianist – whilst waiting staff served morning tea. Klaris ordered a scone and a mint tea.

Charles required some further information about Klaris's involvement with the Trelawney's: when she had met them, what she had made of them initially, when she had noticed a deterioration in the relationship between the mother and youngest son.

He couldn't have been more amiable towards Klaris. If she were not lacking in confidence and if Charles were not wearing a wedding ring, she might have fancied that he was making a little play for her. He seemed a steady man who would be devoted, diligent, dependable. Just the sort of man whom no woman ever wanted to marry – not until thirty years later, given the benefit of hindsight and loneliness.

He made no mention of knowing Klaris's ex-husband

and Klaris formed the conclusion that he knew nothing of it. Demon Man had very little to gain by complicating his own reputation. Maybe he had moved on and the matter could now rest.

Klaris had built the meeting up with Charles to such proportions that by the time they parted company and she walked to the multi-storey car park, she felt faint. She sat in her car, her pulse racing, her hands shaking. She hadn't had a day off in a long while. Flicking through her appointments, she saw that she only had a three o'clock and then an internal departmental meeting. She could rearrange both. She would take the afternoon off.

She headed for home in order to sit out in the garden. It wasn't a bad day – a bit mixed, but fine enough. Yet once home she felt agitated, so she packed up a gym bag and headed for the health spa.

As she drove, she glanced at her reflection. She had changed – was changing. Something was changing.

She found the respite that she was looking for at the spa. She swam fifty lengths; she lay in the jacuzzi for twenty minutes; she almost fell asleep in the sauna. She came out feeling marvellous and congratulated herself on having the self-knowledge to take some time out.

At home, she changed into her dressing gown and pyjamas, enjoying the debauchery of doing so at barely four o'clock on a week day, and poured herself a generous glass of Chablis. She was just ripping off a chunk of baguette and holding it in her mouth whilst taking her wine and library book out to the patio, when there was a knock at the door.

She placed the wine glass down onto the nearest corner table, chewing the baguette thoughtfully. Who could it be? The knocking came again.

"Klaris?" The letterbox flapped open then shut.

She recognised the voice immediately. She reached for the wine and took a long drink. "Klaris? I know you're there."

She looked down at herself, at her inappropriate attire and then decided that she didn't care a hoot about it. She opened the front door, tightening her dressing gown belt. Her brain was fast-pedalling to find a suitable greeting containing just the right amount of sarcasm and acidity.

But then when she saw him she couldn't say anything whatsoever.

"Klaris," he said, hands on hips. He hadn't changed. Just thinner, greyer, more ragged. He was agitated – hopping about, glancing behind him, above him, beyond her. "Can I come in?"

"No," she said.

"Okay then we'll do this here…" He wiped his mouth with his hand and then pointed at her. "Are you going to tell them about Annaliese Payne, or shall I?"

"Tell them what?" said Klaris, tightening her dressing gown belt further. She glanced about to see whether her neighbours were about. She didn't want a scandal.

"You know exactly what. I haven't got time for games. I've got a train to catch."

"Good," she said, folding her arms.

"Now listen up, Klaris." He wiped his mouth again. His jumper was around his waist. He was red in the face. It struck Klaris that there was no car parked outside. He had either taken a taxi or walked. He had probably walked. He looked sweaty. How had he known her address? "You've got till 5pm tomorrow to figure out how to tell them. If you haven't by then, I will enlighten them. I *swear.*"

"Be my guest," she said. "Now, if you'll excuse me…" And she turned and slammed the door so hard in his face that she thought the pane of glass might fracture.

She imagined herself standing there like a cacti, covered in lethal splinters of shiny glass, iridescent for a moment in the afternoon sun before crashing to the floor.

Since Brett had been born, Jacko couldn't remember a time when he hadn't felt a certain sadness. Sometimes it lasted several hours, sometimes even the whole day and into the next morning, a glow of grief crackling away. Looking at his son now, he couldn't imagine what it was all about but thought it probably had something to do with his own ineptitude.

"So how's Beth?" said his mum.

"She's okay, I think. It's the hearing in two days."

"Yes, I know. I'd like to come. I'd like to…" She trailed off. Jacko considered for the first time how fragile his mother looked. She wasn't that old – sixty-one? – but she was tiny and tiny people always looked as though they were built to just get on with it, like clockwork mice. He had no idea what her general health was like, whether she had any friends.

"What would you like to do, Mum?" he asked, looking away from her and fixing his eye upon Brett who was amusing himself with a plastic giraffe and an elephant. He had never seen him play so calmly. If Jacko's mother had to give evidence of such in court, it would be a bloody awful dilemma for her. Perhaps this was what was pressing upon her now – the reason for her fragility.

"I'd like to live nearer Beth and the boys," she said. He had just taken a large bite of apple cake. He held it in his mouth a moment, stunned, before beginning to chew.

"What's brought this on?" he said.

"Oh, I don't know," his mother replied, sipping her tea. "The fact that Beth is in a terrible situation and needs family? Her son is my grandson. I'm all she's got."

"What about me?"

"What about you, son?" she replied.

Jacko stared at his mother. She didn't seem to be trying to pick a fight. Or was she?

"I know about your mistress," she said. "Beth told me

all about it when she was here last."

Jacko took a drink of his coffee, ate another mouthful of cake and thought about his response.

But his mother closed him there and then. "You really should leave now," she said. Just like that.

So he finished his coffee and cake, kissed his son goodbye and left him – like he always knew he would.

When he got back to Bath, he was surprised to see Matt's car parked out the front of Natasha's place. Damn. He really didn't want to talk business at the moment.

He rapped his knuckles on Natasha's front door. He didn't have a key – had no intention of getting one. There was no response. He tried the handle and found that the door was unlocked. He pushed it open, bracing himself for Matt's barrage of questions, inspiration, whatever it was that had driven him here tonight. Until he suddenly realised that Matt didn't know that Jacko was living here.

He dropped his briefcase and suit jacket onto the sofa and moved forward through the lounge, casting his eye about him. No sign of anyone.

Then he heard something. A low grumbling, rumbling sound. He moved towards the sound. As it drew closer, it grew more distinct. It was grunting. Male. And then he heard her moaning *yeah give it to me, that's it big boy, harder, come on!*

He didn't have to open the door to see her face knitted up with ugly pleasure, to see her gritted teeth, her tanned flat stomach crinkling as she contorted to wrap her legs higher, to get ever closer to pleasure, her head grinding up and down on the pillow, her hair spread out around her like a drowned woman floating on water.

A faceless back was pummelling her. A toned torso just like his. Buttocks clenched, sweat causing a sheen that any stag would be proud of, thighs tight and pumping. It could be him. He saw himself in all his glory and in all his revolting depravity. Except that it wasn't him. It was his best friend, Matt Mount, the irony of the surname causing Jacko's mouth to contort into a pained smile.

He envisaged himself launching at Matt, at using his considerable height and stature advantage to pummel the guy into the ground. Or taking Natasha by the throat and holding her up against the wall until her chicken-thin bones snapped. Except that he had no claim to do so. He couldn't tell his best friend off for sleeping with the woman whom he was also secretly sleeping with behind his wife's back. He couldn't tell the woman that he was having a sex-only relationship with that she wasn't allowed to have a sex-only relationship with anyone else.

He had no claims, no holds, no nothing in this room.

They hadn't noticed him. He had managed to enter the room and stand there for a full minute without interrupting them, so enwrapped in lust were they. And it was surely lust. There was no way that Matt was going to fall in love with this girl. Or was he? Jacko didn't know.

He moved away from the door and into the kitchen, where in the dreary light he assembled his belongings. He purposely hadn't put anything in her bedroom or bathroom. And the purpose was clear now. He took the bin liners out to his car and as he slipped out the front door, closing it softly behind him, he heard his friends reach their glorious conclusion together.

He passed Danny in the hallway, who muttered a greeting of sorts before disappearing up to his room. Erland was lying on the lounge sofa playing on his Einstein Touch, unwilling to look beyond it to say hello.

He finally found Beth sitting outside. She was sat on the bench, drinking a glass of wine, listening to classical music through the open window. There were two glass bowls on the bench beside her – one full of pistachios, the other containing their shells.

Jacko stood in the dusky light. He could smell lavender. Beth had a couple of lavender plants in pots that she loved to sit beside. Every now and then she would reach out and brush the leaves to release their aroma, as she was doing now.

A calm had been restored, a civility that had existed before he had arrived and that had returned in his absence. He wanted to be part of the calm, to be part of Beth's cultured life. He wanted to consider everything as carefully as she did, to resist watching television, to be sure of his own self. He wanted to cock his head in thought as deep as Beth's, to go to wherever she went out here in her garden.

"You look nice," was all he could think to say. As soon as he said it, he felt like a moron. And therein lay the problem: he felt stupid in Beth's presence – inadequate, clumsy, uneducated. He had reeled in confusion at her bookshelf in the lounge, itched to find a dictionary to translate some of her words, stared in dull incomprehension at her sons who appeared to want to be every bit as painstaking as their mother.

"Jacko," she said, half-surprised, half-obliviously. "Sit down." She patted the bench next to her, moving the pistachio bowls.

Relieved, he accepted her offer. He was still wearing his work clothes. He glanced down at himself. His clothes felt like a shell – like saggy armour in a fight against an enemy who hadn't made itself known. He had lost his direction, his cause.

"I went to Cornwall," she said. There was no breeze tonight. It was warm again – not heat wave warm, but warm enough that Beth was wearing a summer dress and a cardigan draped around her shoulders. "I met my foster mother, Pammy, the woman who hurt me. And I found out that my mother is dead."

Jacko didn't know what to say. He put his head in his hands and stared at all the stones on the ground – the thousands of stones that had been lying here all this time and that he had never so much as glanced at before. Had he ever joined Beth on this bench? What had he been doing when he had lived here with her?

"And I'm okay," she said, her voice intonating upwards brightly. "There's no magic formula or anything – you can't undo what's done, but I feel as though I have some closure. That's an awful word I know, but it's the only one I can think of."

"Why didn't you ask me to go with you?" said Jacko, looking up. "I'd like to have helped."

She shrugged, her mouth clamped shut.

She had opened up and then the moment was over. It probably happened once a year and if you missed it then you had to wait another twelve months.

Jacko felt angry. He was taking all the blame – for his relationship with his mother, for his relationship with his wife, but both women were at fault too for allowing the situation to develop. No one had asked him to be otherwise. Didn't you owe it to the people you loved to try to improve them, to correct their wrongs?

"Don't you see that everything began to go wrong because you kept pushing me away?" he said. "I..I...have issues with people rejecting me. You never asked where I was or where I'd been, so I thought that you couldn't care less. You seemed to hate Brett and I, and love your other boys so much that I thought maybe you preferred them and their dad more than Brett and I."

Jacko sat back in his seat, shattered with the effort of telling the truth. He felt almost ecstatic. He had done it – he had found his part in all this, found a voice that sounded right to him.

"Well, maybe I do," said his wife.

He shook his head wearily. "I'll be off." He stood up. "I came here tonight with all my bin liners in the car. I don't know what I thought might happen. Maybe I thought you might let me move back in…I won't trouble you any more."

"We shouldn't have got married," she replied.

"Don't say that."

"It's true. I married you because I thought that I wasn't enough for the boys. But I am. I can see that now."

"No one person is ever enough. You're wrong to think that. It doesn't work out…I should know."

"But I'm not wrong about us. We don't fit, you and I." She said this sympathetically, as though she were talking to a teenage boy who had his first crush.

"Okay, that's enough," he said.

"I don't have enough forgiveness in me to go round, if I'm to get over what that woman did to me. I can't. I'm sorry."

"Enough, Beth. *Please.*" He held up his hand, holding his other hand over his face to hide his grief.

He left her, knowing that the sadness that he had felt all along had been merely a glimpse of this one big moment – the moment when he became the absent father that he was always meant to be.

Danny brushed past him in the hallway. Jacko took him by the arm. Danny stared at him with a belligerence that Jacko hadn't noticed before. The kid had changed, grown up, wised up.

"I'm sorry, Danny," he said. "Sorry you and I didn't work out."

"Then don't go," said Danny.

Jacko, who was already stood with his hand on the front door, turned in surprise. "You what?"

"Then don't go," said Danny, louder, folding his arms.

Erland appeared in the lounge doorway, a long skinny shadow. He had grown tall. How was that possible in such a short space of time?

"Fight," said Danny. "If you care about mum and us and Brett then fight her. Don't walk away like a coward. I

226

always hated that about you. Prove me wrong."

Jacko stared in amazement. When did this boy get so ballsy? Were all kids like this now?

"I…" He thought of the bin liners in the boot of his car, of Matt's naked form pounding Natasha, of his mother's dismissal of him as deftly as shaking crumbs from a mat. "Okay then," he said. "Okay."

Danny's mouth tried to form a smile. The Danny that Jacko knew would have smiled like a kid at a carnival. But this Danny couldn't let that happen any more. He went slightly red in the face with the effort of trying to still his emotions.

And so another perfectly well emotionally adjusted male crosses the ragged line into adulthood, thought Jacko, as he left the house. He meant Danny, but it could have applied to either one of them.

CHAPTER TEN

Zoe removed her nose ring and had her braids taken out yesterday in time for the hearing. Her hair was long, spiralling into curls and she had decided to wear it loose today. She had bought a suit also – a proper grown up pinstripe one, although she couldn't completely kiss corporate ass so was wearing lace-up platform boots.

She was packing her bag up with paperwork for the hearing when she heard the office door click behind her.

"Is…?" Ned began. …*Zoe here?* she wanted to say, completing his sentence, swivelling round to reveal her stunning new identity. "…it okay if I use your phone?" he said.

"Huh?" she said. "Uh, yeah. Sure. Whatever."

She turned away, bending back over her bag, grateful for her hair curtaining her face. What an idiot she was. He was no more interested in her new look than he was in what the weather was going to do today. Actually, it looked like it might thunder. The sky was that electric kind of white that looked like something might happen up there.

"You look…" He considered her at length, in Ned-time. "Nice. Yeah." He nodded, affirming his choice.

"Nice."

He sat down on the edge of her desk, crossed his legs and picked up her phone. "Langley's been trying to call me," he said. "Has he called you?"

"Nope."

"Is something wrong?" he said.

Zoe stopped, holding her hands on the clasp of her bag. Sod it. Damn it. Bugger it.

"I am nice," she said, snatching the phone receiver from him and slamming it down onto its stand. "I look nice because I *am* nice."

"Eh?"

"I'm a nice person. I'm even better than that. I'm beautiful. Can't you see that?" She held her face towards him so that he could inspect her in daylight.

He scratched his goatee, his mouth hanging open, his eyes scanning her skin before fixing finally upon her mouth. He was wearing jeans and a shirt with a hole in the elbow.

"I don't make a habit of sleeping with ugly women," he said. "So, yeah, I agree." He folded his arms around him with his shoulders held tight and high in a smug gesture. "But there's one slight problem with your theory about being nice: you're not a stay till morning kind of girl. Your words, not mine."

"I am," she said, her cheeks burning, or was it her eyes? Everything felt like it was burning. She felt like that child again – a child that was so eager to please that she was willing to ignite with the effort.

"Stay with me tonight," he whispered. Had he known the effect that whispering would have he might have chosen to voice the words normally, or maybe he had intended all along to weaken Zoe beyond repair. She moved towards him and allowed every suppressed recollection of him to race back into her mind as she kissed him, with one platform boot raised out behind her.

The phone rang, jolting Zoe away from Ned. She wiped

her mouth and looked about her, trying to remember what she was supposed to be doing. Ned was laughing. She picked up the phone. It was Charles Langley. His usually honeyed tone was abrasive, garbled, agitated.

"Sorry?" she said, frowning. "Who is Annaliese Payne? Run that past me again."

"I knew all along that something wasn't right with this case," Charles was saying. Zoe motioned for Ned to pick up the other phone. She placed her finger over her lips, indicating for him to do silently. "I've known her ex-husband for years. I didn't know he was married to her though."

"Married to who, Charles?" said Zoe. "Slow down. I don't understand." She cupped the phone underneath her chin and held her hands out in a shrug to Ned.

But Ned knew what was going on. He had put the phone down and was searching the Internet, scrolling through page after page until he found what he was looking for. He looked up at Zoe.

She stared at the computer screen trying to read as well as process Charles's words. "Klaris Shaw relocated to Bath after she was involved in the case of two-year-old, Annaliese Payne. Annaliese was suffering from hyperactive behaviour and mood swings," said Charles. "She banged herself unconscious and the mother was charged with abuse. Ring any bells?"

Rosie arrived punctually with Brett for the hearing. It was the first time that they had had a normal set-up at home since everything had begun. Beth dared to imagine a time when it might be even more normal, without Rosie here. She didn't mind Rosie personally, but her presence reminded Beth that the law didn't view her as responsible enough to look after her son on her own.

Brett was wearing a pair of stripy denim dungarees that were a favourite of Beth's – a nice touch, she thought, or perhaps a coincidence – and his hair was combed flat to one side like a 1920's Etonian. She held her arms out to him upon his arrival and he trotted forward without hesitation.

"Mama," he said. It was a pure moment, defiled only by the presence of another household's smell upon Brett's clothes and hair – someone else's soap, someone else's washing powder.

Rosie was stood at the window, diplomatically turned away to allow mother and son a private moment. She had been instructed to not leave them alone together. A lesser mother-in-law might have taken some sick kind of pleasure in the situation, but Rosie had played her part delicately, sensitively, and for that Beth was grateful.

"I see that your neighbour is selling up?" said Rosie.

"Good riddance to the nosy old bag," said Danny, entering the room and sprawling on the sofa, legs wide apart. He opened his arms for Brett to join him. Brett ran over and Danny scooped him up, tickling him. An inevitable emission of wind ensued from the toddler. Danny pulled a mock face of disgust and tossed his little brother aside onto a mound of cushions. Brett reappeared dribbling and laughing, his Eton hair all messed up. Beth smiled. She had forgotten the funny details.

"Ursula's not an old bag," said Beth. "Who knows what she might have going on in her life?"

"Nothing, by the looks of it," replied Danny. "She's too busy watching ours."

"Really?" said Beth, suddenly recalling the anonymous caller that had contacted the children's services. She rose to the window and joined Rosie in looking out. To her surprise, Ursula was there looking back. Ursula jumped, startled, backing out of sight.

So it was Ursula who made the call, Beth thought. But why? And was the reason anything to do with why they were moving away? She could ask her, but it wouldn't achieve anything. Ursula had her reasons and Beth couldn't bear to hear them.

"Do you know what they're asking for it?" said Rosie, keeping her eyes fixed upon the house. Beth glanced over at Danny who glanced at her at the same time. They stared at each other, alarmed.

"I've no idea," said Beth, breezily, picking up the cushions that Brett had strewn on the floor.

Beth went out to the kitchen to put the kettle on. As the kettle wheezed to life, she wondered for a moment what it might be like were Rosie to live next door. She wasn't exactly the mother-in-law from hell – too timid to ever be a nuisance, although over-familiarity could alter that. She was at that age where in a decade she could easily become infirm, need care, twenty-four hour assistance… It would be Jacko's responsibility. Beth didn't have any responsibilities of that kind. It was the way she liked it – the way it had always been. No one had helped her, after all.

"Would you mind terribly," said Rosie, close behind her, "if I were to take a look at the property next door?"

Beth turned to face her mother-in-law. "I can't think about that now, Rosie. I'm sorry. What with the hearing this afternoon…."

"Which is precisely *why* I'd like to be nearer," said Rosie, placing her hand on Beth's arm. "I wouldn't be in the way. I want to help."

"I don't need help," said Beth, knowing how far beyond she was saying anything like that, how hypocritical and ironic it sounded, and yet she uttered the old familiar words nonetheless.

"But I'm lonely," said Rosie.

Klaris knocked at the door tentatively. She had trodden these steps and crossed this threshold so many times and yet today it all felt different, unknown. There was a car outside that she didn't recognise. When Rosie answered the door, Klaris realised whose car it was.

Klaris hadn't expected anyone to be at home except Beth. She had wanted to wish her well before the hearing. She hadn't called to see her as much of late. It wasn't because she hadn't wanted to be there, but because in a way her role had been pushed to the back, now that the children's services were so heavily involved. She would see Beth at the other end as things began to stabilise and Beth became readmitted into normality – as she was confident that she would – back to the ranks of all the other mums whom Klaris classed almost as her family, for want of a more appropriate description.

All this she thought behind Beth's back as Beth led her into the lounge, knowing that she dare not utter such words out loud. One never knew the outcome when the courts were involved. Sometimes things went off at a complete tangent and the law appeared to have gone insane.

Klaris perched on the edge of the sofa, her briefcase on her lap. She smiled brightly at Beth and looked about for the rest of the family. "They're in the garden," said Beth.

"I'll go and check on them," said Rosie, jumping up.

"She seems pleasant," said Klaris, watching Rosie leave. They heard the sound of the back door closing.

"Yes, she is," said Beth. "She wants to move in next door."

Klaris spluttered with laughter. "Goodness, surely you don't want that?"

"I want what's best for my little boy, Klaris. He seems very calm around his grandma."

"Naturally," said Klaris, tightening her grip on her briefcase. "I didn't mean to speak out of turn."

"Is there anything that you need to discuss ahead of this afternoon?" said Beth, standing up. "It's just that my solicitor is due here any minute and –"

"Of course. I mustn't keep you." Klaris stood up to

join Beth. Not so long ago, Klaris's appearance in this household had been heralded by an hallelujah. So much had altered, she thought, shaking her head sadly. Now she was no longer required. Everyone had forgotten that it was her that had brought the case to light in the first place, that had been Brett's salvation. "I'll see myself out," she said.

"Could you?" Beth was distracted by the sound of a mobile phone ringing. "Excuse me," she said, running upstairs.

Klaris paused by the front door, her head tilted to an angle. She could hear the sound of little feet slapping on kitchen tiles. She moved back down the hallway to the kitchen instinctively. It was baby Brett. He recognised her and smiled. She dropped to her knees and held out her hand.

"Hello, my little angel," she said, reaching to touch a curl on the top of his head.

She glanced about her. She could hear the thump of a football being booted about in the garden and the grandmother calling encouragement to the boys. She could hear Beth talking upstairs on her mobile.

She unclipped her briefcase and quickly unzipped a compartment in the lining of the lid and reached for a triangular multicoloured purse. On tiptoe, she reached to the cupboard with the glass door where she had reached so many times before to get the plastic Noddy mug with the chewed spout. Brett was looking at her encouragingly, knowing what was going to happen next.

She got the squash from the bottom cupboard, poured a splash into the mug and added water, with her ear cocked to listen for approaching footsteps.

Then she grabbed the wooden spoon from the utensils jar and used the end of the handle to grind a miniature pill to dust – so miniature that she had to squint to see what she was doing. She tilted the chopping board upright, guiding the powder swiftly into the Noddy cup.

"What are you doing?"

Klaris jumped, dropping the board. It fell to the floor, the powder disappearing into a cloud.

Beth was stood in the doorway, her phone pressed to her ear. "I'll call you back," she said, hanging up. "Come here, baby." She reached for Brett, clasping him to her chest.

Klaris picked up the board and dropped it into the washing up bowl. "I was just fetching Brett a drink. I was on my way out and he –"

"I don't think so," said Beth. "Rosie?" she shouted, looking beyond Klaris to the kitchen window.

"There's no need for alarm, Beth," said Klaris, holding up her hands peacefully. "I know this is a stressful time."

"I saw you," said Beth. "You were putting something in Brett's drink. Oh, my God. Is this what this has been all about? Were you poisoning him?" Beth put Brett down, her eyes wide and staring.

Klaris laughed. "Don't be ridiculous! You're not of sound mind at the moment. We all know that." She moved towards Beth. "Why don't you take a break and I'll see to –"

"Get away from me!" screamed Beth. "*Rosie?*"

Rosie and the two boys came hurrying in from the back garden, staring stupidly at the scene before them.

"What's going on?" said Danny, looking from Klaris to Beth to Brett and back to Klaris again.

"Klaris was inducing the tantrums in Brett. She's been drugging him. That's why he got better at yours, Rosie," said Beth. "It wasn't me. It was her!"

Klaris picked up her briefcase and set it on the oven. "Your mother has taken leave of her senses."

"Wait a minute," said Erland, the scrawny one with haunted eyes. He stepped forward, holding his hands out in front of him, tapping the air as though it were an invisible barrier, his eyes shut in concentration. "You're telling me that all this was *your* fault?" He curled his lip.

Klaris didn't see the next movement coming – the fist rising towards her face. Danny darted forward and grabbed his brother's wrist before it struck her. She lunged backwards, feeling the sharp rim of the oven dash against her.

"Erland, stop it!" Beth was shouting. Brett was crying. The grandmother was trying to pick him up. Erland was pulling at the buttons on Klaris's blouse, flailing about, trying to rip any part of her that he could contact. Danny overpowered him, restraining his arms behind his back. The young boy was so angry he was biting the air, his head thrashing about.

"Get off me! Get *off!*"

"For God's sake, Erland!" Beth said. "Take him upstairs, Dan. Get him to calm down."

Klaris eased herself away from the oven, straightening her blouse with trembling hands. Her face was twitching. All of her felt as though it were twitching, pulsating, about to shatter.

Erland took one last look at her, mustering as much disgust as it were possible to demonstrate, before being pushed out to the hallway. Danny went to follow, but stopped abruptly.

"Hey, come here, buddy," he said, bending down to beckon to Brett. "What's that you've got there, eh?"

Klaris set her eye upon the zipped section at the back of her briefcase, her heart lunging agonizingly.

She thought she had replaced it, but she could see that there was no lump in the lining of her briefcase where the multicoloured purse should be.

"Pretty," said Brett, holding the purse up with delight to his brother.

The amount of times she thought she had been living in hell, but she hadn't; she had been merely close enough to feel the heat. She leaned back with resignation onto the oven and glanced upwards, smiling. Of all people, it was her little angel in the end that had led her straight to hell.

"Rosie, could you please take Brett for a walk?" Beth stood at the bottom of the stairs, listening. She could hear Danny and Erland talking. Things seemed to be under control up there. She turned back to Rosie and Brett. "Just a trip up to the park if you don't mind."

"Of course," said Rosie, reaching for Brett's rain mac. "It's hardly raining."

Rosie pulled open the front door. "Oh!" She called out in surprise. Zoe was stood on the front step, reaching for the doorbell.

"Is that Klaris's car out front?" Zoe said.

"Yes," said Beth. "She's in the kitchen."

Zoe waited for Brett to toddle down the steps with Rosie, before shutting the door and dropping her overladen satchel to the floor.

"I need to talk to Klaris," she said.

"No," replied Beth. "*I* do." Zoe's eyes widened in surprise. "Follow me."

They went out to the kitchen, where Klaris was still standing, face upturned, smiling faintly.

"This woman," said Beth, "has been medicating my child. I caught her trying to administer this." She reached for Zoe's palm and placed the little purse upon it, feeling a surge of satisfaction. There were three pills inside the purse – three tiny pieces of evidence that would make a massive difference to Beth's future.

"Outrageous lie," said Klaris, shaking her head.

"Really?" said Zoe. "Charles Langley seems to think that this has happened before, Klaris. Annaliese Payne was the little girl's name. Your ex-husband brought it all to light."

At the mention of ex-husband, a change came across Klaris's face that intrigued Beth. She looked destroyed, utterly crushed. "Demon Man," she said.

"I beg your pardon?" said Zoe.

Klaris covered her face with her fingers outstretched, as though she were already behind bars, and began to cry. "Oh, Lord," she said with such anguish that Beth felt a temporary stab of pity.

It lasted only a moment. "Call the police," Beth said to Zoe.

As they waited for the police, time seemed to take on the strangest dimension. It was only quarter of an hour in real time, but according to the time-bending clock that had been ticking since Brett was first admitted to hospital it felt like several hours.

Beth thought of the first days when Brett had been taken from them – of how it had felt like weeks, not days. What was it about disaster and time? How she longed for happy flighty meaningless time that was there and gone in a moment.

She glanced sideways at Klaris, who was sat on the sofa with Zoe kneeling at her feet. Zoe's long blue skirt was spread out behind her like a puddle. "It's okay," she was saying, stroking Klaris's knotted hand. "You're ill. You need help."

"I didn't mean to," Klaris said, her breath wheezy, her face etched with distress. "I didn't realise..."

"It's okay...It's okay."

It wasn't okay, Beth thought. There was nothing okay about any of it. She played with her hair in agitation, twisting it up into a knot on her head and then letting it go again. Up and down. Up and down.

"Oh, for God's sake," she said, jumping up and glaring at Klaris. "This is stupid. We must have something to say to each other."

"Yes," said Klaris, quietly, dabbing at her face with a tissue and sniffing. "I do. I want you to know that I care about you and Brett. You must believe me."

"Believe you? You must be kidding!"

Zoe flashed Beth a warning look – an expression that said *she's fragile – have a heart*, but Beth didn't want to have a heart.

She went over to the window. She thought of the amount of times she had stood here in this same spot, wishing so desperately for Klaris to arrive, watching for the flash of her blue car to appear on the bend of the road.

Now there was a flashing blue light coming up the hill, about to turn into their road. The police car was noiseless, insidious as approached, its tyres crunching on the gravel as it parked.

They had come to collect the toll for wronging her. First Pammy. Now Klaris.

"What will they do to her?" Beth said, turning to Zoe. Zoe didn't want to say. She shrugged slightly, as though wishing to change the subject. Beth couldn't change the subject. She wanted to ask Klaris all the questions that she hadn't had a chance to ask Pammy, although really there weren't that many questions. Only one.

"Why?" Beth said.

"I'm sorry." Klaris rose and went to touch Beth's arm.

"Don't *touch* me!" Beth said, rapidly withdrawing.

The doorbell rang. Beth didn't move. There was the sound of footsteps on the stairs. Danny's voice at the door.

"Why me?" Beth said.

Klaris smiled. "I would have thought that was obvious."

"Not to me," said Beth.

"You needed me." Klaris smiled as she said this, as though it were the most simple statement in the world.

"And no one else did?"

"Not like you did. You relied upon me."

Beth thought about that. "Yes, I did Klaris. I trusted you. So what happened?"

"I don't know. I didn't plan it. It just happened. It happened once before too. There was a little girl… I was close to her mum, like I am with you."

"Like you *were* with me," corrected Beth.

Klaris looked pained. There was a cough at the door. A policeman hovered.

"I couldn't have children," said Klaris. "I wanted them of course, but my husband didn't. By the time he left me, it was too late."

Zoe turned to the policeman and gave a barely noticeable nod.

"I'm sorry, ma'am," said the policeman moving forward, his helmet tucked under his arm. "I'm going to have to ask you to come with me." A police woman was behind him, her radio crackling.

"You're the lucky one, Beth," said Klaris. "You've undone the past. Not everyone manages that."

She was escorted from the room. "Can I get my belongings together, please?" she asked.

Beth sat down heavily. "I don't understand," she said, shaking her head.

"It's was about attention," said Zoe. "Klaris was making Brett imbalanced so that she could rescue you. I've seen it before."

Beth nodded, without comprehension. There was a little rap on the door. "She's asking if she can say goodbye to your little boy," the police officer said.

They could hear Klaris crying softly in the hallway. Everyone looked at Beth for her answer. She thought again of Pammy being led off by the police – of her frailty.

"Not a chance," she said.

Danny was halfway down the stairs when he heard Klaris ask whether she could see Brett one last time. He froze and held his breath, worried that his mum was going to waver, or worse – say yes. He would have stopped her –

would have shoved Klaris out of the doorway and into the gutter, police escort or not. To his pleasure, his mum said no as firmly as she could have.

He sat down on the stairs and propped his head on his elbows, watching his mum. She seemed taller. She was stood in the doorway with Zoe, as the police led Klaris down the steps. It was raining. He could smell the dusty summer wet air. Klaris was doddery, unsteady on her legs. She looked nothing like the woman who used to call here. Everyone had changed. Zoe looked prettier. Klaris looked ancient. His mum looked taller – because she was standing tall. She wasn't hunched. She was standing proud.

It was all going okay until Zoe went off in her car and his mum came back and started running about and Erland began to take a shower and Rosie tried to find Brett's favourite toy, Mr Rabbit, and Danny, still halfway down the stairs, realised with a gut-wrenching sensation that the hearing was in less than an hour's time.

"Budge up," his mum said, patting his leg for him to move. He obliged. She was putting her lipstick on using a little mirror. He didn't want to unsettle her before the hearing but….

Jesus. Better out than in.

"Mum," he blurted. "If Klaris was nuts and was medicating Brett, then that explains Brett's tantrums. But what explains you?"

"Oh," she said, quietly, snapping the mirror shut. "We'll talk, Dan. I need to tell you about what went on in Cornwall."

"What, recently?"

"Yes, that and in the past. I…" She frowned at him, trying to find her words. "I wanted to protect you from the ugliness. But I couldn't and I can't and I never will. It's out there and sometimes it's in here too," she said, gesturing around her. "The only way to beat it is to be strong, in ourselves and as a team."

"Like Chelsea?" said Danny.

"Yes, Dan," she said. "Like Chelsea."

That was good enough for him. So long as Chelsea always won.

His mum got up to go. They had to leave now. He could hear Erland blow drying his hair in his mum's bedroom – it would be up on end, as though he'd been electrified.

Danny watched his mum at the front door, patting Erland's hair down. Rosie was reading to Brett in the lounge. His mum put her fingers to her lips. Danny and Erland nodded.

And then they slipped out of the house without saying goodbye to Brett, their heads bent against the rain.

CHAPTER ELEVEN

The courtroom was small and shabby, Beth thought, yet the shabbiness didn't quell the fear that was mounting in her stomach. Zoe was sat behind her. Beside her was Professor Moss's wife, plus the solicitor whom Charles Langley had recommended. Everyone was dark-suited. Beyond them was a bench of three magistrates. There were four other courtrooms in the building, running a conveyor belt of law, making and breaking people's lives five days a week.

There was a creak as the main door opened. Everyone turned their heads to look at the late arrival. It was Jacko in his best suit. Beth wanted to laugh and cry at the same time. She turned her attention to the rain lashing down on the windows outside.

The prosecution was stating that Beth was an unfit mother. The opposing barrister drew upon new evidence proving that Klaris Shaw suffered from Munchausen Syndrome by Proxy – a potentially lethal attention-seeking disorder – and had been inducing hyperactive behaviour in the child through medication. Brett was permanently under the effects of the medication or suffering from withdrawal.

243

The prosecution wondered whether we were supposed to believe that the medication had also slammed Brett's head into the wall?

Naturally, stated the defence.

Beth listened to the ping-ponging action of the lawyers, watching the rain. She thought of school assemblies at her primary school in Pengilly, of the sound of heavy rain on the corrugated iron roof. She would sit there cross-legged on the polished wooden floor, someone's shoe digging into her bottom, someone blowing their nose, someone doodling on their knee with a biro. Back in those days, she felt indelibly the same as everyone else during assemblies – part of a big heart-beating mass of skin and organs. She had hated it. Had she not been singled out by circumstance, she would have striven to have been different anyway.

She glanced back at Jacko. He nodded at her. She looked back at the rain, wondering briefly whether she might ever forgive him.

Her attention was drawn back to the judge. How much time had passed? She tried to watch the judge's lips moving and to listen, but she couldn't concentrate. Instead, she heard the words belatedly as though they were being shouted down a long concrete tunnel. So she reacted about ten seconds later than everyone else – than Zoe, who jumped up to high-five her, than Professor Moss's wife who shook her hand heartily, than Jacko who came rushing forward to hover before trying to hug her.

What Beth heard was that the charges were going to be dropped against her; that she had raised two older children who were well-adjusted and who loved her; that this evidence was even more compelling than the charges against Klaris Shaw, who was going to be brought to trial. The children's services were to monitor Beth until no longer deemed necessary. Brett was going to be cared for by Rosie for another seven days after which he could return to Beth's care, so long as Zoe continued to visit on a daily basis.

It was over.

Outside, Beth stood gulping in the fresh air, not caring that the rain was pouring down.

A car pulled up to the pavement, splashing the puddles and the window wound down. The driver was waving to her. It was Professor Moss. Beth bent forward into the car. "Congratulations," the Professor said.

"Thank you," said Beth. "I can't believe it."

"I can," he said. "You can start rebuilding your life now."

Their eyes met for an awkward moment. "You know… you can come back whenever you wish." He put the handbrake on and looked up, his eyebrows raised speculatively. "It's not the same without you, Beth."

"Well, I don't know…"

"Just think about it," he said.

As he began to pull away, Beth glanced down into his car at the pile of coursework on the passenger seat. There on the top of the pile was Hemingway's *Fiesta: The Sun Also Rises*.

"Wait!" She ran forward and leant back into the window. "You're doing *Fiesta*? You hate that book! You detest Brett Ashley!"

"Detest is a tad strong, Beth. Anyhow," he shrugged with his mouth, "it became a bit of a thing after you left."

She smiled.

"So, might see you back at the faculty then," he said, knowingly, before driving off.

As Beth walked back into the courtroom to find her sons, she realised that Brett Ashley was always going to be a part of her life. Brett Ashley, the little boy who was coming home.

A week later, a letter arrived from Pengilly from Mrs

Gray. She had large sloping handwriting that broke into capital letters mid-word. Beth sat in the garden reading the letter, sipping a cup of tea beside her lavender plants.

In case you'RE wonDering your DAd was a gYPSy who camped up on pentruthen Bay one SUmmer before MOving on. I onLY met HIm the onCe when He visiTed your muM. He was handsome, Beth. I'm Not just SAying that. But I caNT say as I Knew hIM or whether He was your Dad for sure, but Your Mum once Told me he WaS. I'M gueSSing it's true on Account of your DarKneSS.

Beth put the letter down and gazed at her bare arms. So she was a gypsy's child? She laughed in surprise. Mrs Gray had answered a question that she hadn't asked. She hadn't wanted to know who her father was. Why would she? He was merely a man who had slept with a drug addict who had beaten and neglected her. Some family tree.

Still, it was a strange thought – that somewhere out there her father could still be alive. She would be a surprise to him. He might be able to tell her about her background, her lineage. She had no one else to ask.

She looked at the letter in her hand for some time, before finally deciding to tear it up. No more drug addicts, abusers, gypsies. No more Pentruthen Bay. No more past.

She went indoors. The boys were out. The house was silent. In her bedroom, she reached to the back of her wardrobe. There, in a matchbox, was the mood ring. She sat on the bed and turned it round and round in her hand before putting it away again.

She went through to Brett's bedroom and reached up to open the bedroom window to air it. She had spent the week decorating his room with giant mural stickers of jungle animals. She had hung new gingham curtains and bought an elephant rug, plus a little desk and chair and a bookshelf. His name was on the door and over the bed she had hung a plaque that said *Bless this precious child.* She used to hate things like that but now it seemed important to state the obvious out loud.

Brett was coming home to her in a matter of hours. Her stomach was fluttery, she was nervous. It was a fresh start for them all. This time it was going to be different.

The window was stiff. It hadn't been opened since that day.

She turned around and suddenly caught her breath.

She could see Brett stood there in his cot again, exhausted from screaming, his face red and wet with tears, his curls drenched in sweat.

What do you want? she had screamed at him. *Are you trying to drive me crazy?*

He was pounding his fists on the side of the cot. "Out, out, out!" His eyes were bulging in anger, he was pulling on the wooden bars. He was going to break the cot. She was pacing up and down, trying to control her anger, wondering what to do next when he bit her, sinking his teeth into her cheek.

She was shocked. She cried out in pain. She was raising her hand towards him in response, when suddenly the evening sun flashed against the gold letters on his wardrobe door: L O V E.

She had lowered her hand and hurried from the room.

She had been just one sunbeam away from completing the circle.

EPILOGUE

Danny pulled his beanie hat down hard over his head. It had been a long while since he had seen snow – proper snow, not the sort that was flaky and then came to nothing – but big chunky snow that meant business. He couldn't believe that Erland hadn't wanted to come out with him in the snow tonight. Nor his mum, nor Jacko. Brett sort of did, but their mum wouldn't let him. Brett had a cold. Fair enough. But what was Erland's excuse? Chess. Always bloody chess.

Danny got to the end of the street and stood watching the snow fall against the yellow light of the street lamp. There was a spider's web glowing on the lamp. It was amazing what those things could withstand – storms, rain, snow.

Klaris had told him once about a spider's web outside her house that had been there for a whole year. He didn't know whether to believe her. She was doing time now. It made him sad to think of her, despite everything that she had put them through. It was all to do with her husband leaving her for another woman. She had gone cuckoo in the head. Danny made a mental note to never do that to anyone in the future.

Sometimes he wished he was still Lee's boyfriend. She would have told him something to cheer him up, something so stupid about the Klaris situation that it went full circle and almost sounded wise. He had noticed that about life – about things going full circle. Lee had gone full circle too. She had asked him out originally and she had ended things by asking him out again too. He should have been pleased, but she waited until the charges had been dropped against his mum. Danny didn't know much about love, but he had an idea that it wasn't something that you couldn't switch off and on like a mobile phone.

He had one of those now, but not a television. His mum wasn't going to ever have one in the house again, she said. And he sort of respected her for that these days.

He continued along his way, through the gap in the fence and up the side of the hill that led to the huge wasteland that backed onto the council estate. As he walked, he thought of the last time he had walked along here in the snow. It was back when he used to believe that if he swallowed one hundred flakes his father would appear.

He couldn't believe that he used to believe in that crap.

Still, there was no one about…

He stuck his tongue out, just for something to do and walked, enjoying the sound of his boots crunching in the snow.

As he walked, he counted. He got to one hundred and then stood alone in the middle of the wasteland up to his knees in snow. He pulled off his beanie to listen. Silence. It was impossible to believe that there were people all around in their houses, that his own family were just down the hill. It was as though he was all alone in an electric white silent universe. It was beautiful. He tried to take in every detail, every sensation of what he was experiencing so that he might remember it for the rest of his life.

"Don't suppose you're Daniel Trelawney by any chance,

are you?"

Danny swung round as fast as he could, knee-deep in snow. A man was stood a few yards from him, his deep tracks leading all the way to the opposite side of the wasteland in the direction of town.

"Who the hell are you?" said Danny, automatically clenching his fists in his padded gloves – again, not very easy.

The man wasn't looking at him. He was looking down at the city lights that were trying to break through the snow haze. He was wearing jeans and a donkey-type jacket.

"My name's Peter. And I can see now, looking at you, that you're definitely Daniel Trelawney." The man held out his hand to Danny. There was a Chelsea FC symbol on his hat.

Danny held out his glove. The two of them shook hands and then stood looking at the view again.

"Erland said you weren't coming," said Danny, finally. "He said you were a twat."

The man laughed. "Did he now? Well, he's right."

The snow had stopped. It was even more still now. Danny shivered, his feet having gone numb. He tried to stamp them, but they couldn't be shifted they were down so deep.

"Why are you here?" said Danny.

"I don't know," said Peter. "My wife thinks I shouldn't be. I don't know if she's ever going to allow me to come home again. Maybe though…" He turned to look at Danny. "…Maybe I shouldn't be with someone that won't allow me to have you in my life." This wasn't a question. It was a statement. It had been thought about a lot on the journey down here, Danny reckoned.

This guy mulled things over a lot. Danny would turn into him one day if he weren't careful. The two of them were similar – Danny could tell just by looking at him. Which just went to prove – he was transparent, just like

Danny. Peter went round trying to please everyone and in the end all he would have created was a great big car crash. He was like the opposite of Jacko, who never tried to please anyone but still created a car crash. Was there some kind of happy medium to be had?

"I…um…I think I'm still in love with your mum, Danny. I think I always have been."

Danny's body jerked a little in response to this statement. He hoped that Peter didn't notice. If he did, he didn't say anything. He seemed to be waiting for Danny to say something.

"Well, she's with Jacko again now," he muttered. "You left it a bit late."

"Thirteen years too late, to be exact," said Peter.

That was Danny's age. Realising the implication of this, he allowed himself a smile into his puffy jacket.

They stood for a while, until they were unbearably cold. At least, Danny was. He could only guess what Peter felt like, thought Danny, surveying the man before him critically. He was thin-faced and had heavy eyelids like Erland. And like Erland would be, he was dressed for the city and not for a snow storm.

"It wasn't snowing in London," said Peter, reading Danny's thoughts.

"Maybe you should come in for a hot drink or something," said Danny, trying to sound as casual as possible. "Since you've come all this way."

"That would be nice," said Peter, politely, waiting for Danny to take the lead.

"Don't expect Jacko to welcome you with open arms though," said Danny. "The guy's a nutter."

"Duly noted," said Peter.

And the two of them started to make their way across the wasteland towards home, just as the snow began to fall down thick again.

ENJOYED THE MOOD RING?

Leave comments and feedback about The Mood Ring or just say hello on Cath Weeks' Facebook page:
www.facebook.com/cathweekswriter

Find out more about Cath's books at her Facebook page or by visiting her author's page at Amazon.co.uk.

15277311R00153

Printed in Great Britain
by Amazon